She's a dead

Luna Black knows that she's being hunted. The price on her head is astronomical. She was in the wrong place at the wrong time, and she saw some very dangerous people doing some very, very bad things. Now she needs to reach the Feds, stat, and get a new identity *and* a new life. Because her old life? Definitely *over*.

It's not personal. She's just a job.

Ronan Walker lives in the shadows. His job? Simple—to deliver death. And the latest hit has him tracking down the very elusive and unpredictable Luna. But he's not the only hitman on her trail. Luna has valuable intel. The kind of intel that can never see the light of a courtroom. When the other hunters swarm in on her, Ronan has no choice but to intervene.

Death wasn't supposed to be so...dead sexy.

After he defeated the group trying to abduct her, Luna expected to die by the gorgeous stranger's hands. Even as he kissed her, Luna was sure that the tall, dark, and fierce predator would kill her. Only...she woke up, very much *still* alive, and handcuffed to his bed. Before she can even scream, he offers her a deal...protection, but for a price.

Is he a hitman with a heart?

No, he's not. Not even close. His heart never gets involved in a job. Ronan faked Luna's death, and now he has to keep her with him in the shadows until the Feds are ready to use her in order to bring down a massive criminal ring. The problem? He's not exactly used to sharing close quarters with anyone. Especially not someone like Luna...a woman who pushes him to the edge and makes him want to let go of the fierce control that he's kept in place for years.

On the run. Hiding in the shadows. Pretending to be a couple in love...

Sometimes, it's easy to pretend. To act like lovers. But what happens when the pretending starts to feel all too real? The longer they are together, the more Luna realizes there is so much more to Ronan than meets the eye. He protects her, he defends her from every threat, and she...just might be falling hard for the hitman who swears he can never love...

The story of her life. To fall for the man who delivers death.

Author's Note: Ronan deals with death. He's worked undercover as a hitman for years, only seeing the darkest side of life. Then he meets Luna. A woman named for the moon but who feels like sunlight in his arms. No way should he want her as badly as he does. No way should he start to think of Luna as his. But...he does. And anyone coming after Luna will find that Ronan will take "protecting and defending" her to a whole, new level. No one else will touch Luna, no one will hurt her, and he will deliver death to anyone who tries to take her from him.

When He Hunts

A Protector And Defender Romance

Cynthia Eden

HOCUS POCUS
PUBLISHING, INC.

This book is a work of fiction. Any similarities to real people, places, or events are not intentional and are purely the result of coincidence. The characters, places, and events in this story are fictional.

Published by Hocus Pocus Publishing, Inc.

Copyright © 2025 by Cindy Roussos

All rights reserved. This publication may not be reproduced, distributed, or transmitted in any form without the express written consent of the author except for the use of small quotes or excerpts used in book reviews. No part of this work may be used in the training of AI models.

If you have any problems, comments, or questions about this publication, please contact info@hocuspocuspublishing.com.

For all the people who are silently fighting battles that the world knows nothing about...I hope this story gives you a brief escape.

Chapter One

A WOMAN KNEW WHEN SHE WAS BEING HUNTED. AND as Luna Black hurried through the busy New Orleans Street, ducking her head against the surprisingly sharp bite of the wind that blew up from the mighty Mississippi River, she had no doubt that she was the prey...and a very, very dangerous predator stalked her through the night.

I can get away. I've gotten away before. I'll get away again. And then, tomorrow, I'll meet up with the Feds. I'll tell them everything. They'll give me a deal. They'll protect me. Goodbye, old life. Goodbye, terror.

Hello, new me.

She'd get a new name. A new home. Some desperately needed safety. Because for the last few weeks, Luna had been running on fumes and fear. Those two things could only sustain a woman so long. She'd gotten all the way from Atlanta, Georgia, down to the Big Easy. Since arriving in New Orleans, she'd been crashing at a friend's place. A friend who was out of the country and didn't exactly know that Luna was using her home. She'd crashed and tried to plot and plan and figure out a way to escape from the nightmare that held her in its grip only...

Shadows detached from the nearby building as Luna turned toward Jackson Square. Those shadows didn't make a sound, but Luna had the terrible feeling that they'd been waiting there just for her. Watching.

She swallowed and pulled the oversized black jacket that she wore even closer to her body. Her long, dark hair was shoved under the hood of the jacket, but a stubborn tendril escaped to blow across her cheek. Her head remained facing the front as she continued her determined steps. Jackson Square was locked down for the night, so she edged around its exterior. Her steps *might* have accelerated as she made her way toward the old alleyway to the left of the St. Louis Cathedral.

Hurry, hurry, hurry. She had to get out of there. She had to get—

She ran right into a giant, immovable object. An object that had *not* been there moments before. An object that had also detached from the darkness and stepped right into her path.

Sucking in a breath, she tried to take a step back, but it was too late. He'd already caught her. The immovable object—a big, muscled man wearing what appeared to be an extremely expensive suit—locked his hands around her arms. Not a tight grip. In fact, one that was oddly careful. And unbreakable.

"Sorry," he said, though he didn't actually sound apologetic. "Did I scare you?"

Yes. A thousand times, yes. "Let go of me."

The faint light from a flickering streetlamp fell onto him. Shadows surrounded him, but she could make out the firm line of his jaw—a jaw covered by the dark graze of a beard. His thick hair brushed back from his high forehead, and the top buttons on his white, dress shirt were undone. He had her in height by way too many inches and way too many pounds in body weight and strength. Physically, he was dominant and scary, and Luna knew trouble when it grabbed her. She shoved her hand into her crossbody bag to snag her taser because if the stranger didn't release her in the next three seconds, he was going to get the shock of his life.

One.

Two.

Th—

He let her go. "You've got company." He glanced over her left shoulder. "You familiar with them?"

"I-I don't know what you mean."

"The three guys who followed you after you left Café du Monde. They're watching you from the shadows right now. I'm worried they intend to harm you. Thought you could use a hero, so I stepped in."

She didn't want to take her eyes off him in order to look over her shoulder. *He* seemed like the big, bad threat but... "Is that what you are, a hero?"

He smiled. Or at least, she thought that he smiled. In the dim light, it was hard to tell for sure. "Is that what you want me to be?"

She weighed her options. And, dammit, Luna also peeked over her shoulder. Very, very quickly. Yes, crap. Three men were looming in the shadows. *My time is up.* They'd tracked her, and if she wasn't both careful and lucky, there would be no way she'd live to make that eight a.m. appointment with the Feds in the morning.

Her head whipped back to the front, and she made an instant decision. *One is better than three.* Because if push

3

came to shove, surely, she could take out this fancy-dressed stranger in front of her, right? Granted, he was big. Very big. And his shoulders definitely stretched the black suit he wore, but he was just one man. *One versus three. I'll take my odds against one man, thank you.*

Her taser would work on him. She could tase him and run away.

But if she fell into the hands of the *three* men lurking close by...

No way can I take out three guys at once. I'd be done for.

"I definitely want you to be a hero," Luna spoke crisply as she grabbed him. Looped her arm with his. Got way, way close to him. "Act like you know me."

"Excuse me?"

"Act like we're super in love, that you were waiting for me, and that you just can't bear to let me go." The words fired out far too quickly.

"Yes, ma'am." Inclining his head, he pulled her even closer. "I think I can handle that." His voice was deep and rumbly and warm, and it chased away the chill that wanted to wrap so tightly around her and pull her under until she couldn't breathe. Until she was absolutely frozen in ice.

Nope. Keep breathing. Keep moving. Keep fighting. Hadn't that been her mantra ever since that terrible day in Atlanta?

"And let's walk," she urged him. "Fast." Walk, run, whatever got them out of there.

He laughed, like she was playing some great game. She wasn't. She was running for her life, and the stranger in the dark was an answer to a prayer.

Her stranger asked, "Do we have a destination?"

That voice of his...*sex and darkness*. If she hadn't been so very scared, she might have melted. But, nope. She was scared. She was on the run. She was trying to stay alive. No melting allowed.

"St. Peter Street. Let's hit the bars there." Total lie. She did not intend to hit any bars. But her current safe house was close to St. Peter Street, so if she could get there, she'd escape her tall, dark savior and live to fight and scheme another day.

Oh, how she very much wanted to live to fight and scheme another day.

You show up at the wrong place at the wrong time...and suddenly, your life is over.

Tears wanted to sting her eyes, but she blinked them away. No pity parties were allowed. Hadn't she made that rule when she packed up her belongings in Atlanta and raced from the city? That had been *after* the first attempt on her life.

Her mistake had been thinking the cops in Atlanta could help. Correction, one of her many mistakes. But they hadn't believed her—or at least, that was what she'd initially thought. Only to discover they were in bed with the devil. *They sold me out. Watched me. Had me hunted.*

And the first attack on her life had come in the darkness. But she'd been lucky that night. Luna had escaped with a deep slice on her shoulder that she'd had stitched up in Montgomery, Alabama, by a local vet, of all things. The stitches were gone now, she had a wonky scar as a souvenir, but she was still alive. *Lucky.*

"You want to hit the bars?" Her savior seemed mildly surprised by her request. "I told you that I thought the men behind you intended you harm. Wouldn't you rather go to the cops?"

Those men one hundred percent intended to harm her. "Cops can't help." She'd tried that route and failed. Her hopes were resting on the Feds. Or, rather, on one Fed in particular. One man she thought could be trusted to save her ass. Hopefully. If she was wrong about him, she'd be dead.

"Helping is basically their job." Mild.

She kept her grip on his arm. "Maybe the men watching just wanted to steal my bag. But then big, bad you appeared. I bet you ran them off."

"I didn't run them off. They are following right behind us."

Dammit. When she strained, Luna could hear the faint pad of their steps.

But, up ahead, she could also see more lights. More people. That was the great thing about New Orleans. There were always people close by. One street might appear empty and dark, but if you just turned the corner...

Life waits.

And, sure enough, when they reached the corner and turned, she saw a slew of people sliding in and out of the restaurants and bars. A big crowd. Her breath heaved out in a relieved rush.

She started to pull away from her stranger.

"Come now, you don't actually think you'll get away from me that easily?" He angled toward her. Blocked her path.

Her heart kicked hard in her chest.

"Don't I at least get a name before you disappear into the night? That is your intent, isn't it? Now that I've walked you safely through the dark, you want to vanish on me."

If only he really could walk her through the darkness, then maybe she wouldn't be so afraid all of the time. But she *was* afraid. And this stranger had helped—briefly—but there was no way she'd pull him or any other civilians into the madness that was her current life. Still, a name wasn't so much to give in return for the help he'd provided. "Luna."

"Luna." He seemed to taste her name.

She wished that she could see him better. "Do you have a hobby of playing hero? Saving women in distress?" Why wasn't she leaving? Why did she linger with him? His scent wrapped around her. Sandalwood. His warmth pulled at her. She found herself leaning toward him.

"No." A shake of his head. "I'm not really in the business of saving."

"Oh? Then what is your business?"

He let her go.

She started to back away.

But he leaned in toward her. His hand rose and his fingers—slightly callused—pressed lightly to her cheek. His touch made her feel odd. A skittering tension slid through her. She'd noticed it the first time he'd touched her, but she'd attributed it to fear at the time.

Now, she realized that maybe...maybe that intense tension was attraction. Maybe she was attracted to the tall, dark stranger who'd saved her when no one else had—

"I'm in the business of death," he told her.

Her breath froze in her throat. "That's not funny."

"It wasn't supposed to be." His fingers slid down her cheek. Curled under her chin. "You had to know that you couldn't run forever, Luna Black."

He knows my last name.

No. No, no, no. Not him. Not the stranger in the dark. Not the one, tiny spot of goodness that she thought she'd found in this nightmare. She'd even had to give the vet a grand in order to stitch her up. Nearly all of her cash, but she hadn't been able to go to a hospital and...

"Why couldn't you be the good guy?" Luna asked softly, sadly.

His thumb brushed over her lips. "Because that would be far too boring."

Her hand slid toward the front of her bag once again. She had to get that taser. "You're here to kill me?" A crowd was close by. She could scream for help. Maybe they'd help. Maybe they'd ignore her. Hard to say with people.

"I can have you dead in my arms long before anyone hears any scream you might ever make."

Okay, that was terrifying. Soul chilling. And—

She yanked the taser out of her bag. She aimed it toward his stomach, but he moved wicked, wicked fast and knocked the taser out of her hand. His attack was jarring. Her whole hand seemed to go numb for a moment because of whatever he'd just done to her. The taser bounced toward the pavement. Utterly useless. Luna didn't waste time screaming. She'd read a story once about how people ignored screams—seriously *ignored them* unless you were yelling "Fire!" or something like that—and, by the time she screamed, like the jerk had just told her...she'd probably already be dead. Not like it took a lot of time to slit a person's throat.

So instead of screaming, she just rammed her booted foot into his shin as hard as she could. He didn't grunt or make any sound. He let her go, almost as if...as if he was curious to see what she would do next.

Oh, that's easy. I'm gonna run like my life depends on it. Because her life did depend on it. She darted away from him and ran straight into the street. A car horn blared, and she caught the flash of blinding headlights as tires squealed, but she didn't stop. Luna rushed forward. She shoved through the crowd that waited on the other side of the street. Then she was bursting into a restaurant—a seafood place with jazz music filling the air—and ducking out the side of the building a few moments later. Because of the open-air design so many restaurants had in New Orleans, she could go in one side and out the other...and she did that, several times. In several bars and restaurants.

She ran and twisted and hauled ass as she tried to snake her way to safety. In bars. Out restaurants. Through crowds. Past flirtatious men. And drinking women and she—

An empty street.

Silence.

That was so the way of the city. The crowd one road over—on Bourbon—would be toasting the night away. Then...silence. An empty street. Too many shadows.

She hurried forward, jumping over puddles of water that had been left from the last rain and doing her best to avoid the myriad of cracks in the old sidewalk. Safety was at hand. She knew it. She'd managed to escape and survive another night and she—

Was surrounded.

The men came from the darkness. Three shadows that loomed toward her with obvious evil intent. "We missed you at the Square," the nearest man said. Tall and thin.

To the right, another shadow stepped forward. Also tall, but round. Stooped shoulders. Big chest. Thick hands that had fisted at his sides.

Then, shadow number three. He stepped under the lone light. A ski mask covered his face. The others weren't wearing masks. And that was bad, wasn't it? Because if they weren't wearing masks, then they didn't care if she saw their faces. *Because they don't intend for me to ever escape from them.* No, they intended to kill her right then and there.

So why is this guy in a mask?

"You ran from Loverboy," the man in the mask said. "Figured you'd ditch him soon enough. We knew where you were heading, you see. Easy enough to cut you off."

They'd known about her safe house? Her heart thundered in her chest. "Guess you were just waiting for the perfect moment to kill me, huh?"

The masked man nodded. "Yes, we were."

Words that withered her heart. She took a step back, but there was no safety behind her. There was no safety anywhere for her. "Why bother with the mask? Your buddies aren't hiding who they are."

He advanced. Slowly, rather like a snake slithering toward her. "I like the mask. I've found people are far more terrified by what they *can't* see than what they can."

She was filled plenty with terror, thanks so much. "It's because you're not scary beneath the mask, right? A letdown?" She always talked too much when she was nervous. And Luna was way, way past just *nervous*. She was terrified. She'd lost her taser, she had no gun, and there were *three* of them.

They closed in on her.

"You made someone in Atlanta very angry." From the mask. The leader, clearly. "And that someone is going to pay me a whole lot of money to slice you up."

Oh, God. "Any chance I could change your mind?"

"How much money do you have?"

Great question. *Five hundred, four dollars, and seventy-two cents.* "How much money would it take?"

"There's a million-dollar bounty on your head."

What? This could not be her reality. "I'll pay you two million," Luna promised without blinking. "Tomorrow morning, we can meet at the bank and get it all squared away. Does that plan work for you?"

The mask laughed.

Yeah, she took that as a *no*. Unfortunately, the plan did not work for him.

He lifted his hand, and the two men with him sprang for her. She turned to run because it was truly her only option. She whirled, lunged and—once again, hit a very large, immovable object.

He's back.

Her head tilted up. She stared at him. Tried to, anyway. He was in so much darkness—the shadows from the edge of the nearby building covered him. But she had no doubt that it was the stranger who'd so casually told her that he dealt in death. His sandalwood scent filled her nostrils, and his heat wrapped all the way around her again.

And, damn it all, her body got that weird electric charge once more. *Fantastic. You've truly gone off the deep end, Luna. You're attracted to a killer.*

"Darling, did you miss me?" he asked her, voice all tender. "I missed you. Just couldn't stay away, in fact."

"You're crazy," she fired back.

"Crazy good at handling trouble. Why don't you watch and see for yourself?"

Why didn't she *watch*?

He pushed her behind him.

"*Get the fuck out of our way, hero!*" The yell came from the man in the mask.

Hero? Oh, the masked leader was mistaken, just as she had been. "He's not here to save me," Luna announced. "He wants me dead, too."

Her "hero" turned his head to glare back at her. "How about we don't share info with the enemy, hmm? That good for you?"

"Nothing about this night is good for me," she muttered.

11

"He wants to get the bounty!" The man in the mask was clearly enraged. "Destroy that bastard!"

All three men attacked the "hero" who was trying to take their bounty. Luna scrambled back because this was going to be horrible, but...maybe it would also give her the chance to flee. The bad guys could fight each other and perhaps she'd live to run yet another day.

Only...

Only there was no time for running.

Because the "hero" moved wicked fast again. And he knocked out the tall and thin attacker. Then kicked the boofy one in the stomach, jabbed him in the jaw, and had the fellow tumbling into a heap on the ground five seconds later. As for the masked man, he lost his mask. Or rather, he got it ripped away, and when a sliver of light fell on him, she saw his gaunt face. The nose that was slightly off center. The receding hairline.

He lost the knife he'd tried to shove into the ribs of the "hero" who easily beat the crap out of him. When the beaten leader tried to flee, he just got shoved face-first into the pavement.

The man in the fancy suit with the dark, rumbly voice had just taken out three attackers. She didn't think he'd even broken a sweat. And if he hadn't kicked their asses so incredibly fast, she could have used the opportunity to, oh, say, flee for her life.

Instead, he was spinning whirling back for her. He grabbed her wrist even as she tried to surge away, and in the next moment, she was pinned between his powerful body and the hard bricks of the building behind her.

Her breath shuddered out.

"Now," he murmured as his head lowered toward her. "Let me say again, did you miss me?"

A frantic, negative shake of her head.

He inhaled. "You smell like flowers."

What was happening? And she smelled like *roses*. With a side dose of champagne because that was her body lotion. The lotion she'd worn forever and, yes, she'd taken it with her when she fled from Atlanta. "I did not miss you," Luna blurted.

"Too bad." One hand still held her wrist. The other had lifted to press against bricks near her body. He completely caged her. Swallowed her with his size. He'd just knocked out three men like it was nothing. And now it was just the two of them.

"What are you going to do with me?" she asked. Did her voice break? Yes, it did.

"I think I'm gonna kiss you." He seemed surprised by his own words. He even blinked. Then shook his head.

She grabbed the front of his coat—that fancy black coat that made it look like he'd been out at a dinner party before he decided to stop and beat up three men. "Kiss me. *Don't* kill me."

"That a promise you want me to make?" A low rumble.

Somewhere near them, one of her would-be attackers let out a groan. Was he coming back to consciousness? Footsteps thudded a second later, and she knew the guy had fled the scene.

No help is coming. Not unless I can help myself.

"It's a promise I would very much like, yes," she rasped. *Please, please don't kill me.*

How could she catch him unaware again? Maybe if he did kiss her, she could distract him, knee him in the groin, and run like hell? Would that work? It was certainly worth a shot.

"I'm afraid that's not a promise I can give," he replied,

though he seemed apologetic. "I was hired to kill you, Luna Black. There's a big bounty on your head, and, one way or another, you have to die tonight."

Tears stung her eyes. "I should have been less afraid. Done more."

He tilted his head as he studied her.

A tear leaked down her cheek. "It's weird that you think of all the ways you wish you had *lived*, right before you die." But that was exactly what she was doing. Running everything through her mind. Wishing for all the experiences she'd never had.

"Luna..."

"Kiss me." *I'll live before I die.* "Don't kill me." A last plea.

His mouth brushed over hers. Carefully, tenderly. Why would her killer kiss her so tenderly? But he did. She was unprepared for the attraction, the sheer lust, that seemed to explode through her body at the touch of his lips against hers. It was a careful kiss. Gentle. It shouldn't flood need and heat through her entire body, yet it did.

Her mouth opened wider. His tongue thrust past her lips, and the kiss became so much more. Deeper. Rougher. Stronger.

Possessive.

She was holding onto his shoulders, and she didn't remember grabbing him. She was kissing him as if her very life depended on it, getting swept away by a passion that she'd never felt before, and maybe it was the fear or the adrenaline that had her melting against him even as her heart galloped wildly but she had never, ever felt this way before and she—

Pain.

A sharp pinprick of pain in her side.

14

His head lifted. "Sorry, sweet Luna."

His words barely registered. The heat was fading from her body. Fading far, far too fast. Her eyes struggled to stay open and focus on his face. He was back to sounding all apologetic again, and she feared what he'd done.

Her gaze dropped. Her eyes blinked. Narrowed.

She could see the syringe in his hand.

He's already killed me.

"There won't be any more pain," he told her. The words were a promise.

The bastard had kissed her. Drugged her. Kissed her and killed her and she couldn't even speak. Her tongue felt funny in her mouth. Her lips too dry. Her body slumped, and she knew this was the end. No more running.

Another tear leaked down her cheek.

She wished that she'd lived more before dying.

* * *

RONAN WALKER CAUGHT her as she fell. She slumped forward, all of that long, dark hair spilling out around her head, and he scooped her into his arms. The hood of her coat had long since fallen back, and her head sagged against his shoulder as he lifted her up against him. Her arms dangled as she hung—utterly limp—in his embrace.

That was one hell of a kiss, Luna Black.

An unexpected kiss. From an unexpected woman.

He turned and headed toward the groaning man in the middle of the street. The prick who'd mistakenly thought that he'd take Ronan's target.

"It's done," Ronan said as he strode past the fool he'd face-planted into the pavement moments before. Luna's left arm trailed down, her fingers open. "The drugs stopped her heart. The bounty is *mine*."

The idiot swiped out at Ronan, so Ronan kicked the dick in the ribs. He could have just killed him, but Ronan needed a witness to share the news of the kill. "Stay out of my way," Ronan warned him. The guy would get one warning. Just one. "Or next time, you'll be the dead one." The jackass's cronies had both fled. Probably hiding in the shadows and watching the show. Good. Let them watch.

Ronan did love a good show.

He kept walking with his prey. The scent of roses and... was that champagne? He swore it was. The scent of roses and champagne teased his nose. The woman in his arms didn't stir. How could she? The dead didn't stir.

He turned to the right, heading for his car. Almost there.

"Hey!" Two guys in Tulane sweatshirts stumbled toward him. "Hey...what's wrong with her?" One blinked blearily. "I'm pre-med," he said. "I can help..." He weaved on his feet.

The pre-med looked as if he couldn't do jackshit. But he was interfering with Ronan's plans. The last thing he needed was *help* with his prey. "My girlfriend had too much to drink," Ronan told the men. "Gonna take her home. Let her sleep it off."

Even drunk, the two men hesitated.

"She does this a little too often," he continued easily. "Told her that she had to slow things down. Good thing I was there to watch out for her, huh?"

"She...doesn't look like she's breathing." Of course, this would come from the pre-med.

Ronan walked around the college guys. "That's weird. Night, gentlemen." He whistled as he carried her.

Unfortunately, the men might not be *quite* as drunk as Ronan had hoped because he was pretty sure they ambled along after him.

He kept his hold on Luna and hauled out his keys. He pressed the button to unlock the car and also pushed the button to pop the trunk. Then he carried Luna straight to the rear of the Benz. He lowered her inside. Being careful because, with her, he wanted to use care. Odd. Tenderness wasn't typically part of his personality.

Being a blood-thirsty killer who didn't give a shit about anyone? That was more him.

"Hey!" A sharp cry.

Ronan sighed. Why did his night have to keep being interrupted? Satisfied that Luna was all tucked in, he slammed the trunk's lid closed.

"Hey, you can't put your *girlfriend* in the trunk!" It was the pre-med. Rushing forward. Trying to come to the rescue.

Ronan pulled out his gun and stopped the man in his tracks. The gun had been tucked at the base of his back all night. And he'd only needed it now, with a hero. Go figure. "If you want to be a doctor one day, you'll turn around. You will walk away." *And live to save a life another day.*

The pre-med student shook his head.

His friend—looking suddenly way sober—stared with wide eyes. The friend looked like he might faint—or vomit—any moment.

"You can't kidnap her!" Pre-med yelled. He was fumbling with his phone. Probably intending to dial nine-one-one.

Ronan headed for the driver's side. He opened the door. Kept the gun on the men. "You can't kidnap a dead woman."

17

The two guys gaped at him.

"You can't save one, either." Ronan shrugged and then slid into the car. He kept his gun on the men a moment longer. "But it was really nice of you to try." Interesting to know that there were still a few good people in the world. Too bad they'd arrived too late to save Luna Black. If only they'd been the ones to meet her near Jackson Square.

Instead, he'd been there. For just a moment, he'd played the hero for Luna.

And then he'd been her killer.

I can still taste her. Still feel her. Sweet and lush.

He lowered the gun. Slammed the door. A moment later, the Benz's engine growled to life, and he shot through the streets of New Orleans.

His prey was in the trunk.

Luna Black. Current target. A woman who'd had a very large price on her pretty head.

Sometimes, being a hitman was a walk in the park.

A loud thump came from the trunk.

And sometimes, it's a real pain in the ass.

It sounded like Luna was already waking up. He hadn't given her a strong enough dosage. A mistake on his part. He'd have to stop soon and inject her again. Poor Luna.

Unfortunately, some people just did not know how to stay dead.

Chapter Two

HE HAD A DEAD WOMAN HANDCUFFED IN HIS BED.

She let out a low groan.

Correction a...*supposedly* dead woman was in his bed. Ronan Walker continued sitting in the chair that he'd strategically placed a few feet from the foot of that bed. The position gave him a perfect view of one Luna Black. His latest target.

The woman he'd killed hours before.

Her long, dark lashes fluttered. Another groan escaped her, and his eyes remained locked on her face. An intriguing face. Not a face that was classically beautiful, he decided. More...sensual. Sharp cheeks. Slightly pointed chin. Straight nose. Full, plump lips. With her long tumble of black hair, she had a slightly witchy appearance. As in, a wicked witch who starred in men's fantasies. Sexy and dangerous and she—

Her eyes opened.

Green. Emerald. Quite stunning in their intensity. He hadn't been able to see that intensity in the darkness of the

New Orleans streets. But now, well, Luna might just have the most amazing eyes that he'd ever seen.

Only as she stared at him, her emerald gaze quickly filled with horror. Her lush mouth parted. Actually, it more dropped open. He expected her to scream. They were far enough away from civilization that she could scream her heart out, and he'd be the only person who heard her cries. A benefit of having a place in the bayou. Easy to dump bodies and hide victims. Not that he was going to mention that bit of information to Luna just yet.

She jerked upright in bed. She tried to lunge forward, but the handcuff around her right wrist hauled her back. One cuff had been placed around her right wrist, and the other had been locked around the railing of the old brass bed.

Her head whipped toward the handcuff. First to the one bound to her wrist, then to the one locked to the bed. In the next instant, her head snapped back toward him. *"You."*

He nodded. "Me." Ronan continued his relaxed pose. He'd taken off his suit coat. He still wore the black vest he'd had beneath it, but he'd rolled up the sleeves of his white dress shirt. Ronan spared a glance at the watch on his left wrist. She'd been out for a little over four hours. He'd started to vaguely worry. *I hadn't wanted to give her that second dose, but when she'd started to kick the lid of the trunk, I didn't have an option. Couldn't let a dead woman attract more attention than she already had.*

Not that he really minded the Tulane guys seeing him. They would have run to the cops with their story. Given a good description of him and poor, dead Luna. Their story would just be extra coverage for her murder.

As far as the rest of the world was concerned, Luna Black—former drama teacher, budding entrepreneur—had been murdered. Her body would not be recovered. She would not be seen again. Just another tragic case.

"I'm not dead." She tugged on the handcuff but didn't take her eyes off him.

Intrigued by her reaction—because he'd certainly expected quite a few screams by now—Ronan slowly shook his head. "Not dead." His voice came out low and hard. Typically the way he spoke. His shoulders rolled back as he continued to study her.

He'd taken off her shoes, socks, and the big, black coat she wore. He'd left on her shirt and the jeans that fit her like a second skin. Luna was average height, but with full breasts and hips that flared in the best possible way.

Sensual. The word whispered through his head again. The perfect way to describe her.

A perfect problem. He shifted a bit in his chair. *What in the fuck? Am I lusting after a target?* It was probably because of the kiss. A mistake. He'd known it was a mistake even as he bent to taste her.

Why in the hell had he kissed her?

And why did he want to kiss her again so badly?

Luna licked her lips.

Damn.

"This...this isn't some weird sex thing, is it?" Hushed. Trembly.

His eyes narrowed.

"Oh, God. It is." Her breath heaved in. Then out. "I'm handcuffed to your bed. This is about to get weird and kinky, and I don't care how hot you are—*this is not happening!*"

I don't care how hot you are. She thought he was hot? Interesting to know. He filed away that tidbit for later.

But she sucked in another deep breath, and he knew the

21

screams were about to start. To save his ears, Ronan figured he should make a confession. "I was hired to kill you by a certain dangerous individual from Atlanta." Ah, Atlanta. A city he'd been visiting too frequently for the business of death.

Her mouth opened wider.

"I was hired by him to kill you," he repeated, "but the Feds are paying me more to keep you alive."

A strangled gasp was the only thing that emerged from her parted mouth. Then her lips snapped closed. She blinked. Twice. Squinted. "Say again?"

"The Feds are paying me to keep you alive." He rolled back his shoulders once more and got a bit more comfortable in the chair. "It's your lucky night, Luna Black. I just made the rest of the world think that you're dead. That means you actually have a chance to keep living."

"Thank...you?" Luna's words were definitely a question.

But he nodded anyway. "You're welcome."

Another swipe of her tongue over her lips. An unfortunate side effect of the drug he'd given her? Dry mouth. He should probably offer her some water. He'd already put a glass on the table near the bed. Look at him being all thoughtful. His friends would laugh their asses off. Ronan had never particularly been known as the thoughtful sort. "If you're thirsty, there's a drink waiting for you." He pointed to the glass.

She grabbed the drink with her free hand. Downed the water in a couple of fast gulps, then put the empty glass back down with a soft clink. Her breath came fast, and he noticed that her fingers had trembled and made the glass shake. She was clearly terrified but fighting hard not to show her fear.

You just keep intriguing me, Luna.

"I...let me get this all straight." She shoved back some heavy locks of hair that had fallen over the side of her face. "You drugged me."

"Um. Had to do that twice. You just wouldn't stay out. Can't have a dead woman waking up and trying to escape. Looks bad."

She squeaked. Caught herself. Cleared her throat. "Yes." Husky. "Don't want you to look *bad* as a...hired killer?"

He nodded. "Totally bad for the reputation." And he *did* have a reputation to maintain. One that Ronan had carefully cultivated over the years. "You don't get to be the most feared in the business by making mistakes."

"H-how do you get to be the most feared?" Luna pulled her legs beneath her. Tugged on the handcuff around her wrist. She could tug on it all night. It wasn't going to open. And the brass bed might look old, but it was sturdy. Luna would not be getting free until he released her.

And he didn't trust her enough to release her yet. He had to be sure she wouldn't run from him the moment the cuffs were off. That meant they needed to reach a deal. Not like he was in the mood to trail the woman all through the bayou in the middle of the night. Gators were out there. And snakes.

He freaking hated snakes.

But back to her question. A good question. "You get to be the most feared by always getting the job done." Which he did. "I'm not big into blood and gore scenes. Too dramatic." A little FYI for her.

Luna seemed to pale. "Right. Way too dramatic. Don't want that."

"So I execute with a minimum amount of fuss. A quick push of a needle can give vics a sweet, painless death."

Her eyes squeezed shut. "You kill people for a living."

No, technically, he did not. Technically, he worked undercover as a hitman. The people he *killed*? They got shiny, new lives someplace far, far away. But he wasn't ready to share all with Luna just yet. Mostly because he never shared *all* with anyone. Besides, if she feared him, she was less likely to be problematic.

Problems tended to annoy the hell out of him. He liked order. Regimen. Was that too much to ask?

Her eyes cracked open. The green sparkled at him.

Oh, right. He should respond. "Killing pays well."

"That is a terrifying thing to say."

"It's a truthful thing."

She rose onto her knees. Her arm pulled a bit where her wrist hooked to the cuff. "But you are *not* going to kill me?" Hopeful.

"Told you, I'm being paid more to keep you alive." Were the drugs making it hard for her to follow along?

"Do the Feds often make partnerships with hitmen?"

"That's something you'd have to ask them." *More often than you would suspect, dear Luna.*

"How do I know you aren't lying to me? That this isn't some terrible trick?" Her gaze darted around the room. "Maybe you're into torture and this is the way you start. You give your victims hope. Make them think they're going to survive, and then the knives come out."

The knives? Really? "Just told you I wasn't into blood." But he rose to his feet.

She stiffened.

"Relax." He pointed down to his body. "Do you see a knife strapped to me?"

Her stare raked over him. Seemed to really search. "Could be on an ankle strap. I've heard people do that.

Keep knives strapped to their ankles and hidden beneath the legs of their pants."

He showed her both ankles.

"Could be under your vest."

Without taking his eyes off hers, he slowly unbuttoned the vest. He was aware of a sudden, hard tension as he opened the vest and let it fall. The tension seemed to stretch in the air between them.

She swallowed. "You don't have one tucked under your shirt, do you?"

"Luna." Her name came out almost as a caress. "Are you trying to get me to strip for you?"

"No." But she nodded.

And damn if he didn't almost smile at her. "I am not planning to use a knife on you." To mar that perfect skin? That would be a crying shame.

"Good to know. The last attacker did."

Anger burned through him, lightning fast. "What?"

"He got my shoulder. Better the shoulder than the heart, though, am I right? But it still bled like crazy. Couldn't risk going to a hospital, so I paid this shady vet to patch me up. And—wait! What are you doing?" Luna backed up against the headboard.

He'd just stalked toward her. Blazing anger had pushed him closer to her. "Show me."

"Show you...what?"

"The wound," he bit out. And why was he so mad? *Because she was hurt. I don't like for her to be hurt.*

Hell. This wasn't good. Or rational. Maybe he needed to calm down, back off, and sleep.

Instead, he leaned ever closer.

Her left hand rose. She pulled at the top of her shirt, angling it down to show the jagged scar on her shoulder.

"The vet wasn't very good at stitching. Probably because animals don't complain about wonky lines."

Ronan's back teeth clenched. "No wonder you don't like knives." His hand lifted toward her.

"Promise you won't hurt me."

His hand froze. Their gazes collided. He could almost hear the seconds ticking by. Finally, he asked, "You gonna believe the word of a hitman who drugged you and kidnapped you?"

"Well, when you put it that way..." Her lips pressed together. She shook her head. *No.*

"Didn't think so." His fingers reached out to touch her shoulder.

She flinched at the contact.

Silken skin. A scar that enraged him beyond reason. "I promise not to hurt you." The words rumbled from him.

Her breath whispered out. "Does that include not drugging me again? Because I'd really prefer not to be drugged, thank you very much."

How the hell is she this polite? "Are you always so courteous with your kidnappers?" His fingers kept brushing along the scar, almost as if he could take her pain away.

He couldn't, of course.

Why am I still touching her? Why do I like touching her so much?

"You're my first," she said, those incredible green eyes staring at him without a blink. "Figured I could try courtesy instead of hysteria. Thought it might work better."

She fascinated him. He sat on the side of the bed. With an immense force of will, Ronan made himself stop touching her.

Luna continued to crouch on her knees. "How did I get here?"

"I drove you in my car."

A nod.

"Full disclosure," he added, aware that his voice was gruff. "You were unconscious in the trunk at the time. Well, technically, you woke up once, but then I had to drug you again. So, yeah, here we are."

Her delicate nostrils flared. Her only sign of fear. Well, that and the frantic pulse he could see racing along her throat. She was trying very hard to appear controlled and calm, but Ronan realized that was just an act. Luna was completely terrified of him.

And I'm fascinated by her. What. In. The. Hell?

"Where, exactly, is here?" Luna inquired in her ever-so-polite tone.

"A cabin in the bayou. Far, far away from civilization. You know, one of those places where no one will hear you scream."

Silence.

"So there's not much point in screaming. Or running. Because either you'll stumble straight into a gator, or I'll just catch you. And if I have to hunt you through the bayou—dodging snakes and sinking in smelly sludge—I will be pissed. Know that."

"Oh, no." Zero emotion in her voice. "I'd hate to piss off the hitman-slash-kidnapper who drugged me. Who knows what he might do next?" Her eyes had gone extra wide.

Suspicion hummed through him. "You're a good actress, Luna. Guess you had to be, huh? Wasn't that your thing?"

A sniff. "I was a middle school drama teacher."

"Right. So you taught other people how to act. I think that means you're pretty good at hiding your real self." Ronan found that he was quite curious about her real self.

"You're calm while you talk to me, but I completely terrify you, don't I?"

"I'm handcuffed to your bed. You confessed to being a hitman. You *drugged* me. What sane woman wouldn't be terrified right now?"

"Excellent point." He caught her scent again. He was ninety-nine percent sure that scent was roses and champagne. "But I think we need to revisit my earlier statement to you."

"Which statement would that be?" Her wrist casually twisted inside the handcuff.

Cute. Did she think she'd be able to slide her wrist out? Not happening. Unless she was Houdini, she was not getting out of the cuffs. "The statement where I told you the Feds were paying me more to keep you alive than the jerk in Atlanta was paying for me to kill you."

Another twist of her wrist against the cuff. "How do I know you aren't lying to me?"

"Grayson Stone."

A blink of those long, long lashes.

"You were going to meet him, weren't you? He's a Fed and you were desperate to see him. You set up a chat with him here in New Orleans." He glanced at his watch. "It's supposed to happen in about five hours, but you won't be making the appointment. Instead, Grayson will spread the news that you were killed last night. Two witnesses saw your lifeless body get dumped into the back of a BMW. Those Tulane students are definitely coming in handy."

"Who?" Her wrist pulled against the cuff.

"Oh, right. You were unconscious. You don't remember them. College guys who tried to save the day. Unfortunately, they were a bit too late." His hand flew out and curled around the handcuff—and her wrist. "You're

28

going to get bruised if you keep pulling at the cuff. You can't get out. Not until I let you out."

Her breathing came a little faster. "And when do you plan to let me go?"

"As soon as you promise not to run."

"I promise not to run." Her immediate reply. "Let me go now?"

Cute, but no. He didn't believe that fast promise. "Grayson knows that I have you. In fact, he sent me after you."

She didn't look convinced.

"Here's the deal." Ronan should move things along. Stop staring into her emerald eyes. Stop inhaling her scent. Stop lusting after his charge. "I'm being paid a great deal of money to do the following things. One, fake your death. Which I have done. Incredibly well." His fingers slid along her wrist, rubbing the area she'd probably already bruised. "Two, hide your sweet ass."

"Excuse me?"

It is a sweet ass. "Hide you," he clarified. "Dead people can't just stroll down Bourbon Street. Gray—Grayson— wants me to keep you out of sight. You need to stay hidden, and you need someone—me—to protect you *while* you are hiding."

"Is that number three? Protecting me, I mean?"

Sure. Whatever. "Number four, when the time is right, I'll deliver you to the Feds. You'll spill all that you know, and in return, you'll get a new life. Then I'll vanish. Be just a bad nightmare for you. And you can start living a real dream somewhere else."

"You're doing all of this...for me?"

When the hell had he started easing toward her mouth? Ronan caught himself. "I'm doing all of this for the fat cash

29

I'll get paid." He kept his voice hard. "But *you* have to do things in return. There are no free deals from me."

A nod of her head.

His fingers slid along her wrist again.

She shivered.

Fear or...

No, stop it. The shiver has to be fear. You might want to fuck her like crazy, but to her, you're the boogeyman. You drugged her. Put her in a car's trunk and then cuffed her to a bed. She is not thinking about putting that hot mouth of hers against you again.

Unfortunately.

"What do I have to do?" A husky question from Luna.

Do not say what you're thinking, Ronan. Do not. Control the impulse. He'd always had dark impulses that needed to be controlled. With Luna, those darker impulses seemed to be pushing against the normal restraints he kept on them. Ronan swallowed. "You have to follow my rules. Don't be a pain in my ass. We keep a low profile, and you *don't* cause any trouble for me, understand? And you absolutely *must* tell the Feds everything you know about the business in Atlanta. No holding back. I don't care if it destroys the life you had before." Hell, that life was already destroyed. Boom. "You share every bit of intel you have. And then you tell the Feds what an amazing job I did keeping that sweet ass safe. I'll probably get a bonus when the job is done." Total bullshit but...

She didn't know that.

There is no big payday for me. I work undercover. I get the job done. I fight against the scum of the earth. For him, that was payment enough. He did the job over and over because the bad guys out there never stopped. There were always more waiting in the dark.

"I think...as a show of trust, you should uncuff me," she said.

Yeah, he probably should. Gray wouldn't be thrilled to know he'd kept her cuffed this long. But what Gray didn't know wouldn't annoy the guy. Ronan studied his prey. Tried to decide if she was gonna follow all the rules. "No running."

"Because running would make me a pain in your ass. Check. Right. Heard that the first time." Her fingers wiggled. "Uncuff me? Please? Pretty please?"

He shoved his left hand into the pocket of his pants. Hauled out the key and put it at the lock. *Snick*. The cuff popped open. He lowered her hand, rubbing his fingers along her wrist. Was that a bruise already forming? Dammit, he'd have to remember to be extra careful with her because Luna was so delicate—

"You drugged me!" She slammed her whole body into his. Because Ronan was perched on the side of the bed, he tumbled right off the edge and down to the floor where he landed on his ass. Completely humiliating. He had to outweigh her by at least one hundred pounds, but she toppled him and as he fell, she didn't come down with him. Instead, fleet of foot, she danced across the mattress, jumped off the edge of the bed, and hauled ass for the bedroom door.

He leapt up to give chase. *"Luna!"* A roar.

She slammed the door shut behind her. He barreled into it. And—

Locked.

Sonofafucker. He'd been the one to install the lock. Just in case she gave him problems. And she'd just used the lock against him. His fist slammed into the wood of the door.

31

"*Luna!*" Another roar. One that almost shook the wooden door. "Don't do this! You need me! *Luna!*"

No response. Only, hell, had he just heard the cabin's front door slam?

Ronan ran to the bedroom window. The clouds that had hidden the moon and stars earlier had vanished, and he could just make out Luna's form as she rushed from the cabin.

Hadn't he just told the woman he was going to protect her?

Hadn't he just said his job was to keep her safe?

Dammit. He hauled open the window. Jumped his ass out. And gave chase. "Luna!"

At the thunder of her name, she paused just long enough to glance back at him.

Then she took off even faster. Right into the heart of the bayou. Toward the sludge. Toward the gators. Toward the freaking snakes.

Barely free two whole minutes, and already, the woman had broken a cardinal rule.

She is totally being a pain in the ass.

So much for being the nice guy. Time for the evil hitman to play.

Chapter Three

FEAR HAD HER RUNNING BLINDLY.

Hello, story of my new life. Her bare feet sank into the cold, wet ground. She hadn't even realized that her shoes and socks were gone, not until she'd jumped off the wooden porch. As soon as the sludge oozed up between her toes, she'd realized that fleeing without shoes probably wasn't the best plan.

But then the hitman had leapt through the window as he shouted her name, so stopping and grabbing shoes hadn't exactly been an option.

Oh, he sounds pissed.

A pissed, confessed killer. How wonderful for her.

Fleeing without shoes was bad.

But staying back in the cabin, with the big, dangerous, predator who'd kidnapped her? *Even worse plan.* So, yes, as they'd talked, she'd acted for all that she was worth. Pretended that she believed his crazy story, and then she'd *run*.

She was still running, hoping that she'd see some light in the darkness. That she could find some help. That she could get away and survive. But there was just blackness ahead. She could hear insects chirping and croaks that—*please, please be from frogs and not alligators*—and Luna just kept running because there was no alternative. If she wanted to keep living, she had to keep going and—

She hit the ground. Not because she tripped and fell like a horror movie queen, but because a massive hitman had just slammed into her. He fell down on top of her, caging her, and for a moment, terror held her still against the dank earth.

This is it. He's going to kill me right now. The end. This is how I go out. Face down in the mud and muck.

"Pain in the ass," he groused. And he...lifted up. Flipped her over. But he caught her wrists and pinned them to the ground even as his legs went between her spread thighs.

Way, way too intimate.

He was a giant, menacing shadow above her, and his grip on her wrists seemed utterly unbreakable. More unbreakable than handcuffs.

"How does this make sense?" he snarled. "I tell you that I'm the person protecting you. And you immediately run from me. Do you *want* to be gator bait?"

Not particularly, she did not. "You're the person who brought me to a scary cabin in the bayou. *And* you're a killer."

"I haven't killed you."

Not yet. No. Her breath huffed out.

His didn't. He'd been running after her, and he wasn't even breathing hard? How was that not extra terrifying?

I hit him. He's going to be so angry with me...

"Fucking sonofafucker." An enraged growl. And then he...

Let her go?

He did. He let her go. She started to scramble up—

Only for him to grab something that had been right beside her head. He yanked it up. *Wait, what is that? A twig? No, way bigger. A branch? A—*

OhmyGod. It was a crazy long snake that he picked up and *threw* away from her.

"Thanks so much for that," he snapped at her. "Could have gone my whole life without doing that shit. Freaking snake wrangling now. Gray owes me so much for this job."

Did he truly mean Gray as in *Grayson Stone?* The Fed that she'd planned to meet in New Orleans? She was too scared to really hope.

But the hitman was on his feet, and he'd hauled her up. Not just up. He tossed her over his shoulder, and when she squirmed, he—

"I will spank that sweet ass if you don't *stop*. I am not in the mood for more snakes. We're going back to the cabin, Gray will vouch for me, and you *will* cooperate. Or else I'll leave you on your own and you can face the rest of the hired killers that come to claim the bounty on your head."

Definitely pissed.

He stomped back toward the cabin. She didn't fight because—what would fighting do, right then? She'd seen for herself that no one else was close by. Running in the dark had just gotten her nearly bitten by a snake, and her captor had chased her down with crazy, super speed.

But he *hadn't* hurt her.

He was swearing and stomping and holding her tightly. One of his hands was right beneath her ass, clamped along the back of her upper thighs, and each angry step he took had her bouncing and thudding into him.

"This is what happens when you do one good fucking

Cynthia Eden

deed," he seethed. "You have to throw snakes in the dark. Who wants to do that shit? Not. Me."

They were back at the cabin. He kicked open the front door. Stalked inside. Kicked the door closed as soon as they were past the threshold. She'd just levered herself up by pressing down on his very strong back, so she saw the wood of the door slam closed. The whole cabin seemed to shake from the impact.

Then he was stalking forward again. Cursing and muttering and going on and on about snakes. She shoved her hair out of her eyes and figured she should try calming down her captor, if that was at all possible. "Look, could you —ah!"

He'd hauled her off his shoulder and planted her into a wooden chair. His hands clamped down on the arms of the chair as he caged her in place. "That was a water moccasin."

He'd been able to tell that in the dark? He must have phenomenal night vision. She had really shitty night vision.

"It's venomous. It was four freaking feet long, and it was about to bite you because you'd nearly run right on top of it as it came out of the water!"

His eyes were icy chips of blue rage.

Luna cleared her throat. Swallowed hard. "You tackled me, so if I nearly hit the snake, isn't that on you?"

If possible, his eyes narrowed even more. "I tackled you because you were running straight into the water. Could you even *see* the water?"

She'd been pretty frantic so... "Guess you have better night vision than I do."

His nostrils flared.

Wow. This close, there was no denying the obvious. "You are awfully attractive for a hitman."

36

His nostrils flared again. "You think you're gonna charm me now, Luna?"

No, she just thought that she was helluva scared, and she'd blurted out the first thing that came to mind.

He leaned in even more. Was practically nose-to-nose with her. "Not that I'm counting," he gritted out. "But that is the second time I saved your life. The first was when I stopped those *three* assholes from slashing you to pieces in the street."

Another swallow from her. Or more like a gulp. "Sounds like you are counting to me."

"*Luna.*"

"I-I would say your name in return, but you haven't given it to me. So...*hitman*."

His gaze assessed her. A blue that seemed to see right through Luna. A blue that was utterly inscrutable in that instant.

Her breath came out way too fast. Again, he didn't seem to be breathing hard at all, despite the fact that he'd chased her through the night and carried her back to the cabin. "What's your name?" she whispered.

"Ronan." Bit off.

"Ronan...what?" Like a last name mattered, but she still asked the question anyway.

"Ronan Walker." Snapped.

Yep, he was definitely pissed. She'd attacked him. Run. Nearly gotten bitten by a snake. "Is that your real name?"

"No."

Well, crap. "That's okay. I'll still just call you Ronan." Probably a hitman rule not to give out your real name. "Luna is my real name, by the way."

"I *know.*"

She wet her lips.

His gaze immediately dropped to her mouth. Was it her imagination or did the blue blaze even more?

"What are you going to do with me?" Luna breathed. *Don't kill me. Don't cuff me again. Don't drug me. Don't put me in a trunk.*

"Not what I want." He was still looking at her mouth.

What kind of answer was that? "Ronan?"

He jerked back from her as if he'd been burned. Then he was reaching into his pocket, and he was pulling out—oh, God, he was pulling out—

A phone.

He tapped the screen. Then glared at it. After a moment, "She's a pain in the ass," he announced.

Luna frowned.

"But she's an *alive* pain, correct?" A man's calm and deep voice filled the air.

Speaker phone. Ronan must have hit the speaker button so she could hear his call.

"No, she's dead," Ronan returned. "As far as the rest of the world is concerned, Luna Black died on a New Orleans street. Maybe her body will eventually be found. Or maybe it's already been dumped at the bottom of the muddy Mississippi. Who knows?"

Luna realized that she'd fisted her hands.

"She doesn't trust me," Ronan added.

"Well, sure, you probably drugged her. And kidnapped her. A lack of trust is bound to happen," the man said.

"Tell her to stop running from me. I'm not in the mood to chase her ass all over the bayou." Then he turned the phone around so it faced Luna, and she realized he hadn't just turned on the speaker option. It was a video call. She was staring straight at FBI Agent Grayson Stone.

Not that they'd ever met in person. That first meeting *should* have occurred in the very near future. But she'd seen pictures of Grayson before. Watched him do a few interviews on TV. So he was definitely recognizable on sight for her.

Grayson smiled at her. "Hello, Ms. Black."

"Luna," she mumbled. Grayson wasn't wearing his typical suit, one of the dark ones that he tended to sport whenever he gave an interview to the media. Instead, he had on a white t-shirt. His thick hair was tousled, as if he'd been raking his fingers through it, and his gaze seemed worried as he assessed her.

"Looks like you won't make our appointment," Grayson noted.

Yep, looked that way. She pressed her palms to the tops of her jean-clad thighs.

"And I see you've met my...associate, Ronan."

"He killed me."

"No, he *pretended* to kill you. A very important distinction. And a necessary one, I'm afraid. You see, I had intel that led me to believe you would never make our meeting. Time was of the extreme essence. You had to vanish. Too many threats were closing in on you." A pause. "Ronan was already close by. He'd been, uh, well, he'd been—"

"Hired to kill you," Ronan told her. "I'd already taken the hit on you."

Her gaze shot to him. Found those incredibly blue eyes on her.

"I'd been hired to kill you," Ronan repeated, as if she'd somehow missed the words the first time. Spoiler, she had not. "Gray reached out, offered more for me to keep you alive, so here we are."

Grayson coughed. "Yes, right. Indeed, here we are. You're off the radar of the bad guys and that gives me time to solidify my case. I have some operatives that have to be recovered—there is much more at stake here than you realize—so as soon as we can close our trap, I will be contacting you again."

Wait, wait, *wait*. "What do you mean, as soon as you can close your trap?" Her right hand shot up to grab the phone. Except when she did that, she wound up putting her fingers on top of Ronan's and that weird *awareness* pulsed through her again.

What was up with that? Why was she attracted to the man who'd been hired to kill her?

No, not kill you. Grayson is telling you that Ronan is here to protect you.

But...Ronan *had* killed other people, hadn't he? And if Grayson hadn't reached out to the hitman...would Ronan have killed her? Would he have gone through with the hit?

"Why are you looking at me that way?" Ronan asked.

"Uh, *hello?*" From Grayson. "How about someone look at *me?* What is the point of a video call if no one is seeing me? And, look, it's the middle of the night. I should be getting beauty rest. Hell, I should not even be on this call because the last thing I want is for anything to be traced to Luna. She needs to stay dark, understand me, Ronan? Darker than the grave."

Like those words weren't chilling. Goosebumps rose on her skin.

"I'll contact you by secure means when it's time to bring her into the light again," Grayson added. "Until then, you stick to the woman like a second skin. She goes nowhere without you. She doesn't get out of your sight. Because one slipup will mean she's dead, for real, and the case I'm working will go down in flames. Those flames will burn way too many innocent people."

That wasn't such a great visual.

"It would be easier to keep her close," Ronan's growling voice returned, "if she wasn't absolutely terrified of me."

Sorry. That happens when I wake up handcuffed to a strange bed.

"How about you reassure her, Gray? People are always reassured by you and that big, bad Federal Agent BS you love to spout. So spout some now. Tell her to stop running. Tell her that she can trust me to make sure she's safe."

She was still looking at Ronan. She should probably look at Agent Stone. So she hauled her eyes down to the phone.

Grayson stared back at her. "Don't run from Ronan. That will just piss him off."

"It did," she mumbled.

"And he'll still catch you. He's good at catching his prey."

Yes, he'd already caught her. Twice.

But he says he saved my life twice so...

"He'll keep you safe. If you trust nothing else, believe that. His job isn't to kill you. It's to—"

"Kill anyone who comes for you," Ronan cut in roughly.

Grayson winced. "No, dammit! The FBI is not ordering any killing! That is not what is happening here. Ms. Black—Luna—Ronan will protect you. I'm working to get a safe location and cover identities ready to go for you two. You'll blend, you'll hide, and before you know it, we'll be putting a seriously dangerous individual away for life. We'll be putting away all the criminals linked to him. Then you'll be

41

safe—for good—and all this will be but a distant memory for you." He flashed a killer smile.

"Memory, nightmare. Whatever." Ronan's clarification.

Her fingers were still on top of his. Had she just been caressing him? Oh, please, say she had not been doing that. Luna whipped her hand back.

"Is there a problem?" Grayson inquired politely.

There were lots of problems. "Why didn't you tell me this was going to happen? You could have given me a head's up that I was going to be—" She broke off. "You could have warned me that Ronan was coming to *kill me*."

"*Fake* kill you," Grayson corrected her. "And there was no time. Also, I didn't exactly have a phone number for you. Our communications have been rather sketchy, yes?"

Yes, fine, they had been.

"But I believed you when you reached out to me. I verified the info you gave me. I know how valuable you are. So when I received word that you were in imminent danger, I took steps to protect you."

"I'm steps. When Gray says steps, he means me." Ronan kept the phone steady in front of her. He held it with his left hand.

She slowly swept her gaze from the phone to his strong wrist. A wrist covered by a big, oddly intimidating looking watch. But, beneath that watch, she could just see... "A snake?"

Ronan grunted.

"I got the feeling you hated snakes. Why do you have a tattoo of something you hate?"

"*Ahem.*" From Grayson. "Focus, people. Wait, just let me sum up, okay? I get that you're running on adrenaline and fear, Luna, but Ronan is the answer to your prayers."

Was that what he was?

42

"A man who will kill to keep you safe," Ronan murmured. "If that doesn't make you feel warm and tingly, what does?"

Her mouth opened.

"*Jeez. Ronan. Be tactful.* Stop terrorizing her. Put yourself in her shoes. Wouldn't you be scared and distrustful? It's a normal reaction. One hundred percent normal."

Grayson was reasonable. A point she'd always noticed about him. But... "You're asking me to trust a hitman."

"I'm asking you to trust a man who has proven to me, time and again, that he will be there when the world explodes and you need a hero."

"Fuck," Ronan groused. "Watch yourself, Gray."

"He saved my ass not too long ago. I thought for sure I was dead, but Ronan was there for me. He hauled me out of hell."

"You do one random act of charity, and someone can't ever forget it." Ronan's hold tightened on the phone. "Be careful what you say, Gray. You're treading on thin ice."

The Fed was acting like Ronan was a good guy. Could a hitman be good?

A federal agent can be good. Maybe a federal agent pretending to be a hitman... Hope had her breath catching in her throat.

"Ronan is lethal. He's conniving. He's probably one of the most cold-blooded assholes you'll ever meet," Grayson said in the next breath.

Okay, so he was *not* the good guy. Her hope fizzled.

"And he's exactly the protector that you need right now. Because the people coming after you? They are the kind who will torture you and make you scream for mercy. A mercy they won't give. Ronan will shield you from them. Ronan will make sure they don't ever touch you."

He'd done that in the street. Stopped three guys who wanted to hurt her.

"Put your trust in him," Grayson urged her. "He'll see you through the dark."

"Happy now?" Ronan wanted to know. "No more running? Gonna actually let me protect you without a fight?"

Happy wasn't quite the right word. "Promise not to drug me again."

"What if there are extenuating circumstances?"

On the phone's screen, she saw Grayson pinch the bridge of his nose.

"Maybe I have to drug you to save your life," Ronan continued. "Hate to promise not to do that when it could, in fact, be saving you."

Her lips pressed together.

"Don't drug her unless it's freaking necessary, Ronan," Grayson fired out. "Protect her. Keep her real identity secret. And *contact me* at the first sign of any trouble. We've already talked too long. I'm disconnecting."

And he did. The screen went dark. She realized they'd been talking on an app. Probably one of the ones designed by Declan Flynn—the billionaire who had so much untraceable tech. The same billionaire who was rumored to be tied to the mob. Was it any wonder a hitman would use that guy's tech?

Ronan shoved the phone back into his pocket. Then his hands went to his hips as he glowered down at her. "I won't drug you unless it's absolutely necessary."

"Thanks so much." She tucked a lock of hair behind her ear.

"And you...no more running? Promise?"

Considering that an FBI agent had basically just told her that Ronan was standing between her and a very real death... "No more running." She sucked in a deep breath. "And I'm sorry if I hurt you."

"What?" His brow scrunched.

"When I pushed you off the bed. I'm sorry if I hurt you."

"You didn't fucking hurt me."

"But you hit the floor hard."

He surged forward and wrapped his tanned fingers around the arms of the chair once more. "You did *not* hurt me. It takes a whole lot for me to hurt."

He was all up in her space again. That sandalwood scent of his surrounded her. He was big and strong and... dammit, sexy. "Stockholm Syndrome?"

He shook his head. "What?"

"It's where you fall for your captor, right? Only I've been with you for just—what, a few hours? I don't think it's supposed to happen this fast."

"What in the hell are you talking about?"

"I find you really sexy." A stark, unsettling truth. "And maybe it's the adrenaline. Maybe it's the fear. Or maybe it's some weird Stockholm thing."

He growled.

She even found that rumbly sound to be sexy. "Why did you kiss me in the street?"

His stare went to her mouth. It seemed to do that, a lot.

"You could have just knocked me out with your drugs. Done that without the kiss." The kiss that was burned in her mind. "Why did you do it?"

"Because I wanted to know how you'd taste."

"And how did I taste?" Why was she asking these

questions? She shook her head. "No, stop. I just—forget I said anything about that. Forget the kiss."

"Hard to do." He kept right on caging her. "Especially since you're about to share my bed."

Luna felt her eyes double in size. *"What?"*

"You and me, sweetheart. We're sharing a bed."

Chapter Four

"THE HANDCUFFS ARE UNNECESSARY."

"Um."

"*Completely* unnecessary." She rolled toward him. Toward him in the bed they shared. She also dramatically lifted and shook the handcuffs. One cuff around her wrist. One cuff around his. "I told you that I wouldn't run again."

"You did say that, yes." He'd killed the lights in the small bedroom. Locked the window. Shut the door. Stripped down to just his pants and boxers.

She had showered. Those muddy feet had needed cleaning. And her clothes had gotten caked with mud and who the hell knew what else. So when she'd come out of the shower, with her hair wet and her cheeks flushed, he'd given her his shirt to wear.

It swallowed her.

He was pretty sure she still had on her bra and panties. Pretty sure because they were both black, and he'd seen the black bra through the white dress shirt.

Sexy as fuck.

He was finding way too many things about his new target to be *sexy as fuck*.

"I get that you're my hitman bodyguard."

"That's not a thing."

"It seems to be. According to Grayson—Agent Stone—it's a thing. It's a thing that you are. And considering that I don't want to be *for real dead*, I promise, I'm not running from you." She inched a little closer.

A bad mistake. The woman had no idea just how badly he wanted to pounce on her.

How did I taste?

Her question rolled through his head again. *Oh, Luna, you tasted like the best damn temptation ever.*

He should not have kissed her on the New Orleans street. He *never* did shit like that. But he'd wanted her. And for once, he hadn't cared about holding back. He'd just wanted to take something for himself.

He'd wanted Luna.

He still did want her.

So very problematic.

"You can uncuff me."

No, he could not. "Glad that you've started to trust me." Fabulous. Really. Maybe it would prevent him from having to throw more snakes into the air. "But I don't trust *you*, princess. You were batting those long lashes at me earlier. Pretty much in this same exact spot. Acting all innocent and weak. Acting like you'd give me *zero* problems, and you'd follow my orders with no hesitation. Then the next thing I know..." His cuffed hand rose and curled under her chin. His eyes had adjusted easily to the darkness. He'd always been able to see well in the dark. "The next thing I know, you're hauling ass into the night. I don't feel like chasing you again. I need sleep. You need sleep. So the cuffs are staying *on*." She would not move without him knowing about it. "Besides, you heard Gray. You go nowhere without me. You don't get out of my sight. Think of the handcuffs as a security measure. They're keeping you extra safe because they're tying you to me."

"They literally are." Disgruntled. "How am I supposed to sleep in bed with you? I'm not used to sharing a bed with anyone."

Well, that was certainly an interesting bit of Luna lore. "Don't have a lover who is wondering where you are, hmmm?"

"No." Soft. "No one is looking for me."

"Not true. Lots of killers *were* looking for you." And he wanted to know more about how Luna Black had wound up in her current situation. *Handcuffed to me.* But Ronan knew he should let her rest. Hell, they should both rest. Tomorrow, he'd have to move them to a new location. Find out what new identities Gray had set up for them. He had no doubt that Gray was spending the night pulling strings and getting emergency plans in place.

A clusterfuck of a situation had exploded on the Fed. And Ronan had bailed his ass out in record time.

"How did a hitman become such good friends with a Fed?"

"What makes you think we're friends? Hate to be the one to tell you, but Gray can be a straight up asshole. He's super manipulative, by the way. Never forget that fun point about him."

"You *are* friends. I can tell. It's the way you say his name. Gray. Not Grayson. And your tone changes when you talk about him. He might be an asshole, but you like him."

Truth be told, Gray was the closest thing to a brother

that Ronan had. *That would be the reason I'm helping his crazy ass.*

Gray had almost died a few months back. He'd been tortured. Held prisoner. Been an absolute bloody mess by the time Ronan got to him. Ronan would not be forgetting that terrible sight any time soon. "He's all right," Ronan muttered.

"He said you'd saved him over and over again. He thinks of you as his friend, too. I don't think a Fed would do that with a soulless killer. Wouldn't vouch for him so willingly. Wouldn't put my fate in his hands."

Uh, oh.

"So what's the real deal, Ronan? Am I supposed to buy that you are some heartless thug? Or is there far more to you than meets the eye?"

Before he could respond, she let out a soft hum then added, "My gut says there is more to you than meets the eye."

Exactly what he didn't need. Someone blowing the cover he'd carefully cultivated over the years. "Ronan Walker is a cold-blooded killer. He's taken out more marks than you can imagine. His name chills the worst scum out there. He gets the job done, and he one hundred percent *doesn't have a heart.* So don't ever make that mistake."

"You just talked about yourself in the third person." A yawn followed her words. "Like he's a character. Like he's not you."

Sonofafucker—

"You don't have to cuff me to you. I'm not running. I want to stay alive, and I believe the best way to do that is to be with you." She tugged on the cuffs. "Let me go?"

"Not happening."

"Then I hope you won't be alarmed when I crawl all over you tonight."

Sweet hell and heaven, do it.

"Like I said, I'm not used to sleeping with anyone, and I tend to...sprawl."

He swallowed. "I'll manage to survive."

Her hand rose, but not to jerk the cuffs again. Instead, her fingers pressed to his jaw. "Thank you."

For saying he'd survive?

"I could be in a grave tonight. Instead, I'm alive and I'm with you, and...I think I'm safe."

"You are." The words were a vow. No matter what else happened, he would keep her safe.

"Is it safe to sleep in a hitman's arms?"

It's safe for you to be with me.

"I think it is." Soft. Low. "I think I'm safe with you." Slurred, as if sleep pulled at her.

She'd been running for so long. Luna had to be exhausted. He should reassure her. That was the right thing to do, wasn't it? Sometimes, he could barely remember what it was like to do the *right* thing.

His lips parted.

Luna rolled away from him. His arm stretched out with her roll. Curled around her. No choice, the cuff pulled him, so he had to take the pose. *Yeah, right. Keep telling yourself that.*

"Please, don't let me be wrong." Even softer from Luna. "I don't want to die."

"I won't let you die, Luna."

She didn't speak again. Her breathing changed, and a few moments later, Ronan knew she'd drifted off to sleep.

He stared into the darkness.

I won't let you die. What an interesting promise for a hitman to make.

* * *

SHE WAS SPRAWLED on top of him.

Ronan opened his eyes. He'd felt her crawling on him. Not like he could sleep through that particular bit of fun. She'd started by inching toward him. Then she'd slid a leg over him. Then an arm. And now, she was fully on him. Their arms were a bit tangled, courtesy of the cuffs, but she still made it on top of him. Her mouth pressed to his neck. Her breath blew lightly against his skin.

He stared up at the ceiling.

Hello, hell.

His dick was super happy with this new position. Mostly because her spread legs were right over his groin, and his dick was shoving hard and eagerly toward her.

And she kept sleeping.

His teeth locked. Carefully, slowly, he pulled her off him. And he put her right next to him in the bed.

She did not stir.

Dead to the world.

* * *

AND SHE WAS BACK on top of him again.

His teeth were clenched so tightly that Ronan's jaw ached. He stared up at the ceiling. He counted to ten, and that counting crap did zero for him and his aching dick.

She rubbed her hips against him.

Sweet mother of—"Luna!" A growl.

Her mouth pressed to his neck. A definite kiss. So she

sprawled *and* she kissed when she slept? Yeah, one hundred percent, the handcuffs had been a terrible, horrible idea.

How was the woman sleeping this heavily? Dammit, was this from the drugs he'd given her? Ronan had never seen a reaction like this to them. She was boneless on top of him, cuddled so close, and he should not be enjoying the way she felt.

But, jeez, she felt *good*.

Again, he lifted her. Put her beside him on the bed. Several inches away from him. Sweat trickled down his temple. His dick was so hard it was almost painful. That happened when the sexiest woman he'd ever met kept rubbing against him all night long.

Stay there, Luna.

He scooted as far away from her as he could.

Closed his eyes.

And started counting again. Right. Like that shit was going to help.

* * *

SHE. Was. On. Top. Of. Him.

Ronan's breath sawed in and out. His heart thundered in his chest. He'd underestimated Luna Black. Clearly, the woman was a master when it came to torture. And he'd faced some sick and twisted torture games over the years.

He'd never given up. Never let the pain beat him.

Her lips pressed to his throat.

Done.

His hands closed around her hips.

She decided to arch against him. Her breasts slid over his chest.

Sonofa—

His teeth ground together. *You fucking win, Luna.* Round one was going to her. Because his aching dick could not take more of this. He lifted her up. Off him. It took a few minutes of fumbling, but he got the cuff off his wrist. He wasn't a complete idiot, though—just a horny bastard— so he locked the cuff around the headboard once again. One cuff secured to the headboard, and one still around her delicate wrist.

Then he grabbed his pillow and surged off the bed. His breath still came too fast, tension held his whole body in a death grip, and Luna...

Just went right on sleeping.

He threw the pillow to the floor. Then he was on the floor, too. The cold, hard floor. Ronan glared up at the ceiling.

And Gray had thought it would be *easy* to watch over her? He could still hear the bastard's words in his head, right *before* Ronan had agreed to take the job.

"She's sweet as can be, Ro. Seriously. A drama teacher. She got caught in a dark and tangled mess and if she doesn't get a hero soon, the woman will be dead. And I'm not talking easy dead. I'm talking pain and screams and a horror that makes her beg for the men to put her out of her misery. You want that for some innocent?"

"I'm not a hero, Gray. You know that shit."

"Yeah, duly noted. But that's why I'm calling you. In this case, I don't need a hero. I need a hitman. And you just so happen to be in the right place at the right time because I know you've already been contacted about her. Luna Black. She needs you."

Gray could always sound so very convincing.

"You fake her death. You keep her out of sight. Easy. Probably the easiest job you'll ever have. I mean, come on,

what kind of trouble could she possibly be? This isn't like Tyler and his Esme. Not like I'm getting you to watch some world-class thief. This case will be a walk in the park."

Utter bullshit.

There was no park, and he sure as hell wasn't walking in it.

Instead, there was Luna. Lovely Luna. Witchy Luna. Gorgeous, sexy Luna...

Who liked to sprawl when she slept.

Night one...utter disaster. He was aching and needy and turned on for the target. He *never* crossed lines on the job. Never had even been tempted. He had never—

"Ronan."

His body jolted. He leapt up.

She was still sleeping. Only she'd rolled back toward his side of the bed. She'd reached out a hand toward his pillow. And in her sleep, she'd just called his name.

His hands fisted at his sides.

* * *

"Is she dead?"

Kurt Vail yanked a hand over his face as he stared at the crowd on Bourbon Street. Dancing and laughing and drinking. The people in New Orleans truly did party all night long. He could sure as fuck go for a drink. *Had* been drinking actually, until the boss called.

And, of course, the boss hadn't bothered with any greeting. He'd jumped straight to business. "She is." He'd seen the deal go down himself. Part of him even wanted to take credit for the kill because there was so much money at stake but...

I know who that big bastard was. Ronan Walker.

He'd seen the snake tattoo on the inside of the guy's left wrist. For a brief moment, when the lighting had been just right. *When he was taking my ass down.*

"How did she die?"

Hunching his shoulders, Kurt turned from the crowd.

"Did she tell you everything she knew before you stopped her cries?"

There hadn't exactly been a lot of cries. The boss wouldn't like to hear that, though. He always went for pain with his prey. "Someone beat me to the punch." Not really his fault. The boss shouldn't have offered so much crazy money for the kill. "Told you not to bring in other hitters." *I could have handled her. My team was ready to go.*

"You were taking too fucking long. I needed to chum up the waters."

His eyes rolled. The boss loved to go shark fishing. Always used stupid sayings about fishing and sharks and... *Hell, I know the real deal, boss. I know you dump bodies out there. I know you take people out on your boat in the Gulf, and you chum up the waters with their own blood.* Kurt swallowed. "Consider them chummed." He personally hated fishing. Got seasick.

"Who took her out?"

"Ronan Walker."

A grunt. "He always gets the job done."

Give the man a giant cookie. "He also beat the crap out of me and my crew."

Laughter. Right. Like he should have expected anything else from the boss.

"Sounds like Ronan."

It sounded to him like the boss was impressed with Ronan. Whatever. "Guy is damn creepy. He kissed her, and he killed her at the same time. Never seen twisted shit like that before."

Ronan had a reputation for up close kills. Yeah, everyone knew that. But...

The woman never even realized what he was doing.

"Where is her body?"

Another sore point for him. "He carried her away. Heard on the police radio, though, that some college kids saw her being dumped into the back of a car." But that was all he knew. "You'll have to talk to your superstar Ronan and find out where he buried the body."

If he'd even buried it. Maybe he'd tossed her into the Mississippi. That had been Kurt's plan, after he'd finished interrogating her. "Thought you wanted answers from her," he muttered. "Ronan didn't exactly give her a chance to talk."

"I wanted *you* to get answers. I don't trust Ronan enough for him to know my business. When it comes to hits, his reputation puts him at the top of the pack. But he doesn't get to learn my secrets. You do. You're family."

Kurt's shoulders squared a bit. The boss wasn't talking some mafia family BS. They were related by blood.

"It would have been helpful to make sure she hadn't talked to any Feds." A sigh drifted over the phone. "And to be sure she hadn't hidden anything that could incriminate me anywhere but...our drama teacher is dead. There is only so much damage that the dead can do." Satisfaction purred in his voice.

Kurt didn't think the dead could do any damage at all. "Time for me to come home?" He was a little sad on that point. He liked New Orleans. The beignets were damn tasty.

"Not yet." The boss had turned thoughtful. "I may have

one more job for you. Stand down until I contact you again."

Hell, yes. *Let the good times roll.* But curiosity pulled at him. "What's the other job?"

"You may need to kill Ronan Walker."

The phone fell from his fingers. And fear slithered down his spine.

Chapter Five

SHE WOKE UP HANDCUFFED, AGAIN.

When her eyes opened, the first thing that Luna saw was the cuff around her wrist. Her breath blew out on a heavy exhale. Right, because the events of last night had not just been some very, very bad dream. Unfortunately. She was, in fact, cuffed in a hitman's bed.

And maybe I had some slightly sexual dreams about the hitman last night. And his handcuffs...

Slightly sexual?

Ahem. Luna swallowed. She tugged on the cuffs. "Uh, Ro—" Her voice broke off because she'd just realized that the other cuff was hooked to the brass headboard. Not to Ronan. Her body twisted and heaved, and she realized that she was alone in the big bed. Alone, cuffed, and suddenly terrified.

He left me cuffed in the bed? "Ronan!" Luna shouted.

His head popped up beside the bed. Wincing, he demanded, "What?"

She blinked. She'd sat up in the bed but now she hunched over the side to better see Ronan as he glowered at her from his position on the floor. "What are you doing down there?" Luna asked him.

He kept glowering. "Not here by choice, princess. Not by choice."

Well, sure he was there by choice. Not like she'd made the man sleep on the floor, and that certainly appeared to be exactly what he'd done. "Why did you sleep on the floor? I thought you were staying in the bed with me."

His dark hair was tousled, as if he'd raked his fingers through it over and over again. His eyes burned, but he had a slightly haggard—maybe even hungry—look about him as he pinned her with his gaze. "Staying in bed with you isn't exactly easy."

Her cheeks stung with embarrassment. Those words sure sounded like an insult.

"You...*sprawl*."

Her fingers plucked at the sheet. It had fallen near her waist. "I warned you about that tendency."

He shot to his feet. At the move, her head whipped up as she straightened, and suddenly, his bare chest and abs were basically right in front of her face. *Oh, there is no basically about it.* That twelve pack of his was right there.

"Just how often do you work out?" she whispered.

His hands went to his hips. "You crawled on me three times last night."

Another light pluck at the sheet by her restless fingers. "I don't remember that. Sorry?"

"You licked my neck."

She had *not*. Had she? "I tend to be a heavy sleeper."

"You rubbed those tight nipples of yours against me over and over again."

Her cheeks weren't stinging. They were flaming. So hot that she was surprised smoke didn't start drifting in the air around her. Luna cleared her throat. "In my defense, you did drug me, so I was probably sleeping even deeper than I normally do."

"You rocked against my dick."

She bit her lower lip. For a moment, she considered just yanking that sheet up over her head. But hiding wouldn't help things. "I didn't." *Please, say I didn't.*

"You *did*. And then you *moaned* my name."

Considering the snippets of her, ah, sexual dreams that she recalled, that bit of news certainly tracked. "Again, I was drugged."

His expression turned even more savage. "You do that shit with everyone you sleep with?"

A shake of her head. "Told you, I don't sleep with many people."

"Do you *fuck* many people?"

Okay, he'd just gotten extra growly. And very, very personal. "I'm not sure what's happening right now. I would just like to point out that I was drugged by you—"

"You've pointed that out. Noted. Twice noted. No, *thrice*."

Thrice? She soldiered on. "I was sleeping so, clearly, I was not responsible for my actions and I—" Her shoulders dropped. "Why bother having pride with your hitman?"

"*What?*"

"I'm not *fucking* anyone. Haven't for a very long time. That's part of my whole 'Should-have-been-living-before-dying' new mantra, by the way. Another part is that maybe I should just say what I think and feel more often. I was always holding back before. Biting my lip." Which she had literally just been doing. *Break the habit.* "I was always worrying about embarrassing myself or saying the wrong thing." A trickle of laughter escaped her throat. "Don't really see how things can get more embarrassing than this. My captor fled the bed because he didn't want me touching him."

"I'm *not* your captor."

"Fine, my hitman fled the bed because—"

"Consider me your protector, got it?" And his hands weren't on his hips any longer. They were on the bed. Super close to her.

"I want you," Luna blurted those words. "And I had sexy dreams about you so if I was moaning and rubbing, I, uh, I'm sorry. I won't do it again." The moaning and rubbing, anyway. She'd try to avoid those particular acts. As for her dreams? Not like a woman could control her dreams.

He blinked. Ronan had lowered his face so that it was right in front of hers. He had some incredibly thick, dark lashes. And with that beard covering his hard jaw...

Someone wakes up extra sexy in the morning.

"You want me," he said.

She nodded.

"You want to *fuck* me?"

She hadn't said she wanted the man to play cards with her. So, yes. Fucking. "That's probably a bad idea, isn't it?" Hesitant. Husky.

"You have no idea how bad." One of his hands rose to curl under her chin. "This the Stockholm thing again?"

"What?" Then she shook her head. "No, I-I wanted you before. Before I knew you were a hitman and I—*this is a bad idea.* I've never had a one-night stand in my life, and you are not a safe lover."

"I am not a safe lover," he repeated. His eyes were on her mouth. "I will absolutely devour you."

Her sex squeezed. In a good way. A way that had her yearning because maybe all the talk about women falling for bad guys was actually true. Ronan was big and bold and dangerous and so sexy.

It's because of your hot dreams. Settle down. You don't want to make a mistake that you'll regret.

"I will fuck you until you scream, Luna. Until you are begging for release. Then I'll have you coming and begging for more."

She couldn't even think of a response to those words. Except maybe...*yes, sounds like a great plan.* Because she'd never been fucked until she was begging for more. Was that even possible? Did that seriously happen with people? "Sounds fantastic." A quick sigh. "Let's do that."

His mouth rushed toward hers. His lips pressed against her mouth. And—

Ringing. Loud. Sudden.

She jerked.

He swore. And pulled back. "Hold the fucking thought."

Hold the thought about fucking? Sure, right. She could do that. She also yanked up the sheet while he turned toward the nightstand and picked up a phone. He stared at the screen, and whoever the caller was—well, Ronan didn't like the person. His face darkened before he swiped his finger over the screen and put the phone to his ear. "What the hell do you want?" he growled.

Well, Ronan is certainly friendly to his early morning callers.

"I finished the job last night," he added, voice rumbly and deep. "Unless you're calling to offer me a bonus, don't interrupt my beauty sleep."

But he hadn't been sleeping. He'd been about to kiss her. And...*Wait. Back up. I was the job last night.*

She inched the covers a wee bit higher.

He angled toward her as his gaze locked onto hers. "Hell, yes, she's dead."

Her heart squeezed.

"How did I do it? A quick push of too many drugs in her system, and she collapsed in my arms. Died with a smile on her face."

No, she had not. Goosebumps rose onto her arms as she realized just how easy it would have been for Ronan to actually kill her. If he'd given her different drugs, she would be dead right now.

She inched a bit away from him.

His left hand flew out and curled around her arm. He shook his head once. Hard. *No.*

Right. Not like she *could* go anywhere. On account of the handcuffs. The handcuffs had to go. Permanently.

"Pretty sure there were witnesses," he added, sounding bored. "Some idiots who thought they'd get the bounty. Three of them were there. We fought. I kicked their asses." Simple statement. "No one takes *my* bounty."

His expression had hardened. A wave of fear snaked through her.

"I'll expect payment to hit my account today. If it doesn't, we'll have a problem." Not so bored. More menacing.

He's getting paid for my murder. And she'd just asked the guy to fuck her. Obviously, she was having issues.

But the Fed trusts Ronan. There is more going on here than meets the eye. He's not who I think.

Or maybe she just hoped he wasn't.

I'm alive. If he was the bad guy, I would be dead.

"You want *what?*" Ronan demanded. And his hand snaked down so that he was suddenly holding her hand. "A finger?"

Her hand jerked in his grasp.

He tightened his hold.

"You want me to send you a freaking finger from her as proof that she's dead?"

Now she was the one to shake her head. Over and over and over again.

"*Not* happening," Ronan snarled.

Her breath expelled in a rush of relief as her shoulders slumped.

"Why? Why is it not happening?" A rough laugh escaped him. "Because the alligators have already taken care of her body. I went to a cabin in the bayou—friend of mine has the place—and I dumped her last night. She sank fast, and the gators were closing in as I watched. There are no fingers left. There is *nothing* left of her. Luna Black is gone." A brief pause. "And I expect my payment. It had better be in my account by noon, or believe me when I say, there will be hell to pay."

She believed him. He sounded so convincing. Luna truly thought there would be hell to pay. But...

He also sounds so convincing when he says I'm dead. Even though she was sitting and breathing right in front of him.

Ronan hung up the phone. He tossed it back on the nightstand. Then without a word, he went to work unlocking the cuff. The soft *snick* as the handcuff opened seemed extra loud in the suddenly very quiet room.

She kept holding the sheet. Sitting in the bed. Staring at him.

"Still want to fuck me?" Brutal. Guttural.

Luna flinched. "You're a very good liar."

He laughed. The sound was rough and deep and chilling all at the same time.

65

She rose onto her knees. "You *are* a good liar. You lie perfectly."

His lips twisted in a humorless smile.

Her stomach also twisted, but she still forced out the words she had to say. "Is that what makes you such a good undercover operative for the FBI? Your ability to lie? Because that's what you are, isn't it? You're a Fed. You work with Grayson Stone. You're a Fed, not a killer. You're only pretending to be a hitman."

* * *

NO ONE THREATENS ME.

Marcus Constantine Aeros exhaled slowly. He hadn't made it to this position in life just so some asshole thug could threaten him.

And I'm not about to lose everything I've worked to achieve because of some middle school drama teacher. Hell, no.

He dialed Kurt. The phone rang once. Twice. Three times—

"Hello?" Slurred. Sleepy.

"Wake your lazy ass up," Marcus snapped. "You're killing Ronan Walker today."

"What?" More alert.

The dumbass had probably stayed out drinking past dawn on Bourbon Street. If the prick wasn't his cousin...

But if you can't give your dirty work to family, then who can you give it to? "I have an address for you." Not exactly a spot-on address. More like a radius. A search field. Because while he'd been talking to Ronan, he'd been using a new bit of tech to trace the call. Super fast and—*supposedly*—very,

very accurate, the tech had given him a small radius for Ronan's location.

Just like the bastard said, he's in the bayou.

A perfect place for the prick to die.

"Y-you want me to kill him...*now?*"

"I know where he is now." Mostly. Hard to say for sure because it was a dot in the fucking bayou. *Kurt can figure this shit out.* "He won't expect an attack now. You move quickly. You eliminate him. Then you get your ass back here."

"He took out three of us last night. I'm gonna need to get backup. Those bozos from last night left me, so I'm gonna need to find men with backbones."

"There is no time for a team. You move and you move *now*. It's called element of surprise for a reason." He texted the location intel.

Silence on the other end of the line.

"Yeah, um, trying to put that in my phone and get directions," Kurt finally mumbled. "But it's just showing a spot in the middle of nowhere. Like, no roads. Nothing. You sure this is right?"

"I'm sure that if you don't find Ronan Walker and kill him, then *you'll* be the dead one. Figure. This. Shit. Out." He hung up.

No one threatens me. Ronan Walker was dead. He would soon be joining Luna Black in the bayou as bait for the gators.

Another problem marked off his list.

Chapter Six

THE WATER FROM THE SHOWER POUNDED DOWN JUST beyond the closed bathroom door. Ronan glared at the door even as Luna's words played through his head again.

You're only pretending to be a hitman.

No shit. If he hadn't been pretending, she would be dead.

Except...

She thinks I'm a Fed. That I've been working undercover this whole time. And the reason why she thought that? Because Gray had opened his big-ass mouth and talked about how Ronan had helped him, over and over again. Hell. Ronan had known that would be problematic the instant Gray had uttered those unfortunate words. Gray had always been the chattiest bastard in their group.

Now Luna knew the biggest secret that he kept. And if she told the wrong person...

I'll be the dead one.

He stalked toward the bathroom door. Glanced at his watch. Okay, seriously, enough. How long did she intend to stay in the shower? His hand lifted and rapped against the door.

Nothing.

Just the thunder of the shower.

Suspicion curled in his gut. Surely, she wouldn't. The woman would *not* leave the shower water pouring in an attempt to trick him as she fled through the narrow bathroom window. Surely...not. "Luna?" Another pound with his fist. "Luna!"

Shit. She just might have. And I was so blindsided by her charge that I didn't plan for this screwup. He grabbed the knob of the door, twisted it, and threw the door open. "Dammit, Luna—"

"*Ah!*" Luna's scream.

Her scream as she spun in the narrow shower with the glass door and stared at him, wide-eyed. One hand rose to try and cover her breasts. Another dipped down to the V between her legs. The water poured over her. Steam drifted in the air. And, sonofafucker, the woman was the sexiest thing he'd ever seen. He took a step toward her.

"What are you doing?" Luna cried. She kept her hands in place. They did not hide much. "You can't just bust in here! I'm naked!"

Yes. Beautifully naked. And he was gaping. And his dick was way too hard and ready. And this was *not* what any gentleman would do. The problem was that Ronan had not been a gentleman in a long time. "Thought you'd run." Rasped.

"What?" She did a little hop in the shower as the water cascaded over her body. That wonderful body. "And could you look *up*?"

His gaze shot up. "Thought you'd run," Ronan repeated. Rougher. Louder. Would that shower be big enough to hold them both? Because she'd very clearly told him that she wanted him, and he…

Yes, he wanted her. So badly that his whole body ached.

He'd thought the night had been torture. It was nothing compared to seeing her wet, naked body. And knowing that the only thing that separated them? That thin piece of glass.

"I'm naked, Ronan."

Yes. Indeed. One hundred percent naked. And wet. And sexy.

"I'm not running anywhere naked. Grayson said you were my best bet of staying in the land of the living. I don't plan on trying to escape from you."

"You can't." Why was speaking so hard? He pulled in a breath. "You can't escape. I'd just find you."

"I'm *naked*."

Again, yes. Indeed.

"Be a gentleman. Go out. Shut the door."

Yes. He should do that. He actually even managed to take one whole step back. But then he had to warn her, "I'm not a gentleman." Something she should have already realized. Probably when he drugged her. Or handcuffed her.

Their gazes held.

Her lips parted.

Before he gave in to the savage need slicing through him, Ronan finally dragged his ass out of the bathroom. He hauled the door shut. Whirled. Marched the hell out of the bedroom and through the cabin and out onto the porch where he sucked in deep gulps of air because holy hell, the lust that held him in its grip was red-hot. He could not ever remember wanting someone so badly.

She's a target. A target. You are not supposed to cross that line with her. This is just business. His head understood this vital bit of information. His dick? Not so much. But his dick had never exactly been a thinker.

Ronan sucked in another deep, bracing breath. The sunlight trickled through the trees around the property, and he could hear the call of a dozen different insects, as well as the deeper, harder croaks of the alligators that waited nearby.

He still wore the pants he'd had on yesterday. Shoes, socks. An old, black shirt that had been left behind in the cabin. She'd taken *his* white dress shirt into the bathroom. She'd been wearing the damn thing and looking sexy as fuck as he talked on the phone.

The bastard wanted me to cut off her finger and send it to him.

Yeah, that tracked with some of the whispers he'd heard about Marcus Constantine Aeros. The guy was rumored to be cold-blooded as hell. Untouchable. And as sadistic as they came. But the whole finger collecting business? That reeked of being a trophy routine. Did the guy always keep mementos of his kills? If so, that would be one interesting bit of news to pass along to Gray. Because if they could find the bastard's stash, they would be able to tie him to so many crimes.

And finally nail his ass to the wall.

Provided, of course, they could find the stash. In Ronan's experience, the perps like Marcus always kept their precious mementos tucked away in an ever-so-secret spot.

The faint growl of an approaching engine had Ronan tensing. His head tilted toward the sound. Definitely a car. One coming his way.

His borrowed cabin was the only one in this particular area of the bayou. He certainly hadn't thought any visitors would be coming his way...

Fuck.

Was he really going to have to start his day by killing some bastard?

The growl of the engine grew louder.

Sure looks that way.

* * *

IT WAS Kurt's lucky fucking day. And normally, he didn't have lucky days. He'd never been lucky, or he wouldn't be working for his prick of a cousin now. *He'd* be the one calling the shots, instead of following orders and cleaning up the messes that Marcus left behind. Marcus was truly a messy, bloody bastard.

But this time, luck was on his side. That beautiful, sweet lady.

Because he'd been driving into the freaking swamp or bayou or whatever the hell it was, he'd been cursing and grumbling and wiping sleep from his eyes and thinking he'd never find Ronan Walker's hiding spot and then...like a gift from above...

He'd spotted the other car in front of him. Just a quick glint of light on metal as the sunlight hit the vehicle before it turned. But, he'd seen it, and he'd decided to follow the bastard. Why not?

Not like there were a ton of options out there, and he'd wondered if maybe he'd just gotten lucky.

So he stayed far back. He tightened his grip on the steering wheel, and when the other vehicle stopped near a ramshackle cabin, he stopped, too. Stopped far enough away that he wouldn't be spotted by the other driver.

"Holy fuck," Kurt breathed. He'd just hit pay dirt. Because according to the news story he'd picked up, some frat guys had seen Ronan Walker dump Luna Black's body into the trunk of a dark BMW.

A dark BMW was partially hidden under the nearby slope of a willow tree. He could see it from his tucked away position.

My lucky day.

Only...

The driver he'd been following climbed from his vehicle while Kurt continued to watch and wait. *That bastard is big and scary and...hold up. Is he heading right for my prey?* "Shit," he whispered. Was this one of Ronan's buddies? Because Kurt had come alone, on the boss's orders.

He was either staring at one of Ronan's friends—and that would be highly problematic or...

Or are you also someone who came to eliminate the prick that is Ronan Walker?

Kurt pulled out his gun. The weight felt good in his hands.

Time to kill some bastards and get back to Bourbon Street. He'd had one hell of a time the night before. Friend of Ronan's or foe, well, Kurt would just kill the big bastard. Didn't matter how big you were, a bullet to the back of the head would take you right out. And Kurt did enjoy sneaking up on his prey.

* * *

LUNA HAD no choice but to put back on her black bra and panties—and Ronan's oversized shirt. It was either wear the same items or try to use the thread-bare towel to cover herself as she went out and faced off with her new guard.

She'd gone with the borrowed shirt over the towel. At least the shirt provided more coverage.

73

Her wet hair trailed over her shoulders as she pulled open the bathroom door.

He looked like he wanted to eat me alive.

Yes, it had been steamy in the bathroom, but there had been no mistaking the expression on Ronan's face and in his bright gaze. He'd wanted her.

Meanwhile, she didn't know what to do about the needs and emotions swirling inside of her.

Just tell me that you're a Fed. Don't let me think I'm lusting after someone who is evil in his core. Her instincts told her that she was right about him. And Grayson had vouched for Ronan, so that had to mean he was good. Or at least, it had to mean that Ronan wasn't the devil incarnate.

The hardwood floor squeaked beneath her bare feet. "Ronan?" A little too weak. She cleared her throat and tried again. "Ronan, we need to talk." Maybe she should just put on her muddy clothes from the night before. Because walking around just in his shirt made her feel all sorts of vulnerable and unsteady on the inside.

He wasn't in the small bedroom. She walked out, headed into the little den and—still no Ronan. Her hands went to her hips as she turned her head and glanced toward the connecting kitchen.

Again, no Ronan.

She was the only one in the cabin. After keeping her handcuffed, the guy had run out on her? Now? Not cool. She swung for the front door. Took a step toward it.

The door flew open.

Only it wasn't Ronan standing there.

A huge bear of a guy with jet-black hair and a face cut from stone filled the threshold. His shoulders brushed the doorframe, and his hazel eyes glittered as they narrowed on her. He wore all black, and the color choice just made him look extra intimidating. As if he needed any help in the *extra* department.

The fact that he was blocking her exit? *Terrifying*.

And the fact that Ronan wasn't around? *So very bad*.

The stranger's gaze raked her, and, if possible, his expression hardened even more.

Then the guy took a menacing step toward her.

"Ronan!" His name tore from her as a high-pitched scream because what if this man had done something to Ronan? What if he'd killed Ronan while she'd been in the shower? What if this scary stranger was someone else who'd been sent to murder her? *"Ronan!"*

At her cries, the stranger lunged for her. She grabbed a lamp from the nearby table—one that had antlers as its base —and she threw it at the charging man. Then she whirled and tried to dart back to the bedroom. Maybe she could escape through the window in that room. Ronan had gotten out that way the previous night. She could do the same thing. If she could just make it there.

Only, she didn't make it to the bedroom. Because the big guy caught her. He flipped her around and pinned her against a wall. He—

He had a knife at *his* throat.

"Let her the fuck go," Ronan rasped. Because Ronan was standing behind the stranger. Ronan had a knife at the man's throat.

Ronan was still alive. Her breath shuddered out, and a wide smile slid over her face. "I am so glad you're alive."

The stranger blinked. He also didn't let her go, despite the fact that there was a knife at his throat.

"Is that any way to treat a friend? Where are your manners?" A deep, dark rumble from the man who held her. The man with a knife at his jugular. "Here I am, trying to help out, and you decide to play with knives. Bad form, Ronan. Bad."

Wait, wait, wait. Was this terrifying stranger a *friend* of Ronan's?

"Drop the knife," he ordered, "and I'll let your girlfriend go."

"You let her the fuck go," Ronan snapped back, "because otherwise—friend or no friend—we will have a problem."

"Like that, huh? I did wonder, especially when I realized the shirt she was wearing had to be yours. Got to say, I'm surprised at you. Didn't think you were the type to screw a witness—"

He was hauled from her before he could finish. Fast. Jerked away. Shoved several feet, and suddenly Ronan's broad back was in front of her. She pressed onto her toes so she could peek over his shoulders.

"Do not *start* with me right now, Kane." Ronan pointed at the other man. *Kane.* "What in the hell are you doing here? *How* are you here?"

"I'm here—obviously—to help. Because I am a helper." His giant hands spread in the air before falling back to his sides. "As to the how, well, I drove, of course. Not like I flew in on my angel wings."

Ronan growled.

Kane smiled. "It's good to see you, too, old buddy."

Her hands pressed to the back of Ronan's shoulders. "I thought he'd killed you," she murmured.

He stiffened beneath her touch, then whirled toward her. And instead of her hands being on his shoulders, they were now pressed on his chest.

"Thought he was working for..." A swift inhale as her heart raced hard in her chest. "Marcus." His image popped into her head when she said his name, and a shiver skated over her body. "Thought he'd killed you and was coming for me next."

"The day Kane gets the drop on me is the day that will never hap—*Hell*." Ronan's words ended in an angry exclamation because there was a knife now at his throat.

Kane whistled. "What day won't happen? Because I think I just—"

In a blink, the knife was gone. Ronan twisted around, yanked at Kane's wrist, and sent the knife clattering to the floor. Now the two men were eye to eye, glaring and it was just—

"*Stop!*" Her sharp cry. She shoved between them. "You're not enemies." At least, that was what she was getting from the scene and their weird conversation. "You're...friends?" Something like that. "Could we be sane a moment and stop with the knife play? Not a big fan. Super not. I've had enough stitches and don't want more, thanks so much."

The men were much taller than her, so they glared at each other easily over Luna, but, after a tense moment, Kane stepped back. He rolled his shoulders. Then he winked at Ronan. "Got the drop on you."

"Yes, you sneaky sonofafucker, you did."

Kane laughed. "Also got a change of clothes for you in the car." His gaze dipped over Luna. "Clothes for you both because though she looks sexy as hell, I'm thinking she can't go out in that shirt. She'll attract way too much attention."

Ronan growled. Again. A deep, rumbling, primitive sound.

Kane shook his head. "Not hitting on her. Relax. Just stating a fact. You're the one who has been screwing her, not me. So much for that code of yours, huh, Ronan? Not getting involved? Never being tempted? Such a bunch of BS. What was it? One night with her, and you were a goner?"

She felt her cheeks burn. "Nothing happened last night between me and Ronan." She still had one hand on his chest. She dropped the hand as if it had been burned. "I had to wear his shirt because when I ran from him, he tackled me, and I hit the mud. My clothes were ruined."

"You...ran from him." Kane's forehead scrunched.

"I thought he was going to kill me. And he'd handcuffed me to his bed."

Kane choked. His eyes also flared wide.

"But he only tackled me because I think I was about to step on a snake. I wasn't looking down." She'd been looking up, searching for lights. "But he caught the snake and threw it away before it could bite me."

Now Kane's jaw dropped. His gaze slammed toward Ronan. "You *willingly* touched a snake?"

"It was going to bite her," Ronan gritted out. "Couldn't let that happen. The job is to keep her alive."

"Uh, huh." Kane had snapped his jaw closed. "Yep, that's what you do. Keep people alive. Check."

Enough of this. She squared off with Kane. "You're a Fed?" He had to be. Just like Grayson. Just like she suspected Ronan was.

But Kane laughed. In her face.

Rather rudely.

"Oh, hell, no." More booming laughter from Kane. "You think I could survive wearing those shitty suits and stiff shoes? Nah. Not the life for me. I'm freelance. Strictly freelance."

Not reassuring. "How exactly do you know Grayson and Ronan?"

"Semper Fi," he murmured.

Semper Fi. She knew that phrase. "You're a Marine?"

"Former. Strictly civilian these days. Or, mostly civilian." His killer smile—a toothy tiger's smile—came and went. "Can't really say more than that. Classified intel and all."

So that was a bit scary to know. But if he was working classified cases and he was tight with Ronan and Grayson... she whirled back for Ronan. "You're a good guy!"

He blinked.

"Semper Fi." A nod from her. "That means *always faithful*, doesn't it? And you keep saving me. Protecting me. Grayson has you on guard duty." A wide smile spread over her own face. "I didn't want to fuck the bad guy. I wanted to fuck the hero." She threw her arms around him and held on tightly. "That is so reassuring."

He didn't hug her back. He did tense, and, she heard him tell Kane, "Look what the hell you've done."

Kane's laughter spilled from him again just as...

Ronan caught her arms. "I am *not* the good guy."

She disagreed. "I'm living and breathing, and you're protecting me. That makes you good in my book."

"Sonofafucker, it damn well does *not*. It makes me—*gun!*" A bellow.

Then Ronan lifted her up and tossed her through the air. She landed on the couch with a bounce, and he barreled down on top of her.

Gunfire erupted.

Chapter Seven

BOOM. BOOM. TWO FAST AND HARD BLASTS. LUNA screamed because she hadn't even sensed the threat. She'd been too focused on Ronan and Kane.

"*Too distracted,*" Ronan rasped. "Didn't see the bastard coming." His hand slid under the couch.

"You didn't kill her!" A shout. "You lying bastard! I saw her! She's supposed to be dead, but she's alive and she's hugging you—the boss is gonna lose his mind when I tell him!"

She stared up at Ronan, utterly horrified. So scared her body trembled.

His nostrils flared. And...

"*Drop the weapon!*" A clipped order that came from Kane.

Only that order was immediately followed by gunfire, not by the sound of a gun being dropped.

She didn't even have a chance to scream again because in that same instant, Ronan's hand flew up from beneath the couch. He had a gun gripped in his hand, and he lunged off her.

"Stay down!" Ronan barked.

And he leapt away from the couch.

More gunfire erupted.

He'd raised his weapon, and he fired, too, and—

Silence. Sudden and deafening in its intensity. Luna realized that she'd yanked her hands over her ears. Her heart drummed frantically in her chest. She waited, certain that more gunfire would come. Only, it didn't.

"You're hit." From Ronan.

Her hands lowered. Was it safe to get off the couch?

"Flesh wound." Kane's flat voice. "I'll recover." A pause. "He won't."

He won't.

"That was a damn fast shot, Ronan," Kane added.

Her breath sawed in and out. "Ronan?"

"Fucking hell." His disgusted voice.

"He was going to shoot you. There was no choice. He would have killed you—and her. You had to fire." Kane's voice still held no emotion. "And it's not like the guy could have been allowed to leave. Not after he spotted Luna. He would have run back to his boss and told him that your girl was still alive."

She twisted on the couch. "Is it safe now?"

"You don't want to see this," Ronan told her. "Stay down."

"That's not an answer to whether or not it's safe." She crawled toward the side of the couch. "Is it safe?"

"Yes." But the answer didn't come from Ronan. It was Kane who responded.

She inched off the couch. Turned toward the men. Drew up short as she sucked in a sharp breath.

One man was on the floor. Blood covered his chest. A

gun rested in his outstretched hand, and his head was angled toward her.

So much blood.

It was just like another scene. Another time. And Luna found that she was reacting the same way. Freezing.

I walked into Marcus's office. He had a gun in his hand and a dead man in front of him. So silly. So ridiculous. I was supposed to surprise him with a song and a delivery. Stupid singing telegram business that I thought would be a fun side hustle. Only...

Only it hadn't been fun.

Her lips pressed tightly together to hold back the cry that wanted to come from her. Just as she'd done in Marcus's office. Just as she'd stifled her terrified cries even as tears streamed down her face because...

She'd known the dead man in Marcus's office. He'd been her friend. Noah. He'd been the one who hired her to come and sing for the boss on Marcus's birthday.

And he'd been dead. And there'd been so much blood. Marcus had walked toward him and kicked Noah's body even as she'd stood in the doorway with the bright balloons and flowers and...

Ronan walked toward the body in the cabin. He had his gun gripped in his hand. He knelt. Reached out a hand and touched the other man's throat. Ronan's jaw clenched. "Why the hell did you have to follow me out here?" Ronan snarled to the fallen figure. "I left you alive in New Orleans."

Alive in New Orleans. Her gaze was on the dead man's face. Yes, yes, she knew him. He'd been one of the three attackers who came at her on the street. The one who'd worn the mask. After Ronan had fought him in the street, the man had lost the mask. She'd seen his face so very briefly. Briefly, but the memory was burned in her mind. Thin face, an off-center nose. Not nearly as scary as she'd imagined when he still had on the mask. "He wanted to slice me up," she managed.

Ronan rose but kept staring at the body. "Told him to stay out of my way." A disgusted shake of his head. "Told him if he didn't, he'd be the dead one. Bastard should have listened to me."

Ronan had just killed a man.

To save his friend...to save himself...or to save...me?

Kane advanced to Ronan's side. A Kane who had blood streaming down his left shoulder but didn't even seem to notice his own wound. "It was you or him, Ronan. He was the one who came in with guns blazing." A grimace. "And if you hadn't killed him, what do you think would have happened to her?" He jerked his right thumb in Luna's direction.

Ronan's gaze instantly flew to Luna.

And she remembered another time...

I didn't make a sound. I had my mouth pressed closed as tightly as I could to hold back any cries. I was going to back away. To get out of that office. To run as far and as fast as I could.

But a balloon had popped. A silly balloon. A silly job. A silly dream. In an instant, Marcus had yanked his gun up and aimed it at her and there had been so much rage in his eyes. She'd known that he was going to fire that weapon at her. She'd let go of the balloons and they'd flown in front of her, and he'd shot his gun, and the balloons had all erupted and there had been confetti and latex everywhere and she'd run as fast as she could.

She hadn't stopped running.

Not until Ronan had killed her.

But as she stared at Ronan, as she looked into his eyes, there was no rage staring back at her. Instead—

Pain. Sadness.

She crept toward him. "Ronan?"

All emotion vanished with his blink. "We have to get you the hell out of here."

But she shook her head. "We have to get help!" They needed to call nine-one-one. She'd done that in Atlanta. Just in case Noah had still been alive. There had been so much blood, but maybe...maybe—or at least, that had been her desperate thought. *Maybe Noah is still alive.* She'd fled and called for help as soon as she made it to the shelter of an alley. Only there had been no body for the EMTs to find when they arrived. Marcus had already cleaned up the scene.

Just the first step in covering his tracks.

Ronan reached out for her. "You can't help a dead man."

She shoved past him and grabbed for Kane. "I meant we had to help your *friend!*" The one who was bleeding everywhere.

Kane blinked at her. Then smiled. "You're worried about me? That is sweet."

There was a whole lot of blood streaming down his arm. "You need a hospital."

"Nah. I can stitch myself up."

She remembered almost fainting when the needle had first hit her skin. The vet hadn't numbed anything. But Kane was acting like he handled needles and traumatic injuries all the time. "Who are you?" she asked him. Her hands lifted so she could apply pressure to his wound.

But he stepped back. "Kane Harte. And it really is just a flesh wound. Had injuries a million times worse, and they didn't even slow me down." Kane's gaze tracked to Ronan. "You need to take your lady out of here."

Ronan's arm curled around her stomach as he hauled her back against him. "Working on it, but she decided to play Florence Nightingale to you."

She shoved at his hold. "Your friend is *hurt*. We don't leave hurt friends. Or at least, we shouldn't." *I ran and left Noah. No one ever found his body. Now I'm still running.*

Kane threw a set of keys at Ronan. Ronan held her with his right arm still locked around her stomach and caught the keys with his left hand.

"My ride is outside and waiting," Kane informed Ronan. "Got clothes for you and your charge in the back. Also have an envelope in the glove box that has new identities and a destination for you two. Haul ass, and I'll handle clean up here."

Haul ass? "Uh, no," she said. "We are not leaving you with a dead body. We are—*Ronan!*" He'd lifted her off her feet and was carrying her toward the door. "Ronan, stop! Your friend needs our help!" She heaved and twisted in his hold as her gaze remained on Kane. A Kane who seemed to be fighting a grin as he bled.

"The dead asshole on the floor has *friends*, too," Ronan groused. But he did pause on exiting the cabin. His grip remained firm around her as her feet dangled. "Or have you forgotten about the two bozos who were with him last night? I have to get you to safety. That's the priority. Keeping that sweet ass alive. Remember? Priority one. Now, Kane, get moving. You're coming with us, and we'll drop you off when its safe."

"Nope. I'm not going anywhere. Someone has to stay behind and make sure any other gun-happy jerks get what they deserve." He smiled. Then he bent to rifle through the dead man's pockets. Like that was a normal thing. The body was still warm. Also really wet, uh, bloody.

Nausea rolled through her belly.

Kane plucked out a wallet and flipped it open. "Kurt Vail of Atlanta, Georgia. Shocking surprise that he's from Atlanta, am I right?"

No, it was not shocking.

"Didn't hear the prick arrive." Kane tucked the wallet into his own pocket. He arched a brow at Ronan. "Did you?"

"Just heard the growl of your car. Thinking he might have come in at the same time. Would have disguised the sound of his arrival better."

"Shit." Now Kane truly looked pained. "You think he tailed me?"

She felt Ronan's shrug. "Got a call from his boss earlier. The 'Atlanta Bachelor of the Year' wanted me to cut off one of Luna's fingers and send it to him as proof that she was dead."

Weird fact. Marcus had actually been the "Bachelor of the Year"—a title given by one of the high society magazines in Atlanta.

"Told the prick I was in the bayou. Should have realized he was trying to track me with the call. Call me crazy, but I don't think Marcus intends to pay my bill."

Her feet still dangled. "Put me down."

Slowly, he did. But Ronan did not let her go. "Maybe he got an idea of the location from one of those damn new tracers out there."

"Declan Flynn's tech." Annoyance rumbled from Kane. "And then the dead dick on the floor might have spotted me coming in. Not like there is a ton of traffic out here. Hell, Ronan, I should have seen the tail. My fuck up. Not normal at all for me." The blood kept streaming down his arm. "I'm sorry." Stark.

"Uh. Excuse me." Luna cleared her throat. "You're bleeding everywhere. Maybe apologize less and stop the blood flow more?"

"Barely a scratch." He didn't look at his arm. His attention was squarely on Luna and Ronan. "Before you take her out, I need to check the scene first to make sure those other two goons you mentioned aren't lurking around." And then he just—he rushed outside. Blew right past them. As if he wasn't bleeding and needed medical care.

"Let me go," Luna snapped as she heaved against Ronan yet again.

"No," Ronan returned. And if anything, his hold tightened. And he'd made his denial against her right ear. His breath slid over the shell of her ear.

She shivered against him.

"You're afraid of me," he rasped. A rasp that sent a second shiver over her.

She was still staring at a dead body and being held way too easily by Ronan's strength. "You saved me." That was what he'd done. The man on the floor—he'd wanted to kill her the previous night. If Ronan hadn't stopped him then—and now—she would be dead.

"That's the job."

I'm the job.

She twisted in his grasp. "Let. Me. Go."

"Never happening."

She froze. "Never?"

"I—shit, what I meant was—"

"Clear outside." Kane. He was back and standing close to them. "Time to haul her out." He flashed another smile at Luna. "Thanks again for caring. I'll remember that."

He smiled even as Luna threw out her hands and tried to grab hold of the door in order to stop Ronan from carrying her out.

Kane laughed. "She's adorable."

She was freaking out, that was what she was doing. "Stop it! Ronan, seriously, let me go!" The caveman routine had to end. "We can't go rushing out and leave a dead body behind!" That wasn't the way things were done. Like, ever. And shouldn't a federal agent know that stuff?

"Oh, don't worry, I'll make sure the body vanishes," Kane promised. "I'm on it."

Her eyes widened.

"There are gators around, right, Ronan?"

Her nails dug into the wood of the doorframe. "What is happening? Good guys don't feed dead bodies to gators!" That was an understood rule in the world. If it wasn't understood, it should be.

Ronan tugged her over the threshold. "I just killed a man, princess. How the hell does that make me good?"

A bleeding Kane stalked out with them. He had his gun drawn as he trailed them to the SUV. Ronan tucked her in the passenger seat. Slammed the door.

What is happening?

Her breath kept sawing in and out. In and out. Ronan was pausing to talk with Kane. To check his wound. She grabbed for the glove box and hauled out a manilla envelope. IDs—driver's licenses and passports—spilled into her hands.

Information on her. A new name.

Information on Ronan. Only...

He jumped into the driver's seat. "Looks like you found our IDs and our destination."

Yes, a destination had been included with the IDs. And surely, the location was wrong. The IDs had to be wrong. None of this could be happening.

"Where are we headed?"

She swallowed. "Florida."

"Ah. The home of even bigger gators." His lips twisted. "And snakes. Dammit. Gray can be such a prick some days."

Her breath choked out. "We're going to a couple's-only retreat in the Keys." She'd only seen the front of the brochure that had been included, but the text had been big and bold. *Get swept away to an exclusive adult island.*

He'd gotten a look at the IDs and gone still.

She wet her lips. "We're going there because...we're a couple." She'd seen the new name that she had. And *his* new name.

Ronan glanced up at her. *Rock-hard expression. Tense. Glaring.*

"Because we're apparently married," she added.

He swiped the manilla envelope. Shook it. Two gold rings fell out and into his hand. His fingers immediately fisted around the rings. His head tilted as he peered down at his fisted hand.

"Um...congratulations?" Her voice sounded way weak to her own ears.

His head whipped up. Snapped toward her. His eyes glittered.

And this is how I married a hitman.

* * *

ONE DIDN'T DRIVE STRAIGHT from New Orleans to the Florida Keys. Well, you did if you were in the mood for a fifteen-to-sixteen-hour trip on the interstate. Ronan wasn't in that particular mood. All that time on the road would make him tired. Being tired would make him sloppy.

He couldn't afford any more mistakes where Luna was concerned.

That bastard almost got the drop on me. Hell, there had been no *almost* about it. The jerk had gotten into the cabin. He'd fired at Kane and Ronan. He'd discovered that Luna had still been alive. And he'd been intent on killing her.

So I killed him. A shot that he'd had to take because if he hadn't, Ronan knew he'd be the dead man. Not pretend. For real.

Darkness was falling. They needed to pull into a motel. Crash for the night. Then they'd finish their trip in the morning. He also knew he had to check in with Gray and find out what the hell had been done with the scene at the cabin. Talk about leaving a mess behind for Kane to clean up. *Sorry about the blood and death, my friend.* But he'd needed to get Luna away as quickly as possible. He'd driven for hours and hours. They'd passed Tallahassee and were currently heading toward Orlando. Soon there would be plenty of places for them to pick for a safe sleep spot.

The radio blasted in the interior of the car. He'd been the one to crank it up. Luna hadn't spoken much. After the scene at the cabin, she had to be scared as hell, and the silence in the vehicle had been driving him crazy.

I keep imaging that SOB shooting at her. What if she'd walked out of that bathroom and he'd been waiting for her? What if he'd fired while I was busy with Kane? This is what happens when my head isn't in the game the way it should be. I make mistakes. I—

Her hand flew out and turned off the radio. "I can't take it anymore."

Hell.

She twisted toward him. "Talk to me."

What?

"You killed a man, Ronan. That has to be wrecking you on the inside."

He blinked.

"It's okay." Soft. Sympathetic. "You can talk to me. I will understand."

Oh, hell. "Princess, are you sitting there thinking that I'm filled with regret?"

"Ah—"

"Because I only regret that I didn't kill the bastard before he got into the cabin. I should never have let him get that close to you. My mistake. My guard will not be lowered again." His grip tightened on the wheel. "I'm not fucking being eaten up by guilt, if that is what you're worried about. This was not my first kill, not even close." His eyes were on the road, but he could feel her tension. "If I hadn't shot him, do you know what would have happened?"

"He would have killed you."

"Worse, he would have killed *you*."

"Um, I happen to think him killing you and your friend is pretty bad, and my death would certainly not be the goal but—"

"Kurt Vail." He bit out the name. "I was sent his rap sheet before I met you in New Orleans." *Met you.* What the hell? Not like they had a meet-cute or some shit. Ronan cleared his throat. "The guy likes to hurt women, Luna."

She sucked in a sharp breath.

"He prefers to use his knife on them. Takes his time. He wouldn't have made anything quick for you. If I hadn't taken out the bastard—if he'd shot me, gotten me out of the way, then he would have spent a long while making sure you were good and dead."

"He said he was going t-to be paid a lot to slice me up. When he tried to get me in New Orleans, that's what he told me."

"*No one is slicing you up.*" A guttural, savage promise. Just the thought had Ronan wanting to kill Kurt all over again.

"Because of you. Because you're protecting me." Quiet. Thoughtful. Then, "Because you killed to keep me safe today."

Yeah, he had. *And I'd do it again in a heartbeat.* "It's the job." He forced his grip to ease on the steering wheel.

"You mean I'm the job. That it isn't anything personal. You'd do the same for anyone, wouldn't you?"

No, he sure as shit wouldn't do the same for anyone.

"We didn't call the cops." A little sigh escaped her.

"Are you kidding me right now?"

"Will your friend Kane call the cops? Like, notify Grayson, I mean. Because I will tell Grayson that it was self-defense. You did exactly what you had to do. And you—"

A ringing cut through her words. He'd already found the new phone in the console between their seats, and the device was connected to the Bluetooth in their ride. He glanced toward the screen near the radio. No caller name was listed, but he knew exactly who was reaching out. His finger pressed the button on the side of the steering wheel as he took the call. "Figured I'd be hearing from you sooner or later."

"You left me a bloody crime scene," Gray said, sounding

more than a little disgruntled. "Do you know what a pain in the ass that is?"

"*He was saving me*," Luna instantly declared. "That man realized we'd faked my death. He burst into the cabin, shooting! He hit Kane with a bullet. He would have killed me and Ronan. There was no choice. Ronan had to fire back!"

Ronan glanced at her. Her delicate jaw had locked.

"You can't consider locking Ronan up for this. It was clear self-defense," she added, voice breaking at the edges. "It is nothing like what I saw Marcus do. Nothing. Marcus enjoyed the kill. The man he shot was unarmed. And Marcus just—he was smiling while he stared down at the blood. He had the gun in his hand. One with a long muzzle on the end that had to be a silencer because I hadn't heard the shots when I approached his office. I walked in and I saw all the blood. Noah was sprawled on the floor, and Marcus grinned, and I couldn't breathe. I *stood there*."

So much painful emotion filled her words that Ronan had to dart a glance her way again.

"Then the balloons popped, and I thought I'd been shot and—" Tears slid down her cheek. Two long teardrops. "Ronan isn't the same. It *wasn't* the same. He saved me. You can't charge Ronan with any crime. You can't lock him up. You can't take him away from me. You can't. *Ronan saved my life*."

Chapter Eight

RONAN PULLED ONTO THE EXIT RAMP. AS SOON AS HE could, he cut into the service station right off the interstate. He picked a deserted spot—easy to do since the whole building looked shuttered—and then he reached for Luna.

She should not be crying.

His fingers brushed over her cheek. "No one is taking me away from you."

Her eyes locked on him.

"Gray isn't gonna lock me up."

Another tear trickled down. *I didn't realize how close to the edge she was.* He should have realized it. She was a civilian. Life and death—mostly death—tended to be his bread and butter. But she wasn't made for the world of darkness that surrounded him.

"No, not planning to lock him up," Gray's careful voice. "But I do appreciate the eye-witness testimony. It's the same story Kane gave me. Though in his version of events, the only reason Ronan is still breathing is because he was about a half second faster on the trigger than Kurt Vail."

She flinched.

His hand lingered against her cheek.

"I want to know how the hell Kurt found you. And the very fact that he *was* sent after you, Ronan? That tells me that we have a problem."

"Marcus called me." He'd parked on the side of the gas station. "Twisted freak wanted proof of her death. Jerk was telling me to send him one of her fingers." His fingers slid down her cheek. Glided carefully over the curve of her lips. "Told him it wasn't happening." *I will kill anyone who ever tries to slice a finger from her hand. No one will hurt Luna on my watch.*

The brutality of his own thoughts had him tensing and yanking his own hand back. *Way to not keep some professional distance between you and the target.*

"You think that set off his suspicions? When you wouldn't send him her finger?" A humming sound then, "Maybe he doesn't buy that she's dead." Worry threaded through Gray's voice. Gray had recently been promoted at the Bureau. From what Ronan could determine, all the guy did these days was worry.

Well, Gray worried when he wasn't busy slipping into the darkness as he remembered his time being tortured. Ronan knew his friend was trying to keep his growing darkness a secret from everyone. But you couldn't hide darkness from someone who understood it so well, and Ronan was well acquainted with the dark.

"I think Marcus was using a tracker to find my location." The same theory he'd given Kane. "He talked to me just long enough to figure out where I was, probably using that damn new tech of Declan Flynn's."

"That shit is problematic."

"Tell me about it." Someone would need to rein in Declan, stat. Gray needed to handle that job. The problem?

The tech genius had too many connections in this world. Good and bad ones. "Marcus got my location, and then he sent Kurt out to eliminate me. Guessing Marcus didn't want to pay me the money I was owed."

"So you don't think he realizes Luna is alive?"

Ronan hesitated. "He has no proof that she is. I told him I dumped her body in the bayou."

"He'll be finding out soon enough that Kurt is dead."

Ronan smiled. "Good. That should scare the hell out of him. I'll have vanished, and Marcus will wonder if I'm stalking his ass."

"Scared people make mistakes," Gray noted.

"They do."

"If we had Noah Clyde's body, this whole damn case would be so much easier to handle." Annoyance came and went with Gray. "But who the hell knows where he is? Probably cut up into a million pieces somewhere."

Luna made a rough, choking sound.

"And without his body," Gray continued grimly, "the case is so hard to make. I've had agents on Marcus for ages. People trying to slip into his world. But Marcus keeps staying a step ahead. Winning every damn time."

Yeah, about that... "I think the bastard might like trophies," Ronan mused.

Luna's lashes fluttered.

He reached for her hand. A hand so much smaller than his own. His fingers slid over hers. "Marcus wanted proof Luna was dead. Very insistent about the fact. Wanted me to deliver a piece of her to him." *Never happening.* "We all know that some killers sure do enjoy keeping trophies. Might be dumb as hell to keep evidence like that, but with these guys..."

"It's about compulsion. Not about what is smart or

foolish. About reliving the kill. Getting power from the attacks." A random Gray fact? He had a Ph.D. in psychology and had worked intently for a time in the Behavioral Analysis Unit at the Bureau. He knew his killers and their twisted motivations and desires.

Again, you know the dark, Gray. Don't let it pull you in too deeply.

"If he is keeping trophies and we find his stash, then we could bury him." The faintest thread of excitement from Gray.

Better they bury Marcus than have him burying Luna. *Or me.* "Not like it's gonna be easy to find." He released her. Why the hell did he keep touching her? Why did he feel so drawn to her? He needed to stop that shit. Stay focused.

"They never are easy," Gray murmured, but he already sounded distracted. As if he was busy spinning ideas and plotting in his head—which he probably was. "Stay low until I reach out to you again. Only answer this phone and only pick up calls from this specific number."

He could manage that. "We're heading toward Orlando and gonna pick a no-tell motel for the night. Then we'll reach our destination tomorrow."

"No." A sharp retort. "Forget the motel. I've got a safe house close to that area. Near the springs. Isolated and equipped with the best security imaginable. Go there for the night. The last time I had a pretend couple staying in a no-tell motel, well, you know what happened."

I happened. He'd been working undercover on a different assignment. He'd had to rush in and shoot a friend. Not one of his best moments. But he hadn't shot him with real bullets, so his buddy had only stayed down a short time. Eventually, they'd caught the bad guy so...win?

Tyler Barrett was still pissed about the situation,

though. Not that Ronan could blame him. If Tyler knew that Ronan was currently involved in his own pretend-marriage BS, he would laugh his ass off.

Ronan's gaze cut to the gold ring on his left hand. He wasn't quite used to the weight of the thing yet.

"I'll text the address to you. Stay mission focused. Keep Luna alive. And try to keep the body count for everyone else to a minimum, understand?"

He could make no promises when it came to a body count. "Always a pleasure chatting with you, Gray." He started to disconnect the call.

But Luna's hand flew out and curled around his wrist. "Grayson, how many cases have you worked with Ronan?"

"He's not a Fed, Luna." Gray's quiet reply. "He's someone you will never find in any employee database. As far as the Bureau and the CIA and any other government agency is concerned, your new husband does not exist."

You couldn't find the paper trail for a ghost. But you could find one for a criminal.

"Trust him," Gray urged her. "Hasn't he already proven that he would do anything to keep you safe?"

"Yes." Luna's low response.

"Good. Now, Ronan, I'll have some files coming your way. Background. You have to know your prey, am I right?" Then Gray hung up.

Luna's hand was still around his wrist. Her left hand. The plain, gold wedding ring gleamed on her finger. A ring that told the rest of the world they were a couple. A lie, of course. But what if it wasn't?

What if he was really married to Luna?

How would he feel if he was truly married to Luna, and someone was trying to kill her?

The same way I feel right now. Like I want to rip the bastards apart and hear them scream for mercy.

He'd never been particularly big on mercy. A personality quirk. Everyone had them.

"I do trust you," Luna said. "I'm not going to run from you again."

"So no more handcuffs, huh? Good to know." Especially since he'd left them at the cabin. Kane would have handled cleanup at that scene. *And what did that smartass think when he found the cuffs hooked to the bed?*

"I'm not saying no cuffs ever. I'm sure we could use them for other, um, instances."

Did a faint flush tinge her cheeks? "Luna, don't tease." Another quirk. He'd love to cuff and fuck Luna. Any day. Any time. "You don't want to play with me." Not now. Probably not ever. But definitely not in his current mood.

He'd killed a man that day. That kind of act left a savage mark on the soul. It made him too brittle and his control too thin.

"I'm not playing." A swipe of her tongue over her lower lip. "Pretty sure I told you before that I wanted you."

"Then you went running from me." She'd rushed into the bathroom so fast his head had spun. Then, of course, he'd followed. Been afraid she'd fled the cabin. So he'd opened the door.

Hello, naked Luna.

"I won't run again. Trust *me*."

He'd rather fuck her. But, sure, he could trust her. She needed him. She'd seen him kill to protect her. Instead of terrifying her, his brutal act had made her realize that he was her best chance of survival. Check. Understood. "Let's get back on the road." The phone had already jingled with the delivery of the address to the safe house. The sooner they got there, the—hell, the what? *The sooner I can fuck her?*

No, no. Lines couldn't be crossed. Rules had to be followed. He was going to keep his hands off his target.

His distraction with Luna had almost cost them dearly before.

He couldn't afford more distractions.

He could not afford to—

She'd unhooked her seat belt.

"Luna?"

Why the hell had she unhooked her seat belt?

And she...was climbing across the center console. Sliding toward him. Shifting and craning and then she was in his lap. Straddling him. *"Luna."* His hands clamped onto her waist.

"From what I can tell, this gas station has been closed down for a long time." Her hands gripped his shoulders. "I need to prove something."

Prove something? Who the hell did she need to prove something to?

Her mouth crashed down on his.

Bad, terrible, horrible mistake. They should not be kissing. She should not be putting that sweet mouth of hers against his. She should not be rubbing that sexy tongue past his lips. She should not be moaning in the back of her throat. She should not be driving him wild and making him want to cross every line imaginable. Break every boundary and fuck her then and there until they were both shuddering with pleasure. She should not be—

Crawling away from him. Fumbling. Knocking her knee into the console. Rushing back into her seat. Hooking the seat belt. Making the click seem so very loud.

"What in the fuck," he rasped, "was that?" His dick shoved against the front of his pants.

"I want you just as much now as I did before—before you killed a man." Fast. "I trust you. I want you. I know that you aren't some horrible monster, Ronan."

Oh, princess, you have no idea.

"You're the good guy wearing the monster mask, but I see you for exactly what—who—you are. You *killed* to keep me safe. I'm not afraid of you. I still want you just as much as before."

He needed to get them the hell out of there before he did something crazy like say, oh, fuck her in the car. He could do it. They'd both changed as soon as they'd been safely away from the bayou.

She'd slipped into a dress and sandals when they stopped at a rest stop in Mississippi. Items that had been in the suitcase stuffed into the rear of the vehicle. Meanwhile, he'd put on fresh pants and a dress shirt.

He could shove up her soft cotton dress. Yank away her panties and be buried exactly where his eager dick wanted so desperately to be.

Crossing lines. Breaking boundaries. Do not do it. Do not.

"Want a confession, Ronan?" Breathy. "I want you more than I have ever wanted anyone."

His jaw clenched so hard that it ached. He got the location Gray had sent him. Pulled up directions. Reversed their ride. Shot the vehicle the hell out of that empty lot and back on the road.

"Not that I've had a lot of lovers." Another confession from Luna.

He shot onto the ramp that led back to the interstate.

"Three, if you need an exact number."

Had he asked for a freaking exact number? He didn't want to know *anything* about the lucky bastards who'd been able to fuck Luna. If he knew stuff about them, then he'd want to track them down. Beat the hell out of them. Bury the bodies.

I am so far gone. She thinks I'm pretending to wear a mask? Bullshit. The mask is the man.

He'd been this way long before his Semper Fi days.

When he'd become a Marine, he'd just gotten even better at killing.

Kane and Tyler were the heroes. They were the ones with heart. I was the one trying to figure out how to act normal and blend in with everyone else when every instinct I possess screamed for me to let go of my control.

To cross lines.

To break boundaries.

To do whatever I wanted.

To take what I want.

He very much wanted to take Luna.

"The sex wasn't very good with them."

He almost drove off the road.

"Maybe it was my fault. I-I can't quite let go. Can't give up my control."

Her fault? Screw that. "If they didn't make you scream when you came, they just didn't know what the hell they were doing. Not a mistake I'll make. I'll have you coming against my tongue and begging for more long before my dick ever enters you."

She squeaked. Cutest sound.

He seriously needed to ease up his grip on the steering wheel and not say the words that were tumbling around in his head.

But he'd never quite been tempted the way he was with Luna. *Just focus. Don't say anything else to her. Don't lose—*

"I'd like that," Luna breathed. "But only if I get to go down on you."

Yeah. They nearly died in a fiery wreck right then and there. The visual of Luna going down on him? Of her taking his dick into that hot mouth?

Fuck the lines. Fuck the boundaries. Fuck her.

His inner demon. Breaking free. "Turn on the radio, Luna." A flat order.

"I said the wrong thing, didn't I? I'm sorry. I'm not exactly stellar at the sexy talk."

Oh, she was stellar. "Turn on the radio. And...don't talk again." His gaze cut to her. "Because if you say one more damn sexy thing to me, I will fuck you in the car. I don't care if we are on the side of the interstate or at some shady-ass gas station, I will fuck you." Was that enough of a monster thing to tell her? He thought so.

He also meant every word.

Her hand snaked out. Hit the radio.

The blasting music filled the car.

But the image of Luna, of her taking his dick into her mouth, of her sucking him, that image stayed in his head as the car ate up the miles.

* * *

Kurt had not checked in with him.

Marcus stared out at the Atlanta skyline. So many lights. When he glanced down, he saw cars snaking back and forth on the street below.

Night had fallen. All day long, he'd waited for Kurt to check in with him. But there had been no call to tell him

103

Cynthia Eden

that Ronan Walker had been eliminated. No notice to tell him that the job was done.

The silence worried Marcus.

He didn't like to worry.

He pulled out his phone, and, as if on cue, it vibrated in his hand. His gaze darted to the screen, and Marcus saw that he'd just been sent an image from Kurt. A smile began to play at his lips. Was Kurt sending him a pic as proof that the job had been done? If so, he couldn't wait to see the image, though Kurt would know that Marcus liked a more substantial souvenir. Not just a photo.

But a pic of Ronan Walker's dead body will be a phenomenal start.

He tapped the screen. The image appeared.

"What. The. Fuck?"

That wasn't Ronan Walker on his screen. It was Kurt.

With blood all over his chest.

*　*　*

KANE HARTE SMILED as his gloved hand tossed the phone toward the FBI agent. "Let your boss know I just rattled our target's cage."

The young agent frowned at him. "I'm not sure you were supposed to do that."

Kane grunted. Like he spent his time doing what he was *supposed* to do. That would be one boring as hell way to live a life.

"Agent Stone didn't say anything about you making contact with Marcus Aeros."

"He didn't? Odd. Or maybe he just figured you didn't need to know every detail of his operational plans." He ignored the burn in his shoulder. Another day, another bullet wound. At this point, if he wasn't hurting, Kane wasn't sure he was breathing. "Marcus needed to know that he was being hunted. Now he does." *You think you're the one sending out the killers. Well, the killers are about to come for you.*

The young agent bagged and tagged the phone.

Time to get moving.

Kane had places to be. Sociopaths to stop.

Chapter Nine

SAFETY.

She'd craved it for as long as she could remember, and now, when she was on the run for her actual life...when she was supposed to start answering to a fake name and staying with a fake husband...somehow *now*...

She actually did feel safe.

Even though a killer was on her trail.

Even though a hitman was her companion.

She felt safe.

Because the hitman was her companion.

Because he'd kill to keep her safe, and she knew it. Because while Ronan might try to act like the bad guy, he did nothing but protect her.

They were at the promised safe house. His GPS had taken them off the interstate. Away from the crowds. Down a small, twisting road to a house that sat near a spring. It had been too dark for her to see the water clearly, but the moonlight had hinted at the beauty that waited for them.

Without a word, Ronan had unloaded their bags. Taken

her inside. He'd put her stuff in one bedroom. He'd told her to sleep.

And...he'd left her. Gone to the room right beside hers.

After all the hot talk in the car, the kiss, the sensual promise—she'd expected more.

Safety. That was what she'd gotten.

Was it so wrong that she wanted both safety and sin?

Live. Live before you die.

She stared at the closed bedroom door. The house was almost eerily silent. What had she expected, really? For him to rip her clothes off the moment they walked inside?

Um, yes.

For him to pick her up and fuck her against the door?

Would that have been too much to ask?

Instead, she'd had a coldly professional protector leading the way up the stairs. Telling her that she was safe. That he was right next door.

She did feel safe.

She also felt like she was about to jump out of her skin. She wanted Ronan. She wanted the wild release that he'd promised. She wanted to stop being *good* all the time and see what it was like to be bad, just for a night. To not care about consequences or rules.

I could have died again today. If Ronan hadn't been there when the shooter arrived...

Her shoulders squared. She'd put on a pair of black pajamas—soft cotton pants and a matching shirt. They'd been in the suitcase for her. A perfect fit which, yep, that had been a bit creepy. Every article of clothing was exactly in her size.

She figured Grayson had ordered Kane to bring the clothes for her and Ronan. Apparently, the FBI knew everything about her.

Not that there was a whole lot to know.

She'd barely traveled during her life. Never gone out of the country. She'd paid all her bills on time. She'd worked at the middle school since college. She'd just tried to start her new business and that had immediately crashed and burned.

I was always so careful because that's what I was told to be. I had to be careful. I couldn't take any risks.

That had been her world for a long time.

Except...

Maybe I want more.

Her hand reached for the doorknob. It turned easily beneath her grip, and then she was out in the hallway. A quick turn to the right, a few stumbling, nervous steps, and then her fist was knocking at his door. Once, twice, and—

The door flew open. "What's wrong?"

No shirt. Boxers. That awesome chest of Ronan's was on full display. So were his abs. In the soft light of the hallway, she could see the faint, white lines that rose on his tan skin. Scars from long ago wounds. Scars that made him seem even more dangerous and sexier and stronger because he'd survived.

He wasn't the kind of person who'd ever been afraid to live. She knew Ronan certainly wasn't the type to fear death, either.

"Luna." His nostrils flared. "What is it?"

"I—" Maybe this was a bad idea. Maybe she should turn and run. Scuttle back to the safety of her room.

Safety.

There it was again. That word. Her chin lifted. "Promises were made."

"What?" His forehead furrowed. Such a sexy furrow.

"Promises were made," she repeated. Her chin

remained up. "You can't go around telling a woman that you are going to have her coming against your tongue and begging for m-more long before..." She swallowed. "Long before your dick enters her."

His hands flew out. Not to grab her. But to clamp around the wood of the doorframe. "*Luna.*"

"I mean, if you're going to make promises like that, you should deliver on them. Otherwise, it just seems like false hype."

His eyes narrowed. "It's not false hype."

She didn't think it had been. He probably made women come by crooking his little finger. "Then you should deliver."

"*Luna.*"

When he said her name in that growl, it made her stomach twist. In a good way. "I played the radio during the drive. I didn't distract you. I was holding up my end of the deal."

"You distract me by breathing. As far as playing the radio and you not talking—that shit was about me trying not to fuck you in the car."

"We aren't in the car any longer." She tilted a little to the side in an attempt to look around him. A failed attempt because he was so big. "We're in a safe house. One with plenty of beds that we could use right now."

"You don't want to do this."

He was so wrong. "Is making love with me against FBI rules?"

"*I'm not in the FBI.*"

She stared up at him. Then, slowly, her hands lifted so that her palms pressed to his jaw. His beard tickled her skin. "Is it against your rules?"

"I don't tend to fuck good girls and walk away."

"Who says I'm good?"

"You're a line I shouldn't cross." But his head turned. His lips brushed against her palm. The contact did more than tickle. Especially when she felt the lick of his tongue.

Electricity ignited in her veins. "You're a line I *want* to cross."

His eyes squeezed closed. "Fuck."

"Yes, that's precisely what I want to do." But she did have some pride. She'd come here. She'd told him already how she felt. If he was pulling back, making promises he had no intention of keeping, then she would stop. "I'll go back to my room." Her hands dropped from him as she stepped away.

Lightning fast, his hand flew out and curled around her wrist. "Too late." He hauled her toward him. His mouth crashed down onto hers. Intense. Passionate. Possessive. "Fucking in here," he muttered against her mouth. "Fantasizing about you." His tongue thrust deep. Had her moaning. He lifted her into his arms. Kept kissing her, then raised his mouth just enough to growl, "Tried to keep control. Then you showed up. *You came to me.*"

She kissed his jaw.

He shuddered. "You came to me. Remember that." He stalked for the bed. Lowered her right in the middle of the mattress, then stared down at her with a gaze that blazed. "And soon you'll come for me."

Yes, please. She'd like that. Even if she wasn't one hundred percent sure it would happen. Because like she'd told him, she'd never really been able to let go during sex. Too afraid. Too hesitant. But she wanted to try.

Her whole body was tense, and nerves twisted her stomach. She needed him. Wanted him with a desperation that she didn't fully understand. Was it because of adrenaline? The circumstances? Luna didn't know. Didn't care, honestly.

She just wanted him.

She reached for him.

But he caught her hands. Leaned over the bed. Pinned her wrists to the mattress. "I told you how this was going to work. *Warned* you."

He had?

"You'll come for me, begging, long before my dick enters you."

She was wet. Her hips were twisting. And all he'd done was kiss her. This was definitely better than it had ever been for her before. "Ronan!"

"Grab the sheets. Don't move from this spot. Not until I make you come."

What?

He let go of her wrists. Eased back. He stood on the side of the bed, she was in the middle, with her feet dangling over the edge. He caught her legs, and he hauled the pajama pants and her panties away in one fast yank. She gasped because she was completely naked from the waist down, and he was putting his strong, callused fingertips on the inside of her thighs. Pushing them apart.

"So damn pretty."

Then his mouth was on her. Just like that.

His warm, wet tongue brushed against her core. A slow, languorous swipe over her clit. She nearly bolted off the bed. Would have, if his hands hadn't locked around her hips to hold her in place.

"*Delicious.*" A savage rumble. And then he feasted.

Her wide eyes stared up at the ceiling. Light from the

lamp spilled up in a soft glow. Ronan was licking and sucking, and his tongue thrust into her.

Her mouth stretched open wide as she gasped. Even in his hold, her hips surged, but not to get away from him. To get closer.

He lashed her with his tongue. Over and over and over. Her heart drummed in her chest. Her body trembled and ached.

She'd never been more exposed in her life. Never felt more vulnerable. Or more turned on.

Maybe she should tell him this was the first time that a man had gone down on her.

Maybe she should—

He worked her clit feverishly with his wicked, skilled tongue, and she stopped thinking.

Need flooded through her. A knife's edge of desire. She was on the precipice of release. She could feel it. A powerful orgasm built up within her. She was close to coming. So close. Luna wanted to get there so very badly.

She heard her own desperate voice. She was saying his name. Chanting it.

One powerful hand left her hip. Slid between her thighs. His fingers stroked her even as his tongue dipped into her once again. Her mouth opened wider, and her head tipped back more as he raked his fingers over the center of her need—and then she was falling. Falling straight over the edge and into the hottest, longest climax of her life.

"Ronan!"

He didn't stop. His mouth went back to her clit, and he licked and kissed her with a driven and possessive passion that swept away all control. All caution. All she could do was feel. Shudder and tremble and lose her mind to the pleasure that consumed her.

Her eyes had squeezed closed. Even as aftershocks trembled through her sex, she forced her eyes to open again. She looked down. His dark head was between her thighs. As she stared at him, his head lifted. His gaze crashed into hers.

He licked his lips, as if savoring the taste that had been left on him. Her taste.

"What do you want now?" Ronan demanded.

"More." Hadn't that been the deal? That he'd have her begging for more...long before his dick entered her? "I want more, please."

"Such a good girl." He pulled away.

She *hated* for him to be gone. "No."

"Not good? Oh, I disagree." He stood by the bed. His aroused dick saluted in the boxers as he reached into the nightstand drawer. He pulled out a condom.

Who put the condoms in the drawer? Is that like, standard safe house protocol?

He tore open the packet.

"Wait!" Her desperate cry.

His bright eyes raked at her even as his jaw locked. "Changed your mind?" A grim nod. "Run then, while you can. Got a taste of the dark but you don't want to—"

"I want to go down on you." She had zero intention of running anywhere.

He blinked.

"That was our deal, wasn't it?" Luna moved to her knees. Her sex was still quaking in the best possible way, and the rest of her body was shaking with nerves. "I may not be overly good at this, so maybe you can help me out?"

He just stared at her.

She needed to get closer to him. Check. Luna slid off

the bed. Her knees hit the floor. She was right in front of him, and his extremely substantial dick thrust toward her.

"You're...going down on me."

She was about to, yes. That was the plan. Her hand reached for him. Her fingers curled around his cock, and he was warm and hard and thick. Very thick.

We may have a size issue.

One that could be painful.

But she didn't stop. Luna leaned forward. Her breath blew over the head of his dick.

"Why do you think you won't be good at this?" So deep and dark and rough.

"Because I've never done it before." Total honesty. "No one had ever gone down on me, either. Not until you. Thanks for a great first time." Then she licked him. Her tongue slid out and tasted the tip of his erection. And after that little taste, her mouth opened wider. She closed her lips around him. Sucked the head into her mouth.

A moan broke from her because she liked the way he felt and tasted.

Her tongue slid over him. She pulled him in a bit deeper. She sucked on him. She—

Got her ass lifted up and tossed back onto the bed.

"Ronan!" A shocked cry burst from her.

He rolled on the condom. "You think you can tell me things like that?" He caught her ankles. Dragged her right back to the side of the bed. "And not immediately get fucked?"

"Um..."

He positioned his dick at the entrance of her body. "You're getting fucked," he told her definitely. "You're going to come around my dick. You're going to scream my name.

114

You are going to be *mine*." He drove into her. A long, hard thrust.

And she'd been right. There were some size issues. He was way, way more endowed than the other three guys she'd been with in her life. He stretched her. He filled her. And her body did *not* want to let all of him inside.

"Ronan?" Sharp. Worried.

"I've got you." Absolutely certain. His hand snaked between their bodies. Went straight for her clit. He rubbed and stroked, and her breath caught because he did, indeed, have her. He had her in the best possible way. A way that had her arching for him. Softening for him. Taking him deeper into her.

Her head tipped back because he felt good. So incredibly good. "I like that."

"You're gonna love what comes next."

Her lashes wanted to close. She kept them open because Luna needed to see him. All those muscles. The hard angles and planes of his face. The need that blazed in his eyes. Had any man ever looked at her that way before? As if she was the one thing he *had* to have?

No, no one ever had.

Not until Ronan.

He lifted her right leg.

"Ronan?" She shifted a little beneath him.

He hooked her leg over his shoulder. Leaned into her. Thrust deeper.

She thought the new position might hurt. It didn't. Just the opposite. He was going in even more but the angle he was at, the way he was thrusting, the way his fingers strummed her clit again and again...

So good.

Cynthia Eden

The second orgasm soared through her. A scream tore from her lips before she could even think to muffle it.

Then there was no stopping him. He pulled her left leg over his shoulder. He hauled her hips closer to the edge of the bed. He pounded into her. Again and again.

Her hands grabbed for him. Held tightly. He was in her so deep. He consumed her. Seemed to own her body in that instant, and there was nothing she could do.

Nothing, but enjoy the absolute hell out of the ride. "Ronan!"

His body shuddered as he erupted into her.

* * *

HE HAD JUST FUCKED the target.

His body still shuddered. The orgasm still pulsed through his body. The best freaking orgasm of his life.

He'd fucked the target.

The target in question slowly smiled up at him. The most gorgeous, sweet smile. One that made him want to fuck her all over again. Because how in the hell could she be smiling so sweetly and innocently when he was still balls deep in her?

And he could feel the aftershocks of her pleasure all along his dick.

"That was amazing," Luna told him.

Well, yeah. *Same.* He was still in recovery mode and trying helluva hard not to show that fact. Because sex was sex.

Good sex was...well, good sex.

But what he'd just had with Luna...

I want to damn well devour her. Want to fuck her over and over. Sinking into her body had been like sinking

116

straight into paradise. When he'd gone down on her, he'd been obsessed. Her taste. Her scent. Her softness. Everything about her *obsessed* him.

He wanted her again. And again. And again.

Target. She is the target.

A beautiful, sexy, tempting target.

I am so screwed.

Her legs slid off his shoulders. Soft, silky legs.

He slowly pulled out of her. Luna tensed a bit, and he frowned. "Did I hurt you?"

"Oh, trust me on this. The pleasure was more than worth any pain."

His chest ached. In a weird way. "I didn't mean to hurt you." He needed to ditch the condom.

I need to put another one on because my dick is already getting hard again, and I want to fuck her until we can't move.

Nope, way bad idea. Bad.

"It had been a while for me. There was bound to be some...uncomfortable moments. Especially since you are so much, uh, bigger, than my previous partners." She eased back. Scooted into the middle of the bed. Then grabbed for a sheet to cover her lower body.

He turned away from her because he needed to ditch the condom and be a damn *semi-gentleman* and get her a warm cloth or maybe get her a hot bath ready or—

"I really did not expect you to live up to the hype."

Ronan froze right there.

"I didn't think screaming from pleasure would be a real thing. I was *loud*."

Yep, she had been. He'd loved her responsiveness. Ronan looked over his shoulder at her. "I always live up to the hype."

"I'll remember that." Her smile came and went again, and his chest felt even weirder. But he jerked his head forward. He stalked into the bathroom. Ditched the condom. Grabbed the sink a little too hard.

So you fucked the target. Not the end of the world. You crossed one little line.

He wanted to cross that line again and again and again. All night long. He wanted to fuck her endlessly.

Then he heard the click of his bedroom door...shutting.

What. The. Hell?

He yanked open the bathroom door and sprinted across the room. He had the bedroom door open and was in the hallway two seconds later. "Where are you going?" A bit too rough but screw it.

He felt rough.

She looked back at him. She'd hauled back on her pajama pants. *I didn't even take off her top. Hell.*

"I...thought you were done with me."

Done? Hardly. And the next time, that pajama top would be gone.

"You walked away. I-I..." Her lips pressed together. "I didn't want anything to be awkward. So I was going back to my room."

He curled his hand under her chin and tipped back her head so she had no choice but to look at him. "We are way past awkward." His head lowered. His mouth pressed to hers. A soft kiss. But one that was possessive as hell as he savored her. "I'm not done with you." Not even close.

"No?" Her hands pressed to his chest.

"I'm just getting started."

Her eyes widened. "You want to go again?"

More like...*again and again.* "Got to live up to the

hype." Ronan scooped her into his arms and carried her back where he wanted her to be.

In my bed.

He knew it was wrong. He knew it was a mistake. Ronan didn't care. *This is a bad fucking idea.*

But he was going to take her anyway because he'd never wanted anyone more.

Chapter Ten

"THIS IS A BAD IDEA." KANE WAS ADAMANT. "YOU CAN'T do this, Gray. The woman is a civilian. She is not set to handle the kind of nightmare you're planning."

Gray looked up from his laptop. "You need to give Luna Black more credit. She eluded Marcus and his men for weeks. She managed to contact me. To convince me that she was legit. She stayed alive. She stayed hidden. No small task, I can promise you."

Kane slapped his hands on the desk in front of Gray. A temporary desk Grayson had been given at the FBI office in New Orleans. "You are going to use her," Kane accused.

"Um, she is a material witness. She can bring down some very bad people. Not just Marcus, though he is a freaking walking nightmare. But everyone in his web. This could be a major score."

Kane shook his head. "She's a lamb being led to a slaughter. I saw her. I spoke to her. She is not ready for what you're planning."

Carefully, Gray closed his laptop. He'd just sent the intel report to Ronan. In order for the scheme he was hatching to work, he'd need Ronan fully on board. He'd also need to move around a few more pieces on the chess set. "You don't know what I'm planning." He pulled off the glasses he'd been wearing and dropped them near Kane's right hand.

"You think the bastard has trophies. You want to find them. Only in order to do that, someone will have to get very close to the guy."

Yes, that was all true.

"You're gonna leak that she's still alive." Kane leaned forward more. "And when you do, Ronan is going to kick your ass."

Gray straightened his tie. "I'm not leaking anything." *Yet.* "I'm just coming up with options. That's all. I can't have Marcus turning his homicidal attention elsewhere. Better he be focused on the prey that happens to have herself an around-the-clock guard. A very skilled and capable guard, as we both know."

"He will kick your ass," Kane said again. "The worst beatdown ever."

"He's like my best friend." Sort of. Pretty close? "He'll understand. Ronan knows that sometimes, a job can get... messy." Understatement.

"He's won't let anything get messy when it comes to her."

Okay, there was something about Kane's voice that worried him. "You know something I don't?"

Kane sent him an enigmatic half-smile.

Well, that smile told him jackshit. Gray sighed. "I'm not throwing the woman to the wolves, okay? I'm just considering options."

"You'd better reconsider them."

Kane didn't understand the situation. He had no clue

how many murders might actually be tied to Marcus. But, if Gray could get to the truth...

This wouldn't just be about putting Marcus Aeros away for one murder. This could be about—

"Ronan isn't going to let her be put at risk."

"Of course, no one is putting her at risk. Whatever happens, I'll make sure Ronan is with Luna twenty-four, seven." Hadn't he said that already? Or something similar? Gray sent Kane what he hoped was a reassuring smile.

Surprise, surprise, though, Kane didn't appear overly reassured. He looked extra grim as he charged, "You were setting the pieces in motion when you got me to text the pic of the dead man to Marcus."

"You sent that?"

"You damn well know I did. Was that the first part of the plan? You trying to enrage him?"

"Marcus needs to see that there is no one he can trust to do the dirty work for him. His number one guy, Kurt, is cold in a morgue. With a bullet in his chest. Hmmm..." His fingers tapped against the top of the closed laptop. "Just who do you think Marcus will believe sent that text? And killed his cousin?"

"He'll think it was Ronan, of course."

An incline of Gray's head.

"You *want* him going after Ronan?"

"I think that Marcus is probably scared shitless of Ronan."

"Most people are," Kane agreed. "Kurt had his gun drawn at that cabin. He was ready to fire. Ronan was faster." A low whistle. "No hesitation. Just fast as hell."

Ronan had always been fast, and when it came to killing, he never hesitated. "Scared men are dangerous. Scared men are sloppy."

"You *want* him going after Ronan." Not a question this time.

"Ronan is hidden." For the moment. Until Gray was ready for him to step into the light once more. "We don't have to worry about him or Luna right now." Because more plans needed to be put in place first. He was just at the beginning stages. All the players weren't on the board yet. Or, if they were, they weren't in their correct positions. "I sent Ronan intel he needs on Luna."

"What kind of intel?" Suspicion darkened Kane's features.

"Pretty much every detail of her life." Obviously. "Knowledge is power, you know that."

"What the hell do you expect him to do? Manipulate her?"

If it became necessary, yes. "Sometimes, it gets really messy when you're trying to stop a monster."

"And sometimes, you can become a monster if your fool-ass isn't careful enough."

Too late for that warning, my friend. "This isn't Luna's world, but she's in it now. And there will be no easy way out. Not even for a dead woman." He looked pointedly at Kane's hands. Hands that were still slapped on the top of his desk. "Now, do you mind giving me a bit of personal space? It's late. I need to crash."

"Got to have that beauty sleep before you start wrecking lives, check."

His eyelids flickered. "Ronan hauled me out of hell." On more than one occasion, actually. "I love him like a brother. You should know that I would never, ever put him at unnecessary risk."

"Sure, but Ronan lives for risk, doesn't he? That's pretty much the only time he actually feels alive. When he's facing death." Kane yanked his hands off the desk and spun around. Kane started to march away but then stopped. "What about her?"

"Excuse me?"

He glanced back. Gray had already stood. Gray made sure no emotion showed on his face.

"What about Luna? His new bride?"

"That's just a cover story."

"Ah. Right. Sure." Kane scraped a hand over his jaw. "You do enjoy using those stories, don't you?"

It was a convenient ruse. "A man and a woman have been thrown together. They have to stay close to each other, twenty-four, seven. Either they are lovers, or they are brother and sister. You tell me...would anyone in the world buy that Ronan was her brother?"

A sharp bark of laughter escaped Kane. "Not the way he looks at her."

Again...*Problematic.* "Good thing that Ronan knows how to stay professional."

Kane winked at him. "Yep. Keep telling yourself that. Professional. Cold as ice. Hard to the core. That's our Ronan. No heart in his chest. No soul in his body. That's a man who will never get caught up in a woman's web." He faced forward. "Not a man who would throw everything else away because all he wants to do is keep her safe and keep *her.*"

"*Kane!*" Real alarm flashed through Gray. "Kane, are they involved? Is it personal?" But, no, impossible. This time, he was the one to laugh. Kane hadn't even glanced back at him, but Gray laughed. Hard. "Nice one, buddy. But they just met. The woman has practically lived like a nun. She never takes risks. She's safe and dependable. And he *is* ice cold. Not like he's going to meet her and fuck her instantly. Not like she'd ever be the type to do that with a dangerous stranger."

"Uh, huh. You keep right on using that psychology degree of yours, bro. Keep right on impressing me with how much you know about the human psyche and personal interaction." He reached for the door. Paused. And did look back once more. "You've never been in the field, trapped in a life-or-death situation, with a woman who makes you ache, have you?"

Gray frowned. Something was going on here. Suddenly, he wasn't even sure that this was about Ronan and Luna.

"You want her more than anything. Is it the adrenaline? The constant pump of danger? All emotions are heightened, even emotions that you damn well didn't think you possessed. You have to stay with her. You have to be close to her all the time. Sometimes, even a saint would be tempted." Kane cleared his throat. "We both know Ronan is no saint."

No, he was death.

But the way Kane was talking... "I thought you'd gotten over the past." Or maybe he'd just hoped that Kane had.

Kane rolled his shoulders back. "I'm not talking about the past. I'm talking about Luna Black. Obviously. That's the woman Ronan is protecting. I'm talking about Luna."

"No." He hadn't been. Kane had been talking about someone who'd gotten through his careful guard. The one woman who'd been his kryptonite.

"I'm trying to give you a helpful word of warning. I didn't cross a line." Kane turned his head away. "Wish like hell that I had, though." He opened the door. Paused on the threshold. "This is a bad fucking idea."

Unfortunately, it was the only idea that Gray currently had...

The only chance that he had of taking down an individual he deemed a major threat. Someone responsible for too many deaths, with too many dangerous ties.

In order to bring him down, Gray just needed help from one woman.

Luna Black.

A woman with a protector who would kill for her.

Ronan will keep her safe. He will do the job.

He always did the job.

Chapter Eleven

SHE SLEPT BESIDE HIM LIKE SOME KIND OF AN ANGEL. Soft and sweet and innocent. Innocent, after he'd fucked her three times, and she'd screamed for him and came for him and still asked for more.

She'd been like wildfire beneath his hands and mouth. He'd touched and tasted and licked and savored and feasted on her.

And I want to do it again.

After the third time he'd pumped himself into her, she'd fallen asleep. In his arms. The first time he could remember anyone just trusting him enough to curl up and go to sleep with him after sex.

Who slept that peacefully with a killer?

And I am a killer. I've killed more than she'll ever know. Sometimes, he'd killed as a Marine. In battle. And other times...

I worked for the government. Special Ops. Took out high-profile targets that no one else could reach. And then...then the government had found a new way to use him. To get him to live a different life. To become Ronan Walker. The

127

man with the striking snake on his wrist. The hired killer who always got the job done.

What if I'm sick of the job?

His arm had curled around her stomach. Would she sprawl on him soon? If she did, it would just make him want to fuck her again.

Who was he kidding? Just the sound of her soft breathing made him want to fuck her.

My reaction to her is unreal. I need to calm down. Get my control back.

Though, actually, he had been in control. Every moment that he'd fucked her, he'd held onto his control. He'd been far too conscious of his size with her. Hurting Luna wasn't in the cards for him. It was easy to hurt others, especially those who deserved pain.

Not Luna.

He'd held back, even though every part of him had wanted to let his control shred. He'd wanted to just take and take and take.

He hadn't.

You fucked her three times. If that's you having control, what would you do to her if your control broke?

Swallowing, he eased from the bed. She was naked, and one tempting breast peeked out at him. With his jaw locked, he pulled the cover up over her. Trying to hide that temptation. Then he headed for the door.

He *meant* to head for the door.

For some odd reason, he just kept staring down at Luna. He had a flash of her the first night, running in New Orleans. Kissing him. And then him lowering her into the trunk of his car. She'd been so still. So pale.

He'd slammed the trunk closed on her supposedly dead body. He'd left her in the dark.

His hand reached out. The back of his knuckles skimmed over her cheek. Her warm, silken cheek. In her sleep, her head turned. Her lips brushed against him.

Probably reflex. The action didn't mean anything. She liked to sprawl, and she did stuff in her sleep and she—

"Ronan." A soft whisper. Her lips curled into a smile as she slumbered.

A smile for him. His body tensed.

Then her smile slid away as she drifted into a deeper sleep.

He pulled his hand back, but Ronan swore he could still feel her. With more effort than it should have taken, he turned away. He hauled on sweats that he'd unpacked earlier and crept from the room. His steps were soundless as he made his way down the stairs. On the first floor, he turned toward the small desk that was nestled under the staircase.

He'd put the laptop on that desk after their arrival. Kane had packed the laptop in the bag he'd had ready for Ronan. After sitting down, it only took a few moments to get the laptop online and then he was accessing the secure email address that he only used when he was communicating with Gray.

No big surprise, Gray had already sent him intel.

On Luna.

He'd read brief background info on her before. Back when Gray had contacted him and demanded that he move fast in New Orleans. But *brief* had been the keyword. Basic physical description. Her age. Height. Weight. Her job. The interesting fact that somehow an unassuming drama teacher had managed to avoid death for weeks while being on the run and keeping out of sight...

He still needed to ask Luna just how she'd accomplished that vital task.

But this file, hell, this file was like an everything-you-ever-wanted-to-know book about Luna. Including the fact that her father had cut out on her when she was eight years old. At the same time she'd been diagnosed with cancer.

When he read that bit of intel, every muscle in his body locked down. For a moment, he couldn't seem to breathe. His lungs felt frozen. So did his heart.

Cancer. Luna.

Then he was clicking through the files as fast as he could. Reading old medical reports. Feeling his guts twist and his heart now race too fast as he saw all that young Luna had endured. The tests. The treatments. The pain. Over and over.

Her father had left her when she needed him the most.

Ronan's teeth ground together. *You sonofafucker.*

His breath sawed in and out. In and out. Not frozen. Too hard and heavy.

Remission.

His breath exploded. He read through more of the files. Sweet Luna got better. Stronger. There were clippings about her as she grew up. Awards. She'd been some kind of star at her high school. Performing in all the plays. Winning local talent shows for her vocal performances. She'd gotten a scholarship to attend college in New York. Luna had been Broadway bound.

A college yearbook quote—because, sure, why *wouldn't* Gray have been thorough enough to include that? "*I get to be someone else on stage. And I want to be someone else on Broadway. I want to live the biggest life I can.*"

But Luna hadn't gone to Broadway.

Why?

The answer was right there. Thanks to organized Gray.

Her mother had a stroke one month before Luna's high school graduation. Luna had become her mother's caregiver. Two years later, her mother passed away.

Luna had been left alone.

She'd earned her degree at a local college. Begun teaching. Barely dated. Recently, she'd opened her new business. A kind of singing telegram side hustle. The side hustle hadn't lasted long before she'd been put on a kill list.

Pictures were included. Young Luna. Fragile. Small. Dark circles under her eyes. Too pale skin. Thin hair.

Teenage Luna. Still fragile, but with pink cheeks. Thick hair. Wide eyes. On a stage, with lights behind her, and tears on her cheeks.

Luna...

In New Orleans.

At Café du Monde. A picture that Ronan had snapped to confirm her ID before he'd approached her. He'd sent the image to Gray. Her dark hair slid against her cheek. Her eyes were down, staring at the beignets before her. He'd watched her the entire time she'd been at Café du Monde. Seen her quick smiles to the staff. Enjoyed the way she seemed to savor the powdered sugar on her beignets.

She'd hummed along to the jazz music that played on the speakers. But her nervous gaze had kept darting around, as if she feared that someone was waiting. Watching.

I was.

He tapped on the mouse and closed the files.

Even as the screen went dark, Ronan realized that his gut was still knotted. His heart still pounded too fast. And...

Luna nearly died when she was eight years old. She's known death longer than most and better than many, and yet she seems to be the most alive person that I've ever met.

He shut down the computer. Stared in silence at the closed laptop.

She'd been so damn brave. Getting away from me at the cabin. Running into the night.

And she'd told him that she wanted to live.

Because she hasn't gotten to live the life she wanted yet.

With heavy steps, he climbed the stairs and went back to Luna. She still slept in the bed, her chest rising and falling softly. He eased in beside her. Stared up at the ceiling.

And then she snuggled against him.

The twist in his gut seemed to ease.

"Ronan." A whisper of his name.

His breath came a little deeper.

She began to inch on top of him, and Ronan could feel a faint smile tugging at his lips. It didn't take long before Luna was completely on top of him.

Sprawled.

Not hell this time. Heaven. Exactly where he wanted her to be.

* * *

LUNA WAS GONE.

Ronan jerked up in bed. He'd been reaching for her, only she wasn't there. Wasn't sprawled on top of him like she damn well should have been. Wasn't beside him. Wasn't in the room. "Luna!" He bolted from the bed and hurried for the bathroom door. He flung it open.

Not there.

Adrenaline and fear poured through his veins. A half-forgotten nightmare tugged at him. Luna had been missing. She should have been with him, but he'd been running in the dark, and he hadn't been able to find her. He'd woken, reached out—and she'd been gone. *Just like the dream?*

He grabbed his gun—he'd tucked it into the nightstand drawer before bed—and hurried out of the room. "Luna!" Ronan raced down the stairs, and his pounding steps seemed to echo all around him.

There's no way someone snuck in and took her while I slept. No way.

There should also have been no way for Luna to have gotten out of the bed without waking him. He was the lightest sleeper in the world.

She hasn't left you. She hasn't run away. Luna wouldn't have sex with you and then run. It's not some plan to catch you off guard so that she could give you the slip.

It wasn't, right?

"Luna!" Not in the den. Or the narrow kitchen. A sliding door led from the den to a small deck attached to the back of the house. He bounded toward the sliding door. Unlocked. He yanked it open. Rushed outside. "Luna!"

And there she was. Lying face down on the edge of the dock.

Face down.

He could feel all of the blood pouring from his head. His body actually swayed for a moment.

Then she yanked her hands out of the water.

What in the hell?

She shoved up onto the dock. Onto her knees. Then to her feet and even as he raced toward her, Luna spun around with a bright, sunny smile on her face. "Ronan! Ronan, you won't believe them—they are *beautiful!*"

He grabbed her arm with his left hand. Hauled her close. Had to be absolutely sure she was alive.

133

Sprawled face down on the dock. Thought she was dead. Thought I'd lost Luna.

"Ronan?" Her bright smile faltered. Her gaze had whipped to the gun he held. "What's wrong?" She sucked in a breath. "Is there trouble? Did someone find us?"

"You're alive." Gritted.

A blink of her long lashes. "Well, I think I'm supposed to be dead, but yes, thanks to you, I am still very much alive."

"You're alive." Why was he repeating those words?

Oh, right. Because he'd just been scared as hell.

"I'm alive," she said softly. "And you have a gun really close to me."

He shoved the gun into the back waistband of his sweats. "You left the bed."

"I didn't want to wake you. You looked so cute."

What? No, he'd never looked *cute.*

"And I was on top of you again, which, you know, awkward. So I tried to slip out without disturbing you. Then I came outside and saw them. I just had to get closer."

"First, it's not awkward for you to be on top of me." It was awesome. "Climb that sexy ass on me any day. Night. Whatever. And second—*who are you talking about? Who did you see?"*

Her gaze darted to the left.

His followed hers.

The water was incredibly clear. Almost like something out of a dream. Wooden steps from the side of the dock actually led into the water, but she hadn't been near the steps. Instead, she'd been reaching out and touching...

"Manatees," she sighed. "Aren't they beautiful?"

Was that the right word for them? Beautiful? He was

pretty sure they were known as sea cows. And there were about three of them bobbing nearby.

"They are so gentle and just gorgeous." Excitement hummed in her voice. "They just swam right up. This place is incredible." She scampered away from him. Only this time, she did go for the stairs. She didn't sprawl on the edge of the dock in that terrifying dead-body style that had stolen several years of his life away. "It's magical," she told him as she kicked off her tennis shoes and crept down the steps toward the water.

It took a moment too long for the truth to dawn on him. "You're going into the water?"

What was it? Seven a.m.? And she was wearing shorts and a t-shirt.

"I always wanted to visit the springs in Florida. I read that in this area, they're supposed to stay around seventy-two degrees." A delighted laugh escaped her. "This is the clearest water I've ever seen!"

The three manatees had drifted away.

He removed his gun and put it down on the dock. No sense in it getting wet. If Luna was going in the water, so was he. But... "We're supposed to head out this morning. This place was just a stop for the night."

She was already in water up to her thighs. A little shiver skated over her. Because seventy-two degrees really wasn't that warm.

His arms crossed over his chest.

"I just want to swim, really fast." She turned toward him. "It's so beautiful. They are beautiful. The water is beautiful. And I'm here, and you're here and it's just—*why not?*" With those words, she sank beneath the surface of the water.

You're the beautiful thing I see.

Had he seriously been dumb enough not to think she was beautiful the first time he'd spoken with her?

And just how long was she staying under the water?

He edged toward the steps.

She broke through the surface of the water, about five feet from where she'd gone under. "Amazing!" A shiver racked her whole body. "Colder than expected, but *amazing*. You can see forever beneath the water." A grin covered her face. "Come in with me!"

Into the cold water that was making her shiver.

The water that was making her smile.

Ronan hadn't bothered with shoes before he began searching for her, and he just wore his sweats. So...he went in with no hesitation. He didn't sink gently into the water. He cut through it and came up right next to her. Ronan didn't care about the slight cold. When he caught her in his arms, he cared about how she felt against him. How her nipples were hard and pebbled against his chest. How her dark hair framed her face. How her whole expression was lit up. And when he kissed her, her lips were wet and ready, and she kissed him back with passionate abandon.

"Swim with me?" Luna murmured against his mouth.

He shouldn't. They had to get moving. He needed to shave and try to get ready for his new identity. *Her husband.* He already felt plenty possessive of her, so it should be an easy enough role to assume. As for Luna, he'd finally get to see her use her acting talent. He was curious about how she would play the role of his wife.

Wife.

Stopping to swim in the spring wasn't on the agenda, but he couldn't refuse her. What would it hurt? Just a few moments, and it made her happy. So he swam.

When she splashed him, he didn't splash back. He just caught her. Kissed her. Let her go. And did the same routine again. Her laughter rang out, and a heaviness around his shoulders seemed to ease.

Sometimes, you didn't notice a burden you were carrying until it started to lighten.

Her arms curled around his neck. Her legs wrapped around his waist. He did not feel any cold. He just felt her. Her mouth was on his again. Her tongue dipping into his mouth. Her breasts pressed to his chest, and he thought about how easy it would be to slip inside of her.

Because he hadn't gotten enough of her the previous night.

Wasn't sure that he could get enough.

Her mouth pulled from his. "Thank you," she told him.

"For what?"

"You didn't want to come into the water." A shiver skated over her. "But you did it for me." Her mouth skimmed his again. "Now guess what I'm going to do for you?"

"You don't have to do anything. We need to get going, though." The new roles they had to play. Hiding in plain sight.

Her mouth moved toward his ear. She murmured just what she was going to do to him.

Ronan immediately rescheduled their morning. "Okay, absolutely, one hundred percent, you can do that." He wasn't an idiot. If the woman wanted to put her tongue and mouth on him, she could have at it.

Then he would have her.

She pulled away. Laughed. Looked so incredibly happy. "Race you back to the house?"

Oh. Adorable.

She was swimming pretty well, but clearly, she did not understand who she faced. He'd grown up on the sugar sand beaches of Gulf Shores, Alabama. He'd been swimming before he walked. He had even—once upon a time—thought about becoming a SEAL.

Instead, he'd wound up as a Marine.

Semper Fi.

But he could still cut through the water just like a fish, and he was waiting on the wooden stairs to watch her as she walked from the water. What a sight to see. The white shirt she'd worn stuck to her like a second skin. No bra. *No. Bra.* The cold had turned her nipples into tight, hard peaks. The shorts clung just as tightly to her. As she exited the spring, water poured down her body.

Nothing had ever been sexier.

He grabbed the handrail. Held it so tightly he was surprised the thing didn't break apart beneath his grip. "I am going to fuck you so hard."

She stopped in front of him. Ran her hand down his bare chest. "Promises, promises."

Yes, it was a promise.

"But you have to catch me, first." Then she took off. She darted around him, snatched up her discarded shoes, and ran up the stairs. In a flash, Luna flew across the dock.

Oh, he had every intention of catching her. Fucking her. *Owning her.*

The last thought drew him up short as he watched her scamper toward the house. She'd left a trail of wet footprints for him to follow.

This isn't permanent. It's just pretend. She's not really mine.

He reached for the gun. She wasn't really his.

So why did it feel as if she was? Why did part of him

138

wish that the roles were real? He'd never wanted someone of his own before. Not for keeps.

This was *not* for keeps. Just a temporary assignment. Another undercover mission. Nothing was real. Nothing.

He headed for the house. Entered and pulled the sliding door back into place behind him. He'd expected Luna to flee through the house.

Instead, Luna stood right in front of him. About a foot away from the door. The shoes she'd been carrying were now on the floor beside her. "I didn't want to drip everywhere." She bit her lower lip. "Thought I'd just wait here for you."

"You didn't want to drip."

"Didn't want to make a mess. It's someone else's home."

He sucked on the inside of his cheek. "I don't think anyone is gonna care."

"I'll care. So I figured we could strip here." Then she reached down and hauled off her wet shirt. And her shorts. And panties. And was completely naked. As his jaw dropped, she carried the items into the nearby kitchen and put them in the sink. "Less mess."

Fuck the mess.

"Mind putting down the gun?"

He put down the gun. Ripped off his wet sweats. Let them hit the floor. He'd clean the place later. Right then, he had other plans.

His other plans turned and hurried toward the stairs.

He caught her before she could climb the first step. He spun her in his arms. Took her mouth. Not one of the teasing kisses she'd given him in the spring. Harder. Deeper. A kiss that told her—in no uncertain terms—that he would be having her.

Now.

He scooped her into his arms. Didn't waste time with words. There was nothing to say. He had her, and he wasn't letting go.

Chapter Twelve

She couldn't seem to stop shivering. But the shivers weren't from the cold of the spring. She didn't feel cold at all, even though droplets of water still clung to her skin.

The shivers came from something else. Anticipation. Need. A heady desire that she'd never experienced, not until him. Ronan carried her up the stairs like her weight didn't matter. His hold and his steps never wavered. He was warm and strong and the sexiest man she'd ever met in her life.

She'd never thought that she'd get swept away by need. Never thought that someone would want her so much. That *she* would want someone this same way.

Back in high school, the boys had all known about her past. They'd all grown up together, and everyone had always treated her as if she was far too fragile. That she'd break if anyone touched her too hard. Then later, when she'd tried to date a few men after college, nothing had ever clicked. By that point, she'd been the uncertain one.

Ronan carried her into the bedroom.

She didn't feel uncertain with him. Luna felt like she just might go mad if she didn't have him in her.

But he didn't take her to the bed. That knowledge dawned on her a bit slowly. She blinked and her head turned. "Ronan?"

"You're cold." Gruff.

No, no, she wasn't cold. Turned on. About to splinter apart with desire, yes. But cold was the last thing she felt.

He took her into the bathroom. Eased her to her feet and let her go. Instantly, she missed his touch and wanted him back, but Ronan just turned on the water so it pounded down from the shower. As the water flowed and steam began to drift in the small room, his eyes raked over her. Every single inch.

"You should..." He swallowed. "Get warm."

Her hand reached for him. "Come with me." Another thing on her list that she'd never done. Shower with someone else. In the movies, it always looked sexy. Hot. In reality, she'd always thought it would be cramped and awkward.

"Like I have to be asked twice."

Just like that, they were in the shower. It was cramped because it was a super small shower, but it wasn't awkward. As the warm water poured over her skin, he pinned her against the tiled wall and his mouth took hers. Heavy, drugging kisses. His muscular thigh slid between her legs. Lifted her up. He put pressure right at her core as she rode along his thigh and kissed him, and his fingers cupped her breasts and teased her nipples and had her moaning into his mouth.

Not awkward. Not at all. Just hot. Sexy. Like in the movies.

Like it wasn't even her real life because surely that

wasn't her sliding her hand down and pumping his thick dick. Surely that wasn't her tipping back her head and moaning as he kissed a path down her throat. As he licked and sucked her skin, and she felt the slightly rough bite of his teeth against her.

She'd always been shy. Holding back with lovers. But she was rubbing her body against his, riding his thigh, wishing that his cock was inside her as the water poured over them. "Ronan, I want *you.*" Right then. Right there. As desperately as she'd wanted him the night before. Being with him hadn't lessened her desire. It had just made her want him more.

She knew how good it would be.

She wanted that insane pleasure again.

"You'll have me." His head lifted. Droplets of water slid through his hair and down the strong planes of his face. "And you'll come for me, won't you? Over and over."

Beautiful, fabulous plan.

"Right now," she urged. Demanded. Luna pumped him faster. "Now, Ronan."

But he shook his head. Ronan reached out to turn off the shower. When the water stopped, she jerked.

"Condom. Don't have them in here." Each word was a rumble. He pulled away from her and stepped from the shower. He turned back with a towel. Curled it around her and pulled her out.

He takes care of me. Again and again. He's not the villain I thought. Not even close.

Then they were back in the bedroom. He snagged a condom and had it on in moments, and they were in bed. Kissing. Tangled. She started to slide onto her back, but he stopped her. He was the one to sprawl on his back, and he tugged her onto him, making Luna straddle him. Her hands flew to press against his chest as she held her balance.

"Take me in fast or take me in slow, princess. You control it."

Her eyes widened. She glanced down at their bodies. Lifted her hips. One of her hands moved to guide his cock into her. She watched as, slowly, he sank inside of her. Inch by inch. Watching him go inside and *feeling* him fill her was so intense that Luna trembled around him. Her lips parted as she gasped out his name. Her inner muscles clamped around him, and she held herself perfectly still as he filled her completely. "That feels...amazing." No pain. Just pleasure waiting to spill through her.

His hands tightened around her hips. "Heaven and hell."

Her gaze whipped to his face and collided with his intense stare. His expression had turned almost brutal with lust. But she wasn't afraid. Didn't think she could be afraid of him. Still holding his gaze, she lifted her hips up. Pushed high, then sank back down to take all of him again.

She moaned.

He growled.

She did it again. And again. The bed squeaked. Rattled. The desire within her tightened even as she tensed.

His fingers slid from her hip to her clit. When she lifted up, his fingers raked over her clit. Fast. Hard. Just what she needed.

Up and down, she went. His fingers raked and strummed and there was no stopping the explosion that rocked through her body as she came for him. She cried out and slumped forward, and his hips kept thrusting against her. The pleasure wouldn't end. It seemed to ricochet through her, and she knew he had to feel the fierce contractions of her inner muscles around him.

"My turn." He tumbled her back. His hips pistoned fast and hard. She stared right at him when the release swept over Ronan. One moment, his face was nearly feral with need...then with pleasure.

I did that. I made him feel that way.

His lips took hers. A kiss as savage as his need and then, against her mouth, he rasped, "Mine."

* * *

"I always wanted to do that."

They were in bed. They shouldn't be. They had to hit the road. A new pretense waited for them.

So why in the hell am I lingering? Ronan turned his head and found Luna smiling at him. Her sweet, innocent smile.

Yeah, she's always gonna look that way. No matter how many times I fuck her, she keeps that innocence. "Do what? Be on top? Figured that was pretty standard fare."

A rosy blush came and went on her cheeks. "Nothing is standard fare for me. Lots of firsts are coming, thanks to you."

What?

"But I was talking about swimming in the spring. And seeing the manatees. I made up this list a while back. Not a bucket list because I don't want to say I'm dying."

She almost died when she was just a kid. Then she almost died with me at that damn cabin. He realized he'd clenched his jaw. With an effort, Ronan relaxed it.

"An adventure list. That's what I saw them called

145

online. I made a list of all the things I wanted to do but never could."

He knew he should tread carefully. He also knew he was more of a bulldozer than a person who ever treaded carefully, so Ronan just demanded, "Why couldn't you do them?"

Her smile dimmed. "I was sick as a kid."

Understatement, princess.

"Then my mom got sick when I was older. She'd taken care of me, so it was my turn to take care of her."

His brow furrowed.

"She was a great mom." A nod against the pillow. "Sometimes, people leave when things get rough. She never left. So I wasn't going to leave, either."

Your prick father deserves an ass kicking.

"When she passed, I felt like I got...stuck. I don't even know if that's the right word to describe things. I didn't take chances. Didn't go after what I used to want. I read that there's a big difference between existing and living, and I feel like I was just going through the motions. Existing. I made the list because I wanted to live."

They needed to go.

He refused to move. "What did you want to do?"

That smile came again even as she pulled the sheets around her body and snuggled a bit closer. Like they were a normal couple and not one say, on the run for their lives. "You want to know what I put on my adventure list?"

He wanted to know every secret that she possessed. "Yes."

"Swimming with manatees. Eating beignets in Café du Monde while jazz music filled the air."

Well, that explained the late-night snack he'd observed.

"Starting my own business. I'd actually just done that,

but, well, it didn't work so well, did it? Just a side hustle that I thought would bring in extra cash so I could take some of the trips I'd started to hope for—a job that might make some people happy at the same time. Only it pretty much cost me my life."

"So you really did have a singing telegram business." His head angled toward her.

One brow lifted in query.

Shit. Had she mentioned it to him before or had he just read that bit in Gray's file? "Uh, Gray might have told me." That should cover his ass. "Haven't heard about one of those in a while."

She inched even closer. "I can sing," she admitted a bit shyly. "And act. Those were my escapes when I was growing up. Mom didn't want me playing sports. Nothing physical that might get me hurt. She always thought I was too fragile. Everyone thought that."

Hadn't he thought the same thing when he first saw her? That she seemed fragile. *Breakable.* Only, she wasn't.

"The stage was safe. And it let me escape. I could stop being the weak girl. I could be a fighter or a fairytale heroine or a doomed Shakespearean character who loved the wrong man." Her lips curled down, then up again. "I could be anyone else. I could escape and I could be happy, and I could forget the rest of the world when I went up on the stage."

"Is that why you became a drama teacher?"

"I was going to New York." Soft. Wistful. "But my mom got sick. She needed me." He heard zero regret in her voice as she told him, "I love being a drama teacher. I get to help my kids escape and shine and..." A little sigh. "They probably have no idea what happened to me." Now there was regret. "I told my principal I had an emergency, and I ran out of town. I hate to leave the kids. I hope they aren't worried."

He didn't know what to do with her. But he didn't like the sadness that had just entered her voice. *Distract her.* "What else is on the list?"

"What?"

"The adventure list. What else is on there?"

Her lashes fluttered. "I want to sing in a club. Always wanted to do that. One of those bluesy places. I want to dance in the moonlight. I want to wake up and see the sun rise over the ocean. I want—" But she stopped. "This talk is all about me. Hardly seems fair. What do *you* want, Ronan?"

He didn't speak.

"I'm sure you've had plenty of adventures. Something tells me that you've been all over the world, haven't you? Seen all kinds of glamorous things?"

He'd been all over the world. He'd seen battlefields. Seen cafés turned into hollowed-out shells as fire raged and explosions rocked the world. He'd seen death. He'd seen crime. He'd seen friends die. Seen friends betray him. "Yeah, I've seen all the glamorous shit." His hand rose, and he tucked a lock of hair behind her ear. His palm lingered against her cheek. "Anything else exciting on this adventure list of yours?"

"Don't even get me going on the sexual things."

Uh, yeah, he'd like to get her going on the sexual things. One hundred percent.

Her head turned, and her lips skimmed against his palm. "I'm already making serious headway there, thanks to you."

He should not ask, but he knew he would anyway. "What kind of headway?"

"Never had someone go down on me, until you." Another skim of her lips against his palm. "Never went down on anyone, until you."

And his dick was making a tent out of the sheets. Surprise, surprise.

Actually, what *was* a surprise? The territorial high he got from knowing he'd been her first. *I don't want any other bastards ever feeling those lush lips on their dicks.* The urge to murder was quite strong at the very thought.

"Never showered with a man, until you. It was a whole lot less awkward and way more sexy than I thought it would be." A pause. "Never spent the night just sleeping in someone's arms, until you. See, I've had lots of firsts with you. You know what? At this point, I'm pretty much thinking you *are* my adventure list."

Damn if that wasn't the nicest thing anyone had ever said to him.

"I get that you've, ah, done the glamorous shit." Her smile came and went again, lighting her eyes. "But is there anything that I've been the first one for you?'

Too many things. "Never spent the night just sleeping with someone else in my arms." Not exactly his style. He never stayed with lovers. Couldn't, not with his job and his cover. "Until you."

Her eyes widened.

"Never wanted to fuck someone until we couldn't move. Until you." It was all he could do not to fuck her again right then. "Never went swimming in a spring with sea cows, until you."

A sweet peal of laughter came from her. Absolutely musical. "I am proud to be your first." She leaned forward to kiss him.

But a phone was ringing. The new phone he'd been

given by Gray. It was on the nightstand. He should answer it. He would. Dammit. "Reality is calling." Gruff. As much as he'd like to ignore reality, he couldn't. He pulled away. Climbed from the bed. Reached for the phone. He whipped it up to his ear. "Gray. We're about to leave now for—"

"Change of plans," Gray said, voice crisp. "We need to talk. Make sure the target can't hear this conversation."

She was in his bed. Naked. Calling her the target felt wrong as hell. Ronan glanced over at Luna. "You should get ready to leave."

She nodded.

He kept the phone to his ear and headed out of the bedroom. The stairs barely creaked beneath his steps. "She can't hear me." Flat. "What's the change?" He reached the landing.

"We're going to let Marcus Aeros take her."

His steps halted. "What. The. Fuck?" Then, right after that thought...

Over my dead body. No, even better. *Over Marcus's.*

Chapter Thirteen

SHE HAD A GOLD WEDDING RING ON HER FINGER, AND her husband was the sexiest, most dangerous looking man on the island.

Luna glanced down at the white dress she wore. Unless she was on a stage, she would never have worn the dress. Way too revealing and sensual and...uh, not her. But this was not an ordinary day. Did she even have ordinary days—or nights—any longer? The garment fit her like a second skin, the top had a daring V that plunged between her breasts, and the dress stopped mid-thigh. *Maybe* mid-thigh. That was certainly being generous. The dress had been paired with a pair of elegant, strappy sandals.

Her hair had been cut. Her decision because she'd wanted it to match the image on her new driver's license. Gone were the long locks she'd sported before. Now her hair skimmed just above her shoulders in a sleek bob. She wore long, dangling earrings that danced when she moved her head. And bright red lipstick to match the shoes.

I feel like a different person. Because, for all intents and purposes, she was.

She was Ronan's wife.

He hadn't been excited when she told him that she wanted to pause their trek to cut her hair. He'd muttered about her hair being gorgeous. But *he'd* gotten to change things up in order to match his new ID—he'd shaved off his beard—so she'd wanted to blend better, too.

And when she'd come out with the new cut...

Even sexier. That had been his response. It had warmed every inch of her.

Though she could certainly have said the same words to him. Before they'd left the safe house, he'd ditched his beard. And she had loved the beard. But without it...

Even sexier. His square jaw was on full display. Not just sexy, but gorgeous. He even had a little dent in his chin. Not a full cleft, but a dent she had the oddest urge to lick.

Whatever. She'd like to lick all of him.

"What are you thinking?"

His low question had her hand flying out to grab the champagne flute in front of her. "Just thinking I'd like to lick all of you." Yep, she said the words. Because this was her second glass of champagne, and she clearly could not control her tongue.

He blinked. Then glanced around.

They'd made it down to the Keys. Or, specifically, to the couple's retreat on a private island. They'd been taken to the island via boat. Dropped off on the wooden dock, and she'd tried hard not to look as dazzled as she felt. The place was paradise. Pure paradise with palm trees and thatched-roof-covered bungalows. They were currently having their dinner on the beach. A million stars glittered overhead, and a dozen tables had been set up beneath hanging lights. Not that they needed those lights, not with all the stars to light the sky.

A band played about fifteen feet away. Flames twisted in firepits strategically placed around the perimeter. Couples danced in the sand, swaying as they listened to the music. The champagne kept flowing.

Upon arrival, she'd been told there were no televisions in the bungalows. No phones were to be used in the guest rooms or any public areas. There was Wi-Fi on the island, but she'd been firmly informed that any ringing phones were frowned upon by management and the other guests.

Not like she planned to have a ringing phone. She was just too delighted by the escape.

I'm trapped in a nightmare one day. Living in paradise the next. She almost wanted to pinch herself because this could not be real.

Twelve acres of paradise. No distractions. No fears. And the sexiest husband in the world.

His lips kicked into a half smile. "Just how much champagne have you had?"

"Two glasses." She put her empty glass down. "And that means I have to stop."

"A lightweight, are you?"

"You have no idea." Much more, and she'd probably be snoozing on the table. Embarrassing.

"Oh, I think I'm about to find out." He wore a white shirt he'd rolled up to his elbows. Dark khakis. His usual watch that perched over the snake tattoo on his wrist. Though parts of the snake—particularly its twisting tail—peeked out. His hair was tousled by the wind, and the faintest hint of teasing seemed to fill his eyes. "Be right back, princess."

Where was he going? Her head tilted as she followed his stride. Okay, fine, her head tilted as she followed his ass.

It was a great ass. It was also an ass that had just gone toward the stage.

She straightened in her chair. She'd ditched her sandals beneath the table and let her feet sink into the sand. How could she not? She was on a beach, for goodness' sake. If your toes weren't in the sand, you weren't doing the beach right.

Ronan was whispering to the singer. Luna was pretty sure she just caught the flash of cash being handed off. Ronan turned back around, caught her watching him, and he winked.

A stupid, sexy wink.

I'm in such trouble. I think I'm falling for my fake husband. It was all too easy to imagine that the pretense was real. If, ah, she forgot about the dead body they'd left in Louisiana and the fact that a hit had been put on her life.

Ronan headed back to their table. Stopped right in front of her. He extended his hand.

Oh. She smiled. "You got him to play a song for us, didn't you?" Another item on her adventure list. Dancing under the stars and moonlight. How perfect. And crazy thoughtful.

He pulled her into his arms. Eased her into the group of couples swaying slowly. His sandalwood scent filled her nose. His warmth surrounded her. Sure, she'd left her shoes behind at the table. Why not? He seemed extra big and bold and he held her so carefully as they danced. One big hand was on the base of her spine. The other cradled her hand.

"Princess..." His head lowered. "The dance is fun, don't get me wrong. But I didn't pay for it." His breath teased her ear.

Then he bit her ear. A light, sensual bite.

A shiver skated down her body even as yearning spread through her. "I-I saw you hand off money."

They swayed together. For such a big guy, Ronan was very light on his feet. "Um."

"Why did you give him money?"

The music slowed. Stopped.

The singer tapped the microphone. "Gonna take a little break," he announced. "But don't worry. We've had a special request, and someone will be taking my spot."

Oh, no. No. She pulled away from Ronan, just enough to look over at the small stage. Toward the singer who was now pointing toward her.

As in, pointing dead at her. Just in case she was wrong, Luna glanced over her shoulder. There was only a palm tree behind her.

"Your adventure list is waiting," Ronan murmured. "Let's see if you're all talk...or if you're gonna start that living you keep telling me about."

The singer raised his brows and kept pointing at her. Now all the other couples were looking at her, too.

"It's our anniversary," Ronan announced into the slightly uncomfortable silence that followed her body freezing. "Five years tonight. Surprise, sweetheart. I thought you'd love to sing your favorite song for everyone." Then he nudged her toward the stage. "You got this." Soft.

Luna stumbled forward. She didn't know if she should be mortified. Mad. Or...

Thrilled?

He did this for me.

Though she did not know if she did, indeed, have this.

The singer took her hand and helped her onto the stage. "Give Cameron over there your song." He bobbed his head toward the man seated at the piano. "He can play anything." A soft laugh. "Don't worry about this crowd. Most have been drinking all night. You could sound like a chipmunk, and they'd still keep swaying."

Well, that was somewhat reassuring. Not like she had time for any vocal warmups, so she'd be going into this thing raw. Which probably meant the first few notes would be rough. Hopefully, not too rough. She wanted Ronan to think she was good. Was it so wrong that she wanted to impress her fake husband?

She crept toward Cameron. Mumbled her request. Then went back and stood in front of the microphone. It was one of those tall microphones attached to a black pole. The pole was positioned way too high for her, so she pulled the microphone off the pole and held it in her hand. Then she scooted the pole to the side.

The couples were watching her. But she didn't really care about them. She cared about the tall, dark, and dangerously handsome man with his hands crossed over his chest and a faint smile on his face. He had one eyebrow raised, and his head cocked to the right as he waited for her to begin.

The piano player's fingers rolled over the keys. The music drifted into the air.

When you sing or when you act, you can become someone else. Nothing else matters. All the pain leaves. Pain and fear disappear.

Her breath whispered out. Her heart drummed too fast.

And she began to sing. Soulful. Bluesy, because that had always been her favorite style. Her voice was a little husky at first, then stronger. Sweeping around the notes and purring with sensuality as her confidence grew.

Ronan's eyes widened. He lost his faint smile. His lips parted. His mouth might have dropped open. She never

looked away from him. She couldn't. This song was about a
lover she didn't want to leave. A man she couldn't lose. It
was for him.

Because she was falling in love with her hitman.

* * *

HE COULD NOT MOVE.

Couples danced around him. Waiters bustled past as
they kept the champagne flowing.

Ronan remained locked to the spot.

Holy hell, the woman can sing.

He had gone up to the stage on instinct. Some foolish
part of him had just wanted to do something to make her
happy. Especially after that piss-poor conversation with
Gray. He hadn't told her about that talk. Didn't plan to
do so.

*Use her as bait? Throw her into the lion's den and let
him rip her apart?* Dumbass plan.

She'd been sitting at the table, smiling her enchanting
smile, and he'd thought...why the hell not? Why not cross
another item off her list?

It had been easy enough to slip the performer on stage
some cash. The fellow had been heading off for a break,
anyway. And the crowd was small. Couples—lovers—totally
involved with each other. Not like he had to worry about
someone snapping pics or recording Luna.

The island was supposed to be phone free.

So he'd paid the cash. Gotten her on stage.

Only now *he* was paying the price. Because Luna
wasn't just good. She was fantastic. Her voice tempted and
taunted and promised so many things as she sang with
unbelievable control. Lights were behind her, shining

around her, and her body was on perfect display. He'd known the dress would be trouble the minute he saw it.

The haircut suited her. The haircut before had suited her, too, though. This one made her jaw and cheekbones look a bit sharper. Gave her more of that enchanting, witchy vibe that he found far too hot.

Luna had been made to perform. He could see that. She didn't tremble or hesitate. She poured emotion into her voice, and she utterly captivated him. It was all he could do not to stalk toward that stage, pull her into his arms, and carry her off.

She's singing for me. Her deep, emerald eyes were on him, and he could not look away from her.

She held the final note. Held it so long and then let go with a soft sigh.

The couples had stopped dancing. They erupted into applause for her.

He didn't clap. He was too damn spellbound.

Her smile flashed. The nervous, shy one. The one that showed she still had so much innocence about her, despite his best efforts to acquaint her with sin. She did a quick, ducking bow. Waved to the crowd.

People were asking for more, but she shook her head and turned for the piano player. Luna bent to speak quickly with him. As she moved to step away from the pianist, his hand flew out and curled around her wrist.

Ronan immediately took a step forward.

Only to find some blond asshole in his path. "Holy shit," the man proclaimed. "Is she with you? Because that woman can *sing*."

"My wife." The words might have come out guttural and possessive. Fair enough, he was guttural and possessive. Particularly when it came to Luna. The blond was also in his way. The man was a few inches shorter than Ronan, so he had no trouble seeing beyond the guy and noting that the pianist still had his hand curled around Luna's wrist.

You need to let her go, now.

"Dude. I want her."

Ronan blinked. His gaze left the pianist and focused on the fool right in front of him. "You want to say that again?" *Clearly, so that when I beat the hell out of you, you understand why you had the pain coming to you.*

The blond gulped. His muddy brown eyes went very, very large. "I'm married!" He threw up his hand. "Married. Happy. Super happy. Deliriously so." He pointed to the right where a curvy brunette with warm brown skin and laughing, dark eyes sipped champagne. She wiggled her fingers back at him. "Monique and I own a club in Key West and one in Miami. We're holding auditions for new talent soon, and your wife would be perfect."

Too bad his wife was running for her life.

"When I said I wanted her...I meant at my clubs. She'd be a hit. That sultry voice, that control...damn. She probably already has deals somewhere, huh? She's really incredible."

She was also tugging against the hold of the pianist. Why was the man still touching her? "Excuse me," Ronan said, stiffly polite. "I have to go and break someone's fingers."

The blond craned his head to see where Ronan was looking. Then, "Oh, shit." He yanked his hand into his pocket. Pulled out a card and shoved it at Ronan. "Just—ah, keep this, would you? In case she wants to talk."

Performing in a busy club wasn't currently an option for Luna. She could be spotted by the wrong person. Especially in a place like Miami. Too many connections there led back to Atlanta. Word could spread to Marcus that she was still alive...

Exactly what Gray wanted to happen.

Tricky bastard.

Jaw locking, Ronan took the card. He shoved it into his pocket and shouldered past the blond.

"Great meeting you!" The blond called after him, "Name's Harris, by the way. And your wife is—"

He didn't hear the rest of the words. He was in front of the stage. A leap had him *on* the stage. A second later, he was behind Luna. "It's going to be hard to play the piano with broken fingers." Just a helpful observation for the pianist. Ronan could be kind that way. Giving out pro tips left and right.

The pianist blinked at him. Dark hair. Tanned skin. Golden eyes. Hair carefully tousled. White shirt unbuttoned to the middle of his chest. Young, maybe early twenties. "My fingers aren't broken."

Ah. Clearly someone who was not too fast on the uptake. "They will be if you touch my wife without permission again."

The man shot up from the piano and staggered back. His hands immediately flew in front of him. "It's not like that!" He wore thick, leather cuffs around each of his wrists. He looked at his upraised hands and hurriedly placed them behind his back. As if that would protect him. "I was just asking her where she'd performed before. No way is this her first time on a stage."

And Luna hadn't been able to respond because she couldn't tell him that she was from Atlanta and that she was a middle school drama teacher on the run.

"I was just impressed, that's all. She's a hundred times

better than the guy I've been working with. Look, we get drunk people up here singing all the time."

"I'm not drunk," Luna hotly denied. "Or maybe I am. A little." She curled her hand around Ronan's arm. "Let's go to our room."

"No, she's not drunk." The pianist nodded. "She's talented, that's what she is. We could work together. People are always looking for singers around here. I can't sing for shit, but I can play like nobody's business."

"Only if your fingers aren't broken." That pro tip again.

The guy backed up a step. "I don't want broken fingers."

"Then keep your hands to yourself."

Luna's grip tightened on Ronan. "What are you doing?"

His head turned. He stared into her eyes. Kept seeing her as she'd been on stage. Seductive. Passionate. His left hand lifted and skated down her cheek. "Protecting what's mine."

"Your husband is a dick," the pianist muttered. "Controlling asshole. Don't want to tell you your business but...*run*. Run, lady. Far and fast."

Ronan's head turned back toward the pianist. "My wife knows I would never hurt her. But I would destroy anyone who so much as bruised her skin." He reached for the delicate wrist that the man had been clutching.

"Oh, God." Ronan could hear the pianist gulp. "Just was trying to get contact info. That's all I was doing while we talked. I was not hitting on your lady. I could use a good singer. We could partner up—"

"Stop scaring him," Luna ordered. "I'm not bruised." She tugged her hand from Ronan. He let her go. She frowned at the shaking pianist. "Told you, I'm not interested. But thanks for playing the piano for me." Her brow furrowed as she focused on Ronan. "Now, are we going to our room or are we standing on stage all night?"

Shit, were they still on stage? They were. Without another word, he climbed from the stage, then turned to catch her waist so that he could lift her back down onto the sand.

A few people clapped for her again as they passed through the crowd. She blushed a bit more and offered her thanks. Luna scooped up her sandals, and they hurried away from the tables and the lights. They snaked through the palm trees and ambled along the faint path that led to their bungalow. As soon as they were away from the crowd, though, Luna stopped. "I forgot that you now get to play the role of jealous husband. Nice job, by the way. Completely believable. For a moment there, I thought you actually were jealous. Didn't realize you had such strong acting talent."

It hadn't been a role. He *had* been jealous. A very new emotion for him. "I don't share."

"Okay." She swung the sandals in her hand and rocked forward onto the balls of her feet. A large palm tree waited right behind her. "Again, great acting. Because you totally had me believing that you're super jealous and ready to rip apart any man who touched me."

"I am." Flat. Truthful. Completely disconcerting.

She sank back onto her heels. "Excuse me?" A laugh. Nervous. "It's just us. You don't have to pretend any longer."

"Screw pretending." He crowded in close to her.

She backed against the tree.

"I am jealous." Something he would have to deal with. He didn't like the feeling, Ronan knew that for certain. It twisted his guts and made him want to drive his fist into the faces of any men who were lusting after her. "You were fantastic on that stage."

Shadows surrounded her, but he caught the flash of her smile. "You think so?" Her smile dimmed as she rushed to add, "You don't have to lie. I was so nervous that my knees were knocking together. I just kept looking at you, though, because I knew you weren't going to laugh at me."

Laugh at her? What?

"You were my strong spot. I used strong spots starting in high school. Whenever I got nervous on stage, I'd find one person in the audience I could count on. It used to be my mom. Tonight, it was you." She threw her arms around him. Squeezed. "That was nerve-racking and incredible at the same time. Thank you." The sandals banged into his back.

His hands curled around her waist. *She's thanking me, and I just nearly broke a man's hands.* "I don't think you're understanding things properly." She shouldn't thank him for being a jealous asshole.

She pulled back. "You did something really nice for me." A brief pause. "I think your heart is way bigger than you realize."

Something was way bigger than she realized, and growing more so by the second. Not his heart. Nope. Not that.

"The doting husband and then the jealous lover. Two big roles in one night. I think I could learn some things from you when it comes to acting." Her hands—and the sandals she still grasped—fell back to her sides. She started to slip around him.

He raised his hands and caged her against the palm tree. "We have a problem."

"Oh, no. What is it?" Alarm flashed in her voice.

"I *am* a jealous lover. I didn't like his hand on you. You

were trying to get away from him. He didn't let you go. He pulls that shit again, and he'll be dealing with me."

No response. Right. Because he sounded like a crazy person. Ronan cleared his throat. "You were gorgeous on the stage. The light was behind you. Your body was fucking perfection. And your voice—sin and sunshine. How the hell can that even be a combination?"

But wasn't that what she was? Sin and sunshine for him? The best of both worlds with her witchy, sexy looks and the innocence that just wouldn't dim? "What the fuck am I supposed to do with you?" Ronan wondered.

He heard a faint thud. One, then another. The sandals had hit the sand.

One of her soft hands rose to press to his cheek. "Protect me."

Yes, that was exactly what he was doing.

"And, I think *fucking* me sounds like a really good option, too."

She almost got fucked then and there. Right against the palm tree. It would be so easy to lift her up. To shove Luna's short dress out of his way and take her there. But...

No protection. No condom.

If he fucked her and got her pregnant, he wouldn't be able to let Luna go. She'd have to stay with him. Forever.

Why was the thought so dangerously tempting?

Before he could speak, she was kissing him. A soft kiss on the mouth. One that just teased when he wanted deep and hard. He wanted her mouth fully open and crushed beneath his as his tongue plundered past her lips. But Luna was gentle. Careful. And then her mouth skimmed down to the scar that curved under his lower lip and swept partially down his chin.

She hadn't asked about the scar. He knew it was more

visible without the beard. But ditching the beard—
temporarily—had been necessary. An easy enough change
that made a big difference for any jerks who might be
looking for him.

*Gray, you'd better not leak our location. If you do
anything to jeopardize her safety, hell will come calling for
you.* Friend or no friend.

She'd angled her head and was kissing his neck now.
Soft. Light kisses. The delicate lick of her tongue
teased him.

*So easy to fuck her here. Just lift her up. Rip the panties
away. Drive home.*

No, dammit, *no*.

At least, not out in the open. They had a perfectly good
bungalow waiting. One with a big-ass bed. One stocked
with more champagne. One waiting with rose petals and
candlelight because *maybe* he'd ordered the romance
package just for her. Not because of their ruse. Because
of her.

Shit. What was up with him?

"Our room," he growled. Either they got there in the
next thirty seconds, or he'd fuck her wherever they
happened to be. Those little licks and the sweet bite she'd
just given him had pushed Ronan too far.

"Race you there?" she asked.

What? It took a moment too long for her words to
register in his lust-fogged head. By then, Luna had pulled
away. She laughed. Scooped up her shoes and ran down the
path. As he watched her flee, a smile tugged at his lips. One
full of anticipation. A bit of savage need.

She wanted to be chased? She'd clearly come to the
right man. He took off after her. He followed the sweet
sound of her laughter. Followed the flash of her legs under

the starlight. She darted up the steps and into their bungalow. Didn't even stop to unlock the door. Just threw it right open and went inside.

Didn't stop to unlock the door.

Except, the door should have been locked. It one hundred percent should have been locked. After the staff had set up the romance package, they knew to lock the door. Standard damn procedure.

She was inside now. He couldn't see her. A burst of adrenaline and speed fueled him, a burst that might have also been marked by sudden, stark fear as he hurtled onto the small porch that led to the bungalow. "*Luna!*"

He burst inside. Then froze when he saw the man holding Luna.

* * *

You DIDN'T LEAVE loose ends in this world.

Fuck me. Ronan Walker knows that I sent Kurt to kill him. The attempt had failed. Marcus huddled over his computer. He was about to send payment for Luna's kill. Maybe that payment would get Ronan off his back.

I didn't get my proof that she was dead. No finger. No photos. The only photo I got was Kurt's. Bloody, dead Kurt.

Kurt...who led right back to Marcus.

Ronan knows that I wanted to kill him. He knows I sent Kurt to end his life. Even if Marcus hit send on the payment for Luna's hit, would that really stop Ronan from getting his revenge?

Marcus knew the man's reputation. Ronan always got the job done. One word was routinely used to describe him. Relentless. A former military hero turned hired gun, no one escaped from Ronan.

He won't let me escape, either. If I pay him, he'll still come for me. I'll be dead, and he'll just be richer.

The only way out? To stop Ronan. Permanently. To kill the killer.

So maybe, instead of paying for Luna's murder, he could use that cash for another purpose. Surely there would be people out there who would jump at the chance to claim credit for taking out Ronan the Relentless?

And with a million-dollar payday waiting, why not see who could get the job done? What did he have to lose? Marcus knew his life was already on the line.

Determination had his shoulders squaring. He wasn't ready to die.

He knew just how to reach out to the right—and wrong —people on the Dark Web. Time to chum the waters.

And put a hit on the hitman.

Chapter Fourteen

In a blink, Ronan had a gun in his hand and aimed at Luna. Or rather, she figured the gun was aimed at the stranger standing behind her. The stranger who held her in a too tight grip. The man had been waiting inside the bungalow. The space had been lit with fluttering candlelight. She'd rushed inside, still high from singing, giddy with desire for Ronan, and this man had been waiting. He'd grabbed her. Spun her around so that she was in front of him, and now he held her in a too tight grip even as her hands grabbed at the arm he'd looped around her.

"You're scaring her." Flat. Hard. From Ronan. "I don't like it when my wife is scared."

"Your wife, huh?" Soft, mocking laughter. "That is a fun one." He didn't let her go. "Kinda familiar situation, isn't it, Ronan?"

He knows Ronan. When they'd checked in at the island, she and Ronan had used fake names. No one should know their real names. This man did. That meant the situation was very, very bad.

"If I remember correctly," the stranger continued,

almost musing, "I was in a motel with *my* wife, minding my own business, when you burst in and you fucking *shot* me."

Oh, no. Her breath shuddered out. She stared at Ronan as terror clawed at her. This wasn't about her past. It was about his. Somehow, a ghost from Ronan's past had found them. Now they were both in deadly danger.

"You shot me," the man repeated, "and then you abducted *my* wife."

Wait, *what*?

"That pissed me off," the man behind her continued.

Ronan took a slow, stalking step forward. "You know I apologized for that shit."

He'd apologized? For attempted murder? And abduction?

"You. Are. Scaring. Her." Gritted from Ronan as he took another stalking step. "I'd hate to have to shoot you, but if you don't let Luna go in the next five seconds, we are going to have a problem." A pause. "These are real bullets, my friend."

And the others had been, what? Pretend? Wait. Maybe that was exactly what they'd been. The light dawned for her. "Did he pretend to kill you, too?" Luna gasped out her question as she tugged at his grip yet again. Only there was zero give in the man's hold.

"Two seconds," Ronan snapped out. "Then, screw it."

Was he about to fire his gun? With her standing right there? "Ronan!" she cried.

The stranger released her. "Someone is in a trigger-happy mood."

She ran for Ronan. He caught her hand and immediately shoved her behind his back. "You scared Luna," he snarled.

"*Oui.*" A woman's voice. A gorgeous femme fatale type

sauntered from the shadows behind the man. Luna hadn't even known the woman was there until that moment. "I believe we have covered the point that Tyler scared Luna. About three times now." She put her hand on the man's shoulder. "I don't believe that Ronan likes for his Luna to be frightened."

The guy caught her hand. Brought it to his lips and kissed her knuckles almost as if by instinct. His gaze didn't leave Ronan. "Point noted."

"What in the hell are you doing here?" Ronan demanded. He finally lowered his gun. Put it on the nearby table.

Had he been wearing that gun all night? She hadn't noticed it. Not even when they'd been dancing so closely. Or when they'd been kissing beneath the palm tree.

"What are you *both* doing here?" Ronan's question thundered out.

The woman's plump lips pulled down in a pout. "How are you not happy to see me? Everyone is always happy to see me."

"Not true, sweetheart." This came from the stranger. "*I'm* always happy to see you," he clarified. "You are the light of my life. But other people are usually terrified."

She frowned.

Luna poked Ronan in the back. She had questions. "Did you pretend to kill him, too?"

He spun toward her. Glowered. Then kissed her. Hard and deep and possessively.

A whistle split the air. One followed by the man noting, "Oh, this is problematic. Very, very problematic."

Ronan lifted his head. His gaze glittered at her even as he ordered the guy, "Fuck off, Tyler."

"That is *no* way to greet your friend!" The woman's

voice. Offended. "We come all this way to provide precious backup for you. And you don't even offer a thanks? You give us a rude 'fuck off' in response to our generous efforts?" She sniffed. "I thought you had better manners."

He sighed and stepped around Luna. Very firmly, Ronan shut and locked the door to the bungalow.

Luna held herself perfectly still. There was a trail of candles leading from the bungalow's front door to the bedroom. Super romantic and mood inspiring. She could also see rose petals sprinkled along the path.

"You did not think I had better manners, Esme," Ronan denied. "You've told me before that I lack manners."

"That was when you kidnapped me. Kidnapping a person is rude. Everyone understands that fact."

Ronan hit the light switch. Immediately, more illumination flooded the area, and Luna could see the man and woman clearly. The woman was truly gorgeous, while the man...

Big, strong, scary.

The typical guy she now associated as being...friends with Ronan? "You're his friend," she said, testing out her theory.

The man rolled one powerful shoulder. The shoulder that the woman was not currently touching. "Like friends can't be horrible enemies at the same time? You clearly do not understand the world in which Ronan and I live."

Ronan grunted as he stalked toward his *maybe* friend. "Your entrance tonight was way too dramatic. You could have just knocked on the door like a sane person."

"I thought you deserved a dramatic entrance." A quick smile curved the guy's lips. The smile didn't do anything to make him look less intimidating.

"Are we even now?" Ronan wanted to know. "Going to

stop roasting me over the coals for shit I had to do in the past?"

"I don't know about even. I mean, have I shot you in the chest? No? Then...not yet."

"Stop it!" Luna marched to stand between the two arguing men. "I have been under a *lot* of stress lately, and I would appreciate fewer intense, ambiguous statements and more just honest talk. Can we manage that, please?" Her head swiveled between Ronan and... "Who are you?"

"Tyler. Tyler Barrett, and this is my lovely wife, Esme."

"*Enchantée*," Esme murmured. She took her hand off her husband and wiggled her fingers toward Luna.

"Uh, sure. Enchanted to meet you, too." No, she was not. She was a bit scared. Probably more than a bit. A lot more. "*Why* are you both here?"

Tyler stepped forward. "Because I'm the man who's here to take you away."

He was there to do what? She must have misheard. "Ronan?" Her head whipped back toward him.

A muscle jerked along his clenched jaw.

"I think I like you better with the beard," Esme announced thoughtfully. "You're a little too polished now."

The muscle along Ronan's jaw jerked again. A harder jerk. His gaze was on Tyler. "Gray sent you?"

"Um. That is my job, after all."

Her head whipped back to Tyler. She was starting to feel dizzy. "What's your job?"

"I'm a U.S. Marshal. I'll be the man escorting you to your new life and giving you a new identity."

She already had a new identity. "I'm Ronan's wife."

Tyler shook his head. "That's only a temporary cover. I'll be giving you the real deal. When you leave this island with me, you'll never be seeing Ronan again."

Her heart seemed to wither in her chest. When was this event supposed to happen? Was he taking her away from Ronan right then? Why did the idea of never seeing Ronan again hurt her so much? They'd just met days before. He'd saved her. They'd had insanely incredible sex. But—but emotions weren't involved. Right?

Right?

If emotions weren't involved, why did her chest ache so much?

"She's not leaving." A guttural vow from Ronan. Then he was taking her hand. His fingers threaded with hers. "You try to take her, and we'll have a problem."

Her lips parted. Only no words would come out. Was he saying that he wanted her to stay with him? Hope flared. Her withered heart began to bloom—

"Or at least," Ronan continued grimly, slanting a fast look in her direction before focusing on Tyler again, "she's not leaving until I get the all clear from Gray. So stand the hell down, my friend. Because until I receive word that I am officially off-duty, I am in charge of Luna's protection. She stays with me. And that is a non-negotiable detail." A lift of his chin. "I am sure you understand all about non-negotiables."

"Those non-negotiables can bite you in the ass," Tyler murmured.

"Do I look scared?" A challenge.

"No, but you do seem a bit obsessed. Better watch that." Tyler saluted. He took his wife's hand. "Come, sweetheart, I think our own bungalow is waiting."

"Will it be filled with candlelight and rose petals?" Esme batted her eyes at him. "A perfect lair of seduction?"

Tyler glared at Ronan. "Asshole. Now you're making me look bad in front of Esme." His head tilted as his stare narrowed in suspicion on Ronan. "Just why do you have the full romance package?"

"Because I believe in a thorough cover." An immediate reply from Ronan. "We're celebrating our fifth anniversary. What else would a caring husband do but splurge on the full package?"

"What else, indeed." Tyler sucked in the side of his cheek. "Got to keep up those appearances."

Esme elbowed him. He gave no reaction to the jab.

Tyler's stare remained suspicious as he mused, "Interesting, though, the way she came running in this place. Why *were* you running, Luna? Were you scared of something?"

She felt heat sting her cheeks. She hadn't been scared. Turned on, but not scared.

"I don't think she was scared," Esme pointed out.

An unnecessary point.

"I don't think so, either," her husband agreed. He inclined his head. "Night, you two. And, of course, Ronan, I don't have to warn you about the danger of crossing lines, do I?"

"Considering that you married the last line you crossed, I'm thinking the warning isn't one you should give."

Luna was lost.

"I am not a line." A dramatic announcement from Esme. "I am a star. A supernova. The light of his life. Did you not hear him say that very thing just moments before? I heard it. Incredibly romantic."

"Absolutely. You are a light. A blinding supernova, no doubt." Tyler nodded. "He used the wrong word. Ignore him."

Esme sniffed again.

Luna did not know what to think of these people.

"In public, we'll be strangers to you," Tyler said. His voice had turned flat. Maybe his getting-down-to-business tone? "Thus, the secretive meeting. Sorry we had to lie in wait for you, but we didn't exactly want the world hearing our business."

Luna did not think he sounded particularly sorry. Just matter of fact. Like he had zero regrets for terrifying her.

"We already know the assumed names you're using, and you can count on us to be professional when we are in public."

"Professional is my middle name," Esme declared.

"It is not," Tyler returned. "Chaos is."

She smiled at him.

Tyler tugged her toward the door, but Esme paused near Luna. "I heard you sing."

Luna hadn't seen the other woman during the performance, but, then again, her eyes had been glued to Ronan. She'd barely seen anyone else at all.

"You have talent."

"Thank you?" Yes, she said the words as a question because Esme had stated hers like an accusation.

"Talent should not be hidden in this world. It should be celebrated. Enjoyed by others. There is enough darkness that we all could use some light." Her eyes assessed Luna. "Why aren't you on a stage all the time?"

"I—"

"Back off, Esme," Ronan ordered. "You don't know her story. And she doesn't have to offer it up to you on a silver platter. I get that you love digging and scheming, but she's off-limits."

"Is she?" Esme did not seem convinced. If anything, she just appeared intrigued. "Is that why you hold her so possessively? Because she is off-limits? Why do we always want the things that we are not supposed to have?"

He *was* holding her. His grip was tight on Luna's hand, and his body stood right beside hers. Protective. Possessive?

"My mother was an opera singer," Esme confided as she leaned a little closer to Luna.

"Among other things," Ronan muttered.

Esme frowned at him. Then she focused on Luna once more. "Her talent was phenomenal. Because of her, I've been around my share of performers. You have something. Potential never dies. Though we can let it languish when life gets in our way. An unfortunate state of affairs." A shrug. "I sound like a croaking frog when I sing."

"You do not," Tyler immediately denied.

"Love is blind, and sometimes hard of hearing." Esme inclined her head toward Luna. "I know talent. I hope to hear you sing again soon. So do me a favor and try to stay alive, would you? Because I think I like you, Luna."

With that parting shot, Tyler and Esme exited. Swearing, Ronan followed in their wake. He locked the door behind them and then stood there for a moment with his hand pressed to the frame and his back to Luna.

She finally took a deep breath even though her heart still raced far too fast in her chest. "Those were your friends?" Slightly scary. Seemed right that they'd be his friends.

"Yes."

"And he's...going to take me away?" A U.S. Marshal. Yes, yes, that tracked. The marshals handled witness protection. Her arms wrapped around her stomach. She'd wanted this outcome originally. Protection. A new life. It had been the whole reason for her New Orleans meeting with the FBI and Grayson Stone. But...

I'm not ready to leave Ronan. Not yet.

He shoved away from the door. Spun and stalked back to her. Ronan stepped over the sandals she'd dropped when Tyler grabbed her. His hand rose and curled under her chin. "Not yet," he vowed, and his words echoed her own thoughts. "No one is taking you away from me yet." His mouth claimed hers.

Chapter Fifteen

Tyler shut the door to his bungalow. A bungalow that just happened to be right beside Ronan's. Gray tended to be obsessive with organizational points like that, so the location was hardly a surprise.

"I don't see any candles." A pout pulled at Esme's lips. "Or rose petals." A forlorn sigh. "However will I cope?" She glanced back at him. Whatever she saw on his face caused all amusement to vanish. In a breath, she was in front of him. Her hands rose to press lightly against his chest. "What is it? And how can I help you?"

She helped him by breathing. By being in his world because he couldn't imagine life without her. His deceptive and dangerous but ever-so-lovely bride.

"You're worrying me, Tyler. You know I don't like to worry. Worry wastes valuable energy."

No, Esme didn't like to worry. She liked to live in the moment. One hundred miles an hour, that was her. Living life to the fullest and usually terrifying him in the process. "He's possessive of her."

"I did notice that."

"He was pissed as hell that I'd scared her."

Her hands darted up to curl around his shoulders. "I noticed that detail, too. I like to be observant."

"Ronan is *never* possessive."

"There's a first time for everything."

"They're involved." He could see it in the way Ronan watched her.

She nodded. "I saw her face whenever she looked at him. The woman has fallen, fast and hard."

Yeah, and Luna Black would be hurt. "Ronan will not fall in love. He might be fucking her, but..." His words trailed off. Five minutes ago, he would have said that Ronan would never fuck a target. He would have been wrong about that assessment.

"Anyone can love. Even the darkest villain can have one person that touches something softer inside of him." Her head tilted. Her hair trailed over her shoulder. "What is it about Ronan that makes you so sure he can't love her? After all, he loves you."

Tyler frowned at Esme.

"He's your friend. Your family. You might still be a wee bit pissed about what went down between the two of you, but the bond is there. Unbreakable. Isn't that why you're here? Because Grayson called you and told you that he wanted someone to watch Ronan's back?"

Yes.

"And in a blink, you dropped everything. Here we are."

He wanted to tell her more about Ronan. About why he was so sure Ronan would not give in and love Luna. About the wall that Ronan had always put up. Hell, Ronan hadn't wanted the ties of friendship. They'd been forced on him.

Tyler remembered when he'd first met Ronan. The guy had smiled plenty, but the smile had never reached his eyes.

That was the thing about Ronan. He could seem open. Even easy-going at times. But it was a lie. Nothing really got past Ronan's guard.

A guard that had been put in place when Ronan was just a teen. The time he'd gotten the scar on his face. After that horrible day, Ronan had become far too good at pretending.

And maintaining outward appearances. Hell could be brewing inside Ronan, and the rest of the world would never know it.

Tyler exhaled.

"I don't like it when you keep secrets. Aren't we supposed to share everything?"

Before he could answer Esme, his phone rang. Right on time, of course. Gray was always punctual. Unless, of course, he'd been kidnapped and subjected to a long torture spree. That recent event had been the only time Gray had gone off the radar. Like his buddy Kane Harte, Tyler was increasingly worried about what that time in torture had done to Gray. Not that Gray would share his secrets or his pain with them. The man tried to act invincible.

No one was invincible.

"Saved by the bell. We will revisit this chat. Secrets bite everyone in the ass." She released him and stepped back.

"Sweetheart, you are the queen of secrets." She lived and breathed them.

She blew him a kiss and turned away.

He put the phone to his ear. "Don't know if you're aware," Tyler began, "but phones are frowned on in this establishment." He was using the Wi-Fi calling option on his phone because regular cellular coverage was pretty much shit on the little island. Or key. Or whatever the hell it was supposed to be.

"Yes, the very lack of phone usage in your location is why the retreat makes for such a perfect hiding spot. But even seemingly perfect things have flaws." Gray's voice was tight with tension.

Tyler felt his gut twist. Something was wrong. "I'm in position. Made contact. He knows backup is close."

"We have a problem."

"Already?" Way too fast. "I haven't even unpacked."

"A hit has been placed. One of our techs just passed along the news. We monitor the Dark Web and—"

"Yeah, yeah, save me that particular explanation. I get that the Feds have their naughty fingers in all sorts of places. Get focused on the hit."

Esme slanted him a frown over her shoulder. "Did you mean for that to sound X-rated? Do tell Grayson to keep his fingers to himself."

"I am focused on the hit," Gray groused. He'd obviously overheard Esme.

The hit should not have come so fast. "I thought Marcus Aeros believed that Luna was dead?" He'd been briefed before his arrival so Tyler understood what he was facing. Or at least, he'd *thought* he understood.

"Oh, Marcus does believe she's dead. Currently, anyway. Despite the plan I previously threw out to Ronan."

What plan?

"This hit isn't for Luna. That's what makes it problematic."

Uh, hits tended to be problematic by their very nature. Someone was being paid to kill someone else. A bad thing. A problematic thing. "Who's the target?" Tyler asked.

Silence.

"Gray, I'm not in the mood for games."

"Ronan."

"What?"

"There's a hit on Ronan's head. He's the target. I'm thinking Marcus fears he's in a kill or be killed situation. As I told you before, Marcus sent his goon after Ronan. Only instead of dying, Ronan killed the bastard."

Yeah, he'd heard all about that. Not just from Gray. Kane had been spilling details, too. Kane was particularly worried about Ronan. And after seeing Ronan with Luna, Tyler understood his concern. *He's not going to be unemotional where she's concerned.*

But Gray wasn't done talking. "And now, I think Marcus is panicking. I believe Marcus is trying to take out Ronan before Ronan comes for him."

"I didn't know Ronan was going after Marcus. Thought he was supposed to stay close to the woman." Unless there had been a change in plans that he didn't know about?

Silence.

"I can't work blind," Tyler snapped when the silence went too long.

"Ronan is supposed to stay close to Luna. And they're both supposed to stay alive. Let's see if we can make that happen, shall we? Double win."

"Gray..."

"A hit has been placed on the head of our hitman. Priority one right now? It's for you to make sure that Ronan keeps breathing. I'm rather fond of that bastard."

Chapter Sixteen

IT WAS JUST TYLER. LUNA WAS SAFE THE WHOLE TIME. Just Tyler. Not a real attacker. Not some goon sent by Marcus to take Luna's life. She was safe.

Ronan forced his head to lift. The kiss had been too hard. Too raw. Emotions seethed inside of him, and he needed to calm his ass down.

He actually needed to put distance between himself and Luna. Only that shit was not going to happen. He had to keep sticking to her like glue. At least, he did until the moment came when Tyler took her away.

Until Tyler swept her out of his life, gave her a new identity somewhere else, relocated her in Witness Protection, and Ronan never saw her again.

Never saw her sweet smile. The innocence that just would not die. Never heard her laugh. Never saw her again on stage as she sang with the sexiest voice imaginable but only looked straight at him. Never had her beneath him as she held him tight and she came for him. Never had her telling him more items on her adventure list so they could mark them off because Luna wanted to live before she died and he was—

Kissing her again. Even harder than before. He could feel his control splintering. A dangerous thing. He should stop. Back away.

"Don't," Luna whispered.

Fuck. Had he rumbled his words out loud? Just how much had he said?

"Don't you dare stop." Her hands were around his shoulders. Her short nails bit into his shirt. "I want you, Ronan. I will always want you."

He felt the same. Always. When she was gone, he'd still ache for her. But she'd be out of his reach. Too far away for him to touch and take.

All too soon, she would be gone from his world.

And he'd be back to death and darkness.

He lifted her up against him. Wrapped his arms around her and plastered her to his chest as he headed for the bedroom. He crushed rose petals beneath his feet as he walked. Rose petals were so delicate. So easily destroyed.

Luna is delicate. I will never, ever let her be destroyed.

"You are so strong," she breathed against his lips. "Have I told you how sexy I think you are?"

He lowered her beside the bed. A massive bed. One covered with more rose petals. Champagne chilled on the nightstand. Candlelight flickered all around them.

"You are the sexiest man I've ever met," she told him as she stood so close to him.

That was Luna. Honest. Stark.

Turning him on all the more as she smiled at him. Innocence. When all he knew was sin. He could fuck her a million times—*and I want to*—and she'd still give him that smile of innocence when he was done.

"I should get naked, right? I mean, we should." She twisted to reach the zipper on the back of the dress.

He stopped her. Turned her around. Slowly lowered the zipper. The faint hiss lingered in the air. His fingers trailed down her spine. His fingers, then his mouth. He loved to kiss Luna. Loved the way she shivered and moaned against him.

Soon, she would be gone from his life. There would be no more touching her. No more tasting her. No more enjoying the way she shivered against him.

The dress fell to the floor. She wore a white bra. White panties.

She looked over her shoulder at him. Her breath caught at whatever she saw in his eyes.

Ronan unhooked her bra. Let it fall. "Get on the bed." Guttural. A dark, dangerous tension filled his blood. He'd always been so careful with his control. Even as he'd taken her before, he'd been *in* control.

But...

Luna will be taken from me soon. I won't have her again. I'll go back to death while she has a life somewhere else.

She hurriedly perched in the middle of the bed. The rose petals fluttered around her. She still wore the white panties.

He was still completely dressed.

He stood beside the bed, staring down at her. Feeling too rough. Too dangerous. Knowing he should never have put his hands on her in the first place because she wasn't meant to belong to him.

He'd fucking shoved her in the trunk of a car.

Drugged her.

She reached for his hand. "This works a lot better when you're in the bed with me."

Her touch burned through him. "I could destroy you, Luna."

She blinked. Tilted back her head. "I'm pretty sure that you're just here to save me."

He didn't want to just save her. He wanted to own her. Too many dangerous thoughts swam through his head. Dark, tempting. *I could take her away. Make her vanish in a blink. Tyler wouldn't be able to find her. Gray wouldn't. The rest of the world could think she was dead. I could keep Luna.*

He could finally have someone of his own. Weird. Because he'd never wanted someone that way, not until Luna. Ties hurt. They made you weak. Especially when...

When the people you needed really did die. When gunfire came at night. When everyone around you died and you were the only one still left standing. When a bastard put a knife to your face and told you that you were going to be next and...

"Ronan?"

He blinked.

There was Luna. Beautiful Luna.

"You are here to save me," she said again.

Right. Save her. *Save her from myself.* Because she should never be around the monster he kept caged inside. His breath slid out. He reached for the champagne. Ronan could feel her eyes on him as he popped the champagne cork. The explosion of sound was loud, and the bubbly poured over his hand. Screw a glass. He raised the champagne bottle to his mouth.

Then had a far better idea.

"Ronan, what's wrong?"

Oh, the usual. He was going to stay in darkness while his one bit of light was taken from him. The champagne dripped over his hand. "I have an idea." He turned back for her.

Her nipples were tight. Her breasts firm and round. Her eyes stared at him. Wide. Her lush mouth was swollen from his kiss. *She's mine.* "Get flat on the mattress."

Hesitating just for a moment, she did.

He eased down on the bed. Then, lifting the bottle and holding it so carefully, he poured some of the champagne onto her left nipple.

She gasped and shivered against the bed. "Ronan!"

"Did I ever tell you, the first time we met...I thought you smelled like champagne and roses?" And now they were surrounded by champagne and roses.

"It was my body lotion," she whispered.

"I thought it was fucking delicious." He lowered his head toward her wet nipple. Took a long lick. Sucked. Tasted. "Delicious."

She moaned beneath him. Her hands grabbed for the sheets.

He licked up every bit of champagne. Then it was only fair to taste the other nipple. Not like he could have that one feeling left out. He held the bottle over her. Poured the bubbly onto her breast.

"*Ronan.*"

He licked up the drink. Savored it on his tongue the way he liked to savor her. Lapped up every single drop of the champagne. She twisted and heaved beneath him.

"I am so fucking thirsty," he told her. He eased down the bed. Caught her panties and started to haul them down her legs.

The panties tore. "Whoops." Totally unapologetic. He'd wanted the panties gone. Now they were. Perfect. He tossed the panties. Kicked off his shoes and climbed between her spread legs. He parted her legs wide so that he could enjoy the view.

Then he brought his champagne bottle close.

"Ronan!"

His gaze lifted—reluctantly—from the prize that he couldn't wait to taste.

"You're not...are you seriously going to—"

"Going to lick champagne from that sweet pussy?"

Her eyes widened.

"Absolutely. Consider this an item on *my* adventure list."

Then he poured the champagne down on her.

She jerked beneath him. Her eyes widened even more. His head lowered, and he put his mouth right where he wanted it to be. Then he licked. Lapped. Felt his control shatter because he was tasting champagne and Luna.

His Luna.

The taste was intoxicating. Better than anything in his whole life. She was better. She was his, and he didn't want to let go. Not fucking ever.

He poured more champagne on her. In her. Sipped it from her. Licked and sucked and he could taste champagne and her pleasure as she climaxed against his mouth. A powerful wave of pleasure that made her whole body quake.

That wasn't enough for him. There was still more champagne left. He poured more. Let the liquid drizzle onto her. Followed it with his tongue. Into her. Sweeping over her folds. Lapping at her clit. Again and again and again.

She gasped his name. Came a second time on a powerful shudder that shook her whole body.

He poured more. He could not get enough of her.

Would never get enough. He wanted her to come for him until she couldn't move. Until she could barely breathe. Until she knew that no one on this planet would ever give her more pleasure than he could.

"Ronan!"

Between her legs, tasting her, he looked up.

Her breath heaved in and out. "I want *you*. In me."

His cock ached. Hard and full and so eager.

He shot up. Shoved the champagne bottle back into the ice bucket. Pieces of ice hit the floor even as he yanked open his pants and pulled down his underwear so he could haul out his thick dick. Ronan put the head of his cock against her straining core. Dipped inside of her. She was wet and tight, and he was *in* her.

Without a condom.

Fuck. He was in her bare. She felt incredible. He wanted to slam deep. To take and take. *Selfish bastard. You're trying to keep her.*

The thought blasted through him.

Tempted him.

Keep her.

"Ronan, that's not enough!" Her head tipped back against the pillow. "All of you. *In me.*"

A primitive growl broke from him. His control held by one thread. One fucking thread. *This is Luna. You protect Luna. Always.*

He withdrew.

"Ronan!" A sharp cry of disappointment.

He grabbed for the top nightstand drawer. Condoms were inside. This resort kept them fully stocked. He'd noticed them earlier when he checked the drawers. He yanked open the drawer. Nearly had the thing falling out and onto the floor. His fingers fisted around a condom. In record time, the condom was on his dick, and he was back at her core.

And control was gone.

He slammed deep inside of her. Luna gasped, not with pain, but with pleasure. She wrapped her arms and legs around him as he pistoned inside of her. He plunged hard and deep even as he kissed her. As his hands swept all over her. He wanted to touch and taste and claim every single inch of Luna.

She is mine. She will always be mine. Even when she was gone, even when some other sonofafucker had her—

She will be mine. "No one else, Luna," he snarled as his head lifted. Another growl tore from him and the room seemed to darken.

She was coming beneath him. Her inner muscles clamped tightly around him.

A hard thrust. "No one else will ever make you feel this way."

Pleasure flooded over her features.

"No one else will fuck you the way I do." In and out. Relentless.

"Ronan!"

"No one else will taste you the way I do." Her taste was the best in the world. Unforgettable. His favorite.

Her breath panted in and out.

"No one else, Luna." His release was too close. He couldn't hold back. *"You're mine."*

His release exploded. A powerful orgasm that thundered through his blood and wiped away everything else. Wiped it all away except...

I'll kill any bastard who tries to take what's mine.

Chapter Seventeen

"THAT WAS..." A ROSE PETAL DRIFTED IN THE AIR around her. Landed really close to her right nipple.

"Too rough?" Ronan raised up onto his elbows as he stared down at her. His jaw had locked, and his eyes glittered.

"I was going to say it was really pretty amazing." She smiled at him.

He blinked. Then groused, "That fucking smile."

Her fucking smile dimmed as he pulled out of her. Some of her bright, happy glow began to dim a bit, too.

He climbed from the bed. Marched away. "What the hell am I gonna do without that smile?"

Had she just heard him right? Luna sat up in bed and, realizing she was stark naked, she grabbed a sheet and hauled it close. Clutching the sheet against her chest, she cocked her head and stared after him. "Ronan?"

He appeared in the bathroom doorway. Looked extra grim. "I was too...intense." He'd already righted his clothes. Not like there had been a lot to fix. He'd been mostly dressed while he sent her into delicious oblivion.

"I thought you were perfect." She started to smile again, but caught herself. "The champagne was cold." A remembered shiver darted over her. "But your mouth was so warm." The two opposites had ignited her. There'd been so much pleasure that she'd wondered if it was possible to die from insanely powerful orgasms.

Talk about a way to go. That would certainly be her preferred method for leaving this world.

He took a step toward her. "I'm not...rational with you." Another halting step. As if he was being pulled toward her against his will.

"Is that a good thing or a bad thing?"

"Bad." Another step. Then another. More steps until he was beside the bed and staring down at her. "I'm a bad thing, Luna."

She would not believe that. The open champagne bottle was back to chilling in the ice bucket near her. She would never be able to look at champagne without remembering this night with him. And blushing violently. "I think you're a pretty good thing, Ronan. The best thing that has happened to me in a long time."

Laughter came from him. But it was rough. Almost mocking. "People don't make the mistake of calling me good, Luna."

"Maybe they should." Still using one hand to hold the sheet in place, her other reached for him. She curled her fingers around his wrist. "You're good, Ronan. Someone should have told you that a long time ago. You've saved me. You've helped me." *You've given me the best orgasms of my life.* "You are good."

He looked down. Seemed to focus on her hand as her fingers curled around his wrist. "A good man wouldn't want to do the things I do. Not to you."

Her heartbeat had just managed to reach a normal level. At his words, her heart immediately began to race again. "Just what do you want to do?"

"Keep you."

Her lips parted. Had he just said—

"Fuck you into oblivion."

Well, he actually *had* pretty much done that.

"Destroy any bastard who ever thinks he can touch you the way I do. That he can claim you. Have you. Take you from me."

She had to be gaping at him.

He sent her a hard smile. "Scared yet?"

Scared wasn't the right word. "I want to keep you," she blurted.

His body seemed to turn to stone before her eyes.

"I also really, really like the idea of fucking you into oblivion." Just so they were both being as clear and as honest as possible. "I don't want to fuck anyone else. After you, it just—it would seem wrong." Because any other lover wouldn't be Ronan. He'd marked her, far beneath the skin. All the way to her soul.

"No other woman will ever be you."

She wanted to smile at him. And if she wanted to smile, then why was she having to blink away tears? Probably because it felt like they were already saying goodbye, and she didn't want to do that. "I want to keep you," Luna said, meaning those words with her entire heart. Couldn't there be a way? A chance? "I don't want to be taken from you." Hope twisted and churned within her. Maybe, just maybe...

He stepped back. Pulled his wrist from her. "The job was to keep you alive."

But weren't they way past the point of the situation between them being just a job?

"You'll have a new life. One that doesn't include a hitman. You'll be better off without me."

Her hair slid against her cheek as she watched him. "Are you trying to convince me or yourself?"

"Luna..."

"Because I happen to like you, Ronan." No, way more than that. She just needed to woman up and say the words. "I think I'm falling in love with you." There. Done. She'd never been in love, so she wasn't exactly an expert on the emotion but...

I'm happy when he's near. I feel safe when he's close. I want to hold his hand and have a million adventures. I want to see him when the darkness lifts, and he can smile like he really means it.

But Ronan shook his head. "You don't even know me." He turned away.

Anger had her jumping from the bed. Bringing the sheet with her, wrapping it around her because this was not a naked kind of conversation. Especially not with him pretty much being completely dressed and her being stark bare. "I know you." Certainty. She hopped after him. "I'm starting to think I might know you better than you know yourself."

He glanced over his shoulder. "You know what you *hope* I am. Some idealized version of me."

"What does that even mean?" When a woman told a man that she was falling for him, a different response was expected. Any response other than this rejection that chilled her to the bone.

"Go to bed, Luna."

"I just got *out* of bed, Ronan!"

His hands fisted at his sides. "I usually have perfect control."

"Well, give yourself a cookie. Make it a chocolate chip because those are the best ones."

He whirled toward her. Frowned.

"Life is messy, Ronan. It's not about perfect control. Actually, I think it's about losing control and letting yourself feel real emotions. About not boxing yourself away and being afraid to care." She surged toward him. Kept right on holding her precious sheet. "I've been afraid for most of my life. Afraid first that I'd die long before I could reach my eighteenth birthday. Afraid I'd never graduate high school. Or fall in love. Afraid I'd die before I could get married. Before I could have a family." A heave of her breath. "I was busy being afraid, and it never hit me that I could lose my mother. The woman who was my core. Until the day I found her having a stroke. Then everything realigned, but you know what I did? I went right back to being afraid even after I lost her. I was hiding. Playing things safe. And then..."

Well, okay, maybe not the best example to add...

"Then you tried something new and got a hit placed on your head." He quirked a brow. "Didn't work out so well, huh?"

"Then I met this gorgeous, dangerous man who kissed me like he couldn't breathe without tasting me on a New Orleans street." She waited, practically daring him to deny the charge.

His nostrils flared. He did not deny her charge.

"He protected me, even while trying to make me believe he was the worst thing I'd ever faced." She wanted to reach for him. "But he didn't get it. I'd known death since I was a kid. This man—he wasn't death. He was hope for me. He made me feel alive. He gave me pleasure and laughter, and he put me on a stage because he knew that was what I wanted. He gave me one of my dreams. Yet he thinks he's some bad bastard."

"I *am*."

She stepped forward. Their bodies nearly brushed. "Not to me. You're the hero to me. And I am falling for you."

His gaze searched hers. "You shouldn't."

"Too bad. I am. I'm not asking you to love me back." Though, yes, fine, that would be fantastic. Her chin notched up. "I'm asking you to stop seeing yourself as the devil."

"I killed a man when I was fifteen years old."

Her mouth opened, but no words came out.

One of his hands rose and skimmed over the scar near his lower lip. "My dad made the mistake of getting involved with bad people. Hell, he spent most of his life doing that shit. Petty thefts led to higher stakes. More connections with the wrong crowd. Borrowing money from people he shouldn't. *Stealing* from the wrong person."

She closed her mouth.

"He was going to be a lesson. Used as an example for others. A hit was put on him. On his whole family."

Oh, no. "Ronan..."

"They came into the house while I was sleeping. My parents were downstairs. It was my mother's scream that woke me."

She shook her head. No, no, she did not want to hear this story. She could already feel a teardrop sliding down her cheek.

"Why the fuck are you crying for me?" Now his hand was on her cheek. Wiping away the tear.

"Because I'm so sorry."

"You didn't do it. Hell, Luna, you've probably never

hurt a person in your entire life." His hand lingered. Then fell. "But I have."

"You were defending yourself." She knew he must have been. He'd woken to a scream. He'd stayed alive. He'd done what was necessary.

A shrug. "Then, sure. If that's what you want to say, I defended myself. I ran downstairs and saw the man over my mother. He was pulling the knife out of her chest. My father was running for the door. *Running* to leave her and to leave me. The guy dropped the knife. He took out a gun instead, and he fired at my dad's back. I swear the gunfire seemed so loud that I felt like it shook the whole house." A shake of his head. "I'd never heard gunfire up close like that before."

Another tear leaked out. She swiped it away. Luna almost lost her sheet but managed to keep it up with a frantic grab.

"My dad fell right there, and I ran into the bastard with the gun. Hit him from behind."

"You stopped him." She nodded.

"He got loose. Swung at me. And laughed."

Luna blinked.

"Then he put the gun to my forehead. Told me that my dad was a fuck up, and I had to pay the price."

More tears. She couldn't stop them. There was no emotion in his voice. But he must have been so afraid back then. Terrified.

"But this guy, he liked a personal touch with his kills. That's what he told me. As he held the gun to my head, he told me that knives were better. They were his favorite. He smiled, and he put the gun down. I backed the hell away as he picked up the knife that still had my mother's blood on it. This fucking freak could have killed me with a pull of the trigger, but he got off on slicing up his prey. My mom wasn't dead, you see. I could hear her breathing. Gasping. And his eyes kept sliding back to her."

Luna shook her head.

"He was going to torture us both. My prick father had gotten off easily. When he ran and left us, he got a swift trip to hell. The bullet blasted through his head. His brains were on the door."

She put a hand to her mouth.

"Disgusting, isn't it?" Flat. Still so emotionless. "Brutal? Welcome to my world. Welcome to my life. That's what I am, Luna. I'm brutal. Because that's what I had to be. He came at me with the knife, and I tried to dodge. The blade sliced down my chin. The freak said something about drawing first blood. Like it was all a game. Like life and death were a game to him."

Her hand fell back to her side. "How did you get away?"

"Wrong question. Don't you mean, 'How did I kill him?'"

She waited. Then, nodded. "Yes." That was what she'd meant.

"I ran at the bastard. I was a defensive end on my high school's football team. Always bigger than everyone else but still damn fast. Bastard was laughing. Twirling that damn knife in his hand, and something broke inside of me. All I wanted to do was *hurt* him. Rage consumed me. No, more than that, I lost myself in the rage."

"Ronan..."

"I slammed into him as hard as I could. Then I started beating the hell out of him." His hands fisted again. "Over and over again. And when he swung back, I barely felt the blows."

Her feet were rooted to the floor.

"I thought I'd knocked him out. I rose. I found the gun because, hell, I figured I needed some kind of weapon. I was calling for help when I heard the floor creak behind me." He swallowed. "I whirled, and he was coming at me. I fired. He went down." Brittle. "By the time the ambulance and the cops arrived, my mother was long gone. I was holding her in my arms. My dad's body was just where he'd fallen. They had to step over him in order to get to me."

A slow exhale. "That doesn't make you a killer, Ronan. You were defending yourself. Trying to protect your family."

His lips twisted. "He was only the first, Luna. After we buried my parents, I went to live with my grandfather. I even tried the whole college routine, but it wasn't really for me. I finally wound up as a Marine."

"Semper Fi," she murmured.

"Uncle Sam taught me to be a better killer. When my service was up, the government was already recruiting me for...other things."

"I knew you worked for the government." What she'd suspected after the very first call with Grayson in the bayou. "There was no way you were some cold-blooded hitman."

His eyelids flickered. "You are not listening to me. That is *exactly* what I am. What I became. I've taken out killers—"

"*Killers,*" she pounced on that word, and she pounced on him, too. She jumped toward him. Grabbed both of his arms, and, yes, her sheet slithered to the floor. She'd worry about the sheet later. "You stopped bad people. You weren't out there killing innocents."

"A life is a life."

"Were the people you stopped getting ready to hurt others? Getting ready to hurt you?"

He didn't speak.

"I've been on the receiving end," she said. Been there, done that. "They wanted to kill me in New Orleans and again in the bayou. When that guy with the gun tracked us to the cabin, you had to make a split-second decision. You made a decision that saved Kane and that saved me. You fired your weapon to stop him. Without you, I would be dead. So don't expect me to jump on the Ronan-is-evil parade, because I won't. Ever. You saved me. I'm betting you've saved plenty of innocent people in your life, too."

"My life is soaked with blood."

"Then let's change that. You've given the darkness enough of your soul." Her grip tightened on him. "You have shouldered enough pain. Let's see what happens if you try for a different life."

His gaze searched hers.

Hope stirred in—

"There is no different life for me. Soon enough, Tyler will take you away. *You* will have a different life, and I'll be sent on another hit."

Ice skated over her skin. "Is that what you want? For me to get a life that's far away from you?"

"You'll be safe. I want you safe." An inhale. Then his gaze darted down. "You lost your sheet."

"Fuck the sheet."

He blinked. "Such naughty language from you. Shocking, drama teacher."

"You just bared your soul to me, and now you're trying to shut down and block me out. That's not going to work. I'm not scared of you, Ronan."

"I didn't think you were or else you wouldn't come for me so easily."

Her eyes narrowed. "You're not going to piss me off."

"Are you sure? I've been told I have a talent for pissing off plenty of people. That I can do it pretty effortlessly."

"You're trying to put up a wall between us because you think you just revealed too much about yourself to me."

"You're naked, princess. There is no wall. And you're revealing everything to me." Lust heated his stare.

"Stop it. Be real with me again. Let me in *again*." She stood on her toes. "I can handle your secrets. I'm not going to turn away in horror." But, maybe... "Is that what you wanted? Did you think I'd be horrified, and it would make me leaving you easier?"

His lips thinned.

Oh, adorable Ronan. One of her hands rose, and her finger skimmed over his faint scar. "Nothing is going to make leaving you easier. Didn't you hear me before? I'm falling for you. I've never been in love, not until you came along. I'm pretty sure it will break my heart when I lose you." *Shatter it into a million pieces.* "I'm not asking for you to love me back."

"I *never* get personally involved in jobs. You can't get involved in this line of work." His gaze seemed to burn. "People die. They leave. They vanish. There is no room for a personal connection. People don't get to know the real me—"

"I do," she interrupted. "I have. I know the real you."

"I can't love you, Luna." Stark. "I'm not capable of it. I hunt, I kill, and I wait for the next target. There is nothing more in my life."

That might have just been one of the saddest things he'd told her. *No, hearing that he'd held his mother's dead body was the saddest thing.* She pressed onto her tiptoes. Her hand moved so that she could pull his head toward hers. Luna's lips feathered over his.

"I said I can't love," he gritted against her mouth.

"And let me say..." Luna returned even though her heart hurt, "I love you. I don't need you to love me back. It doesn't change the way I feel."

"Luna..."

She didn't think anything could change the way she felt. Staring straight into his blue eyes, she told him, "This is me, telling my arrogant, growly protector that I would do anything for him. Telling the man who has saved me, made love to me, who helped me cross adventure items off my list...I'm telling him that he is so much more than he believes himself to be. You aren't some cold-blooded killer. You're a good man. Whatever happens, wherever I go, I won't be forgetting you anytime soon."

His hands clamped around her waist. He lifted her up, and her feet dangled off the floor. "I will never forget you," he vowed.

Good to know.

Then he was kissing her. His mouth took hers in a deep, drugging kiss that promised to sweep everything else away. The doubts and the worries. The sadness and the pain that lingered in her heart. With the kiss, he was telling her that he couldn't give her love.

Maybe he was right. Maybe he couldn't love anyone.

But he could give her passion.

He *would* give her passion.

He lowered her onto the bed. Crawled on top of her. Began to unbutton his shirt. But her hand rose to his chest in order to stop him.

"Luna?" Fear flashed for just an instant on his face. "You don't...you don't want me anymore?" His Adam's apple bobbed. "Now that you know what I've done..."

"Don't be silly. I'll always want you. If *you* want the

truth, I wanted you the first time we met. Back when I really did think you might be some cold-blooded hitman. What does that say about me?"

A furrow appeared between his brows.

"I will always want you," she repeated because she realized Ronan needed to hear the words. So tough on the outside, but Ronan carried so much pain within him. Her left hand reached out and snagged the neck of the champagne bottle. "I just thought it was my turn to enjoy a drink."

His eyes widened. "Luna?"

"Get out of those clothes, Ronan. I want to taste you."

Chapter Eighteen

"*I LOVE YOU.*" LUNA'S WORDS RANG IN HIS HEAD. THEY played over and over even as she dripped the chilled champagne on his eager dick. He'd stripped off his clothes, lightning-fast, because what sane man wouldn't strip that quickly when a woman offered to lick champagne off his cock?

Uh, hell, yes. Hell, *yes.*

But this wasn't just any woman. This was his Luna.

I love you.

She couldn't mean the words, right? It was the high intensity of the situation. She was grateful to him because he'd saved her. Because he'd killed to protect her. Because he'd—

She licked away drops of the champagne.

His hands flew out, then up, and slammed into the headboard. The whole bed jerked.

Her head lifted.

Princess, do not stop.

"You good?" Luna asked in her husky, breathless voice.

Good didn't describe him. Hadn't he tried to warn her

about that very fact? Good had nothing to do with who he was. Or the life he'd led.

She poured a bit more champagne on him. Cold bubbly that she immediately bent to sample. Her warm tongue curled over the head of his bobbing cock. She sucked the tip inside. Pulled him in and moaned around him.

His heels dug into the bed.

He wanted to let go. To explode into her mouth.

I love you.

He'd never had a partner say those words. Not that sex with anyone else had ever come close to the intensity he had with Luna. Everything was different with her.

He was different with her.

I love you.

Hearing those three words from Luna had been almost painful. His chest had grown heavy and tight. His whole body had locked down in instant denial. *You can't love me. I'm not good enough for you to love.*

Luna was wide smiles and innocence. She was adventure lists. She was songs on a sultry night.

She deserved to live as much as she could. To laugh as often as possible. To be with someone who didn't know so much about death.

She licked her way down his dick.

Yeah, he stopped thinking.

I love you.

Her tongue skated along the side of his dick as she licked back up toward the head. Then she opened wide again. Pulled him in deep. Moaned around him once more.

I love you.

He moved in a blur. Had her on her back in two seconds. Pressed his fingers to her, in her, because Ronan had to make certain she was ready for him, and, oh, she was. Wet and hot and so tight. His Luna.

His hand grabbed for a condom. Luna would not leave him with his child in her.

A child. A child with Luna. A life with Luna.

His breath sawed in and out. In and out. He rolled on the condom. Drove into her. They both gasped. He was in so deep. She was so incredibly tight as she squeezed every inch of him. Nothing in the world felt as good as Luna.

A life with Luna.

He withdrew, only to thrust harder. Deeper. She arched up toward him eagerly. Met him with no hesitation. Pulled him closer.

He grabbed her legs. Threw them both over his shoulders so he could get inside her as deep as he could possibly go. He needed to be connected to Luna. To mark her. To bind them. When she was gone, hell, no, he never wanted her to forget him.

He didn't want some other bastard trying to take his place in her world.

A life with Luna.

Her inner muscles clamped greedily around him. Held him in a fierce grip as she cried out his name. Her pleasure just pushed his forward. A chain reaction as Ronan's climax flooded through him, and he pumped into her on a seemingly endless wave of release.

A life with Luna.

His teeth snapped together to hold back his roar.

A life with Luna was exactly what he wanted, and it was the one thing he would never have.

* * *

Uh, oh.

Luna knew she wasn't curled up on a mattress. Mattresses were soft and cushiony. She was on top of something hard. Strong.

Her eyes cracked open. She became aware of a faint drumming. Steady. Powerful.

His heartbeat.

She was sprawled on top of Ronan.

Embarrassment flooded through her. She began to scamper away.

One powerful arm locked around her lower back. "Stay." Sleepy. Rumbled. "I like you this way."

She could see the trickles of light coming through their window. In the distance, she could hear the roar of the ocean. She'd missed the sunrise. She'd catch it tomorrow. Something she'd always wanted to do. Watch the sunrise from a beach.

Something else she'd always wanted to do?

Fall in love. And she had.

She snuggled back against him. One arm stayed around her lower back. The other was stretched out to the side, reaching toward her empty pillow. The arm that stretched toward the pillow was his left arm. He'd taken off his watch at some point, and the faint light fell onto his inner wrist. She could easily see the dark lines of the snake tattoo that marked him. "Did I ever thank you for saving me?"

"Which time?" A teasing growl.

All the times. "One day, I'm going to save you."

His heartbeat pounded beneath her head. "Unnecessary. Just watch that sweet ass of yours. Keep yourself safe."

Her eyes were still on the snake. "Thank you for saving

me from the snake in the bayou. I never even saw it coming."

"Most people don't see danger until it's too late."

"But you're not most people, are you? I feel like you might always see danger." Almost like he never shut off or relaxed completely. She'd noticed that about him. The way he would survey every room they entered. The way his gaze would track to each face. During their long drive, they'd stopped at a diner for a quick meal. He'd taken the booth in the back so that he could see each person who walked through the door. Always alert. Always looking for trouble.

"Danger is always there, so, yeah, I see it."

"How did you get the tattoo?"

"Initiation."

Surprised, she turned her head and lifted up so she could see him.

"Ronan Walker needed a beginning," he explained.

Talking about himself in the third person. But he'd told her from the start that Ronan Walker wasn't his real name. Just another deception. *I love him, and I don't know his real name.*

"I needed to infiltrate a gang. My first undercover mission. Make or break, you know."

She shivered.

So he pulled the covers over them. But she hadn't been shivering from the cold. "The tattoo was part of the initiation ritual?"

"Turned out, those pricks had a very unusual initiation routine."

Did she want to know?

"To be fully included in their gang, you had to fucking shove your hand into a tub of snakes. A key waited beneath them. The key to your new life—and, by the way, a key to the motorcycle you got when you were fully initiated."

Her mouth opened and a little squeak came out. "You're...no. No. A tub of snakes? You had to fish through them for a key? But—but the snakes could kill you!"

Soft laughter. "I think that might have been the point. You had to prove you weren't afraid of dying. That the gang meant more than your life. It was also one of those situations where you only thought you had a choice. If you didn't put your arm elbow deep in the pile of writhing, hissing, fucking snakes, then you were going to get a bullet to the brain."

She flopped to his side.

"I liked you where you were," he grumbled.

She needed to see him better. This was a better angle. Fear had her practically vibrating. "So you were facing death one way or another?"

"Not all the snakes were venomous. A point the leader made of saying. We were being judged. If we weren't worthy, we'd be taken out."

"That's...that's insane."

"Don't worry, my handlers promised they had antivenom at the ready for me."

Uh, yes, she worried. "How were they supposed to get it to you in time?"

"You don't die right away from a snake bite. That's just in the movies. A lot depends on the type of snake that bit you and where you were bitten. Best case, you have two to three days before organ failure and death set in. So I knew I had time on my side."

That wasn't time. That was horrific. She sucked in a deep breath and then shoved it out. "I feel like you might be sugarcoating here."

Cynthia Eden

"Even with a black mamba, it can take up to twenty minutes for a man to die."

Her breath got stuck on the second long exhale. She choked, gasped, and managed, "You're a snake expert?"

"Had to be. I knew what I'd be facing. Knowledge helped to increase my odds of survival."

Her temples began to throb. "I know what will now be on my nightmare reel over and over again." For eternity.

"I got treatment during the golden hour. I was fine."

"What is a golden hour?" It actually sounded like he was a snake expert.

"The first hour after a bite." His head rolled a bit on the pillow so he could see her better. "That's when antivenom is most effective."

Most effective, check. "Really good to know." She was on his arm. The arm with the snake tattoo on his wrist. She squirmed and twisted and brought the arm in front of her. "You shoved your arm in a tub of snakes."

"Honestly, it was more like a big, glass aquarium. They dumped all the snakes in and got them in a striking frenzy."

OhmyGod. "And the tattoo?"

"After the bite, you were initiated. The tattoo proved who I was. The gang had a reputation. Just having the tattoo opened doors. Made a certain set of people trust me."

"And then the hitman was born."

He nodded against the pillow. "Born from a pile of twisting, hissing snakes."

And he hates snakes. She sucked in a deep breath, then let it out. No choking this time. Bonus for her. "Have you saved them?"

His eyes narrowed.

"Your parents. A hit was placed on your parents, and now you go out, over and over again, and you save people who've had bounties put on their heads. Are you saving your parents, over and over? Trying to atone for something that wasn't your fault?"

"It's not about them."

"No? It's not exactly a typical job choice, Ronan. You saw firsthand how devastating a hit can be, and now, you stop hits. You couldn't save your parents, but you're saving other people."

Silence. A little too long. Then, "Didn't realize you were a shrink. Thought the analysis BS was Gray's area of expertise."

Now that was interesting. "Has Grayson told you the same thing?"

"I don't have a fucking hero complex. I have a killing complex."

"With you, they just might be one and the same." She wet her lips. "Your parents' deaths weren't your fault. You were a kid, Ronan."

"I killed the bastard, princess. If I'd gotten up faster, if I had heard him enter the house, I could have done *more*. Sooner."

"Or maybe if you'd gotten up faster, you would be dead, too. Maybe you would be dead and all the people you've saved over the years—people like me—maybe we'd all be dead, as well."

He blinked.

"Do me a big favor, would you, Ronan? Stop thinking you're only about death. Try seeing you're also about life."

Chapter Nineteen

"CLEARLY, YOU WERE MADE FOR THE PROTECTION business. You just can't take your eyes off your target."

Behind the lens of his sunglasses, Ronan did, in fact, have his eyes on his target. She was currently snorkeling about ten feet off the shore. Every few moments, she'd bob up, let out a delighted laugh, and call out to him as Luna raved about some amazing fish she'd just seen.

She'd wanted him to come in the water with her. And, oh, but she had certainly been tempting in that little black scrap of a bathing suit that she wore. How could a one-piece be described as a scrap? Fine, it probably wasn't. Probably was meant to be demure and covering, but her breasts filled the top and her hips curved in the bottom so damn temptingly, and every single thing about her was sexy to him.

He'd stayed on shore, the better to watch over Luna. If his fool head was underwater, he might miss a threat.

Ronan couldn't miss a threat. Especially because...

I don't trust Gray. I think he sold her out. Sold us out.

And now I'm about to learn the truth. A truth he'd get from Tyler, one way or another. He'd expected this meeting. Had, in fact, been surprised Tyler hadn't approached him sooner. It was nearing noon. What had his buddy done? Slept the day away?

"My wife is the most gorgeous sight on this beach," Ronan responded. "Why would I want to look anywhere else?"

Without an invitation, Tyler lowered into the chaise next to his. Luna's chaise.

"I thought we were going to be strangers," Ronan noted, voice lower. Only for Tyler.

"We are. We're strangers who are quickly becoming fast friends."

Ronan turned his head toward Tyler. Tyler—also wearing sunglasses—saluted him with a giant pineapple drink.

"What the fuck is that?" Ronan demanded. The top of the pineapple had been cut off and a straw perched inside it.

"Esme insisted we buy one. Then she took one sip and hated it." Tyler sipped. Considered. Then announced, "I don't mind it."

"Fantastic for you." Ronan's head turned back to the best view just in time for Luna to pop up. She waved at him as a broad smile curved her lips.

"Someone seems to be having the time of her life," Tyler murmured. "Or, is that the time of her death?"

"Fuck off," Ronan replied pleasantly.

Instead, Tyler just spread out on the chaise and got more comfortable. "There's a new hit." Mild, like they were talking about the weather.

Only there was nothing mild about the reaction that blasted its way through Ronan's body. Fury filled every cell, and a red, killing haze covered his vision. "That bastard let it leak that Luna was still alive." Damn Gray. He would pay for his betrayal. "I *told* him I wasn't going for that plan. Warned him that it would be carried out only over my dead body." He leapt up. "I'm taking her away." Done. Decided. Choice made. "I'll hide Luna, and no one will ever find her." Luna would have to stay with him now. Forever. He didn't have to fight his instincts. This would be about her protection. Keeping her safe. Doing what was best for Luna.

He fucking *had* this. He took a step forward.

Tyler's hand reached out and lazily curled around his wrist. "Slow your roll. You're looking a wee bit too desperate and dramatic on this beautiful day."

Screw that. "A hit is on my *wife*." Low and guttural.

"First, not really your wife. Did you forget that part?"

Luna disappeared beneath the water.

"Second, I never said the hit was on her."

Once again, his head whipped toward Tyler.

Tyler smiled at him. "Try to look less ferocious, would you? I know that you've been the cold-blooded killer a while." Barely a whisper. "But you're playing a new role. Get with the program." He tugged on Ronan's arm. "And maybe get back on the chaise?"

Slowly, Ronan lowered onto the chaise. "If the hit isn't on Luna..."

Tyler let go of his wrist, only to slap him on the shoulder. "Yeah, sorry to tell you, buddy, but it's on you."

"Someone put a hit on *me*?"

"Considering that you offed his cousin-slash-goon, Gray thinks Marcus now believes you must be coming after him. Apparently, he hasn't paid you for services rendered."

Tyler hadn't checked the offshore account. He left stuff like that to Gray and the federal crew. They were the ones who tracked down the charges and sent people away for paying killers. He stuck with the dirtier work.

The bloody work.

"The hit is on you. Gray thinks it was offered because Marcus now wants *you* to be the dead one. So, I hate to be the one to tell you the news but..."

"But if I'm with her, I'm the one putting a target on Luna's back." Because there would be plenty of people eager to take down Ronan the Relentless. Fuck. Stupid moniker. That name had been Gray's idea.

Tyler didn't speak. His silence was agreement.

The waves crashed into the shore. Ronan tried to unclench his fists, swallow his rage, and *think*.

"I learned about the hit last night. That was long *after* I'd been told to haul ass down here. So I'm thinking Gray had a different plan in the works, one where he was going to use me as your backup, then he got word of the hit."

Yeah, there had been a different plan, all right. Gray had wanted to bring Luna back into the land of the living and wave her like a red flag at Marcus. *Not happening*.

Tyler let go of Ronan's shoulder. Settled comfortably against his chaise. Sipped his drink. "Pretty sure Kane is on the way here, too. Whole team assembling thing, you know."

"We haven't been a team in a long time." Tyler worked with the U.S. Marshals. Gray worked with the Feds. Kane worked with—well, hard to say for sure.

And I just deal with death.

"We'll always be a team, Ronan." Low but adamant. "Time doesn't change that. You need me, I'm there. I do what you want, no questions asked."

Shit. Now the guy was getting all sentimental. But usefully sentimental.

Luna broke the surface of the water. She wore her face mask. The snorkel tube poked out and bobbed near her ear.

"Gray was going to use her as bait," Ronan spoke slowly as he came to a decision. "He needed someone to get close to Marcus. An up close opportunity for a kill."

"He *wants* Marcus dead?"

I want him dead. Gray probably just wanted the prick in prison. "We think Marcus keeps trophies. If that's the case, then we can link him to a shitload of kills." And now Ronan had the perfect means to provide Gray with an up close opportunity to find those items. Only Luna would not be the bait in this scenario. Luna would be safe. Protected.

I'll be the bait. Or, even better, he'd be the predator who turned the tables on Marcus Aeros. "No questions asked, huh?"

"Ronan..."

"That better not be a question coming because you just said *no questions asked.*" Maybe his voice was too harsh. He didn't care. His eyes were on Luna. She'd stood in the shallower water and was staring toward the sailboats in the distance. She'd talked about them renting a sailboat. Or going kayaking. And getting up early to watch the sunrise the next day.

All adventures he would not have with her.

But Luna? She would have every single adventure she wanted. All he had to do was eliminate the threat that dodged her steps. Then she could sing on any stage she wanted. She didn't have to hide her talent from the rest of the world. She could live as big of a life as she wanted.

Only it will be a life without me.

"I just don't want you to make a mistake," Tyler warned softly. "No need to act all irrationally."

He was being stone-cold rational. He could handle killers. She couldn't. "Keep her on the island. It's safe here. You're here. Esme is here." Tyler's lady was hell on wheels. Ronan would never, ever bet against her. "And you just said Kane is on the way." He considered his friend's arrival. "I can meet up with him." Probably in Key West. "I'll get him to cover my six." It was always better to launch an attack with backup. But before he left the island, he had a few more instructions for Tyler. "Make sure Luna gets to go kayaking."

"What?"

"And she'll want to get up early in the morning. Seeing the sunrise is important to her."

"You know Esme doesn't do mornings."

"Seeing the sunrise is important to Luna." Grim. "Set an alarm."

"If it's important, then show her the damn sunrise yourself!"

Ronan's head turned. He stared at his friend. Tyler was one of the best men he'd ever met. Talk about having a true-blue core. Esme had originally sought Tyler out just because the guy *was* so good. Someone who couldn't be bought. Or bribed. One of those few individuals who always did the right thing.

Ronan knew that was the reason Gray had sent Tyler to him on the island. Because Tyler would do what was right. He might not like it. He might want to fight Ronan, but in the end...*you'll keep her safe for me.* "I'm leaving." Words that he absolutely hated to say.

But they had to be spoken.

This will hurt Luna. Because she truly did believe she loved him, and he was going to leave her. Just as her father had left.

Leaving without a word. Dick move. A move he would never want to make. Never. *Fuck.* But if he stayed, if he told her his plans...

She would worry. She would fight him. She would refuse to let him go. *He* was the hitman, but he didn't trust that Luna wouldn't try to blow their cover and sacrifice herself in order to keep him safe. "It has to be this way."

"Yeah, no. I'm pretty sure this deal can go down in a thousand different ways. So how about you slow your roll, take some breaths, and let's talk."

"Marcus wanted me to cut off her finger and give it to him as proof of her death."

Tyler put down his drink. "Bastard."

"Now he's sending heavy hitters after me. Per your intel."

"Uh, per *Gray's* intel. I'm just passing along the info that he gave to me."

"They hunt me, they get near me, and they see *her?* It will be over for Luna. And I happen to like her damn fingers." He liked everything about her. "You can't tell her I'm in danger."

"I have never liked lists of things that I can and can't do."

"Yeah, I know. You're more about giving orders than getting them. Noted." An exhale. His gaze tracked back to Luna. She'd turned toward him.

For a moment, he didn't move. He couldn't. He wanted to remember her this way. The sun shining on her. That dark hair wet around her smiling face. The waves brushing lightly against her from that gorgeous water.

She waved to him once more. Then turned around to look down in the water before pulling up her mask again.

"If you only could see your face right now," Tyler murmured.

Immediately, he locked down his expression. "She'll fight if I explain why I'm leaving. So I'm not explaining." He had to act, fast. *Cut the ties before they are too deep.* Hell, he already feared they were too deep. "Watch her. She's a runner."

"Fantastic."

"I've had to cuff her a few times."

"I do not need to hear about your kink."

He'd never had that pleasure. Cuffing Luna during sex? That would have been great. So many things with her would have been great. "Some things are better left in fantasies."

"Yeah. Like you and your cuffs. Say less, man. Say less."

He wasn't talking about cuffs. He was talking about the life that he might have been able to envision with Luna. But...it wouldn't have been a life of safety. His gaze slid to the stupid snake on his wrist. He'd left his watch in the bungalow. "I hate snakes." What if one of the enemies from his past came after him?

The same way Marcus is coming now?

If he tried to have a life with Luna, a real one, danger would always stalk them. Ronan Walker had made too many kills. Too many enemies.

"Yeah, well, if I'd been bitten after shoving my hand in a freaking tub of snakes, I'd probably hate them, too. Glad I could get you that antivenom in time."

Because Tyler had been there. When he shouldn't have been.

A man Ronan could always count on. "Keep her safe."

"You need backup. Don't do this alone."

"I'll contact Gray." His lips hitched into a half-smile. "He'll be waiting for the contact. It's the whole reason he told you about the hit. He knew I wouldn't serve her up as bait, but he knew I'd—"

"Put your own fool self on the chopping block in order to protect her? Yep, noted. Gray is a sneaky SOB that way. I've always hated his mind games. One day, he's gonna find a woman who is even better at mind fuckery than he is. When that blessed day happens, I will be laughing my ass off."

They both would.

The waves rocked gently against the shore. "Maybe..." Ronan stopped. Maybe what? Maybe he'd trap Marcus, find the evidence to absolutely bury the creep for the rest of his life, and then Ronan could come back and live happily ever after with Luna?

Hitmen didn't get happily-ever-after endings.

More than that, Luna deserved better. She didn't deserve a fake life with a fake name. She deserved a stage. A crowd clapping for her. She deserved all of her adventures. A husband who worshipped her and touched her with hands that weren't blood-stained.

"Okay, so now you're looking all pissed and grim. Want to tell me what you're thinking about?"

"Killing Luna's husband." An honest reply.

The wind blew lightly against him.

"Uh, aren't you her husband?"

He was her pretend husband. One day, she'd have a real husband. Someone who kissed her and loved her and gave her kids.

Ronan had been thinking about killing the faceless bastard.

"Bro, you have some issues."

Some? The wind blew against him once more. In the distance, it seemed like the sky was darkening. If a storm was coming, travel off the island would be harder. They might have to suspend the boats. Good. He could get out now, before the storm hit. Then Luna wouldn't be able to leave even if she *did* manage to get away from Tyler and Esme. Which she would not do. The storm would trap her. "Tell her..." He stopped.

"I think you should tell her yourself. No one likes to be abandoned."

Fuck. "It wasn't real. It was all just pretend."

"Yeah, that is *not* what I want to tell the woman. I don't like breaking hearts."

Those words hadn't been for Luna. He'd said them to convince himself. Their relationship had just been pretend, though it had certainly felt like the most real thing in his life. "I'll never forget her. She should have every adventure she wants. And soon, she'll be safe. No more worrying about the darkness. I'm taking it out of her life." He stood. She was snorkeling again. Having the time of her life.

Luna, I think you were the best time of my life.

His hand rubbed over his chest. Fuck. He was going soft. Maybe it was time to get out of the business. After he eliminated one final problem. "Either I'll get the evidence to lock Marcus away for the rest of his days or I'll bury him in the ground." A roll of his shoulders even as his hand dropped back to his side. "One way or another, Luna will get her life back."

It would be a life without him.

One final look, and he turned away.

"I think this is a mistake." Tyler's low voice.

Ronan stilled. "If someone was sending a parade of

Cynthia Eden

eager killers after you, would you *want* Esme close by? Or would you keep her the fuck away?"

Tyler didn't speak. But Ronan knew the truth. Tyler would live and die for his Esme.

After a moment, Tyler said, "She'll stay safe."

Ronan's breath released. When had he started to hold it? "Thank you."

"Don't thank me. I'm pretty sure I'm helping you to make one of the worst mistakes of your life. That woman... she loves you, doesn't she?"

The pain knifed into his chest again. "Worst mistake of her life," he said, tossing those words back at Tyler. "She'll be much better off when I vanish. And when I make all the threats to her vanish." He wanted to look back. To glance back at her one more time. But if he glanced back and she happened to be looking his way...

Would he be able to go?

Why the fuck was he not moving already? Why did it feel like his feet were glued to the spot? Was he sinking in the sand or something?

"Do you love her?" Tyler asked him. Words so soft that the sound of the waves rushing to the shore almost hid them.

Ronan didn't speak. He took a lunging, slightly staggering step forward. Then another one. Another one and he...

Nodded.

* * *

RONAN WASN'T on the beach.

Luna had just seen the most amazing sea turtle. It had been graceful and gorgeous, and it had darted right beneath her. She'd been so excited, and she broke the surface because, okay, Ronan *had* to come into the water. He'd love to see all the beauty with her.

Except, this time, when she broke the surface and turned eagerly toward him, Ronan wasn't there.

The other guy was still there. Tyler. The man who'd nearly scared the soul right out of her body the previous night. He was lounging in a chaise and sipping out of a giant pineapple. He waved to Luna.

Her gaze drifted to the left. To the right.

No sign of Ronan.

Maybe he'd just gone back to their bungalow.

Or gone to get one of those fancy pineapple drinks for himself.

The woman appeared—hadn't her name been Esme? She took the empty chaise that had belonged to Ronan. She spoke with her husband.

Luna pulled off her mask. Headed toward shallower water. Kept going forward until her feet touched the sand beneath the waves. She hadn't bothered with the flippers that were offered at the snorkeling booth. Maybe she should have used them, but—

Esme's face had just flashed with anger. Now she was looking back toward Luna.

Only the anger was gone. Wait. Did she look *sad?*

Luna hurried forward. As she burst onto the shore, water rolled down her body. The mask and snorkel banged into her thigh. "Where is Ronan?"

Esme and Tyler looked at each other. Then Esme peered at Luna once more.

No, no, no. Why was that pity on Esme's face?

Luna stopped right in front of them. The day didn't feel so warm or beautiful any longer. She sucked in a breath.

She could feel her wet hair sticking to the side of her face. Sand covered her feet. She shoved away the sticking hair even as she kept a grip on the mask and snorkel. "Where is my husband?"

But she knew, the giant aching in her heart told her the truth even before Tyler softly answered, "Gone."

Chapter Twenty

RONAN COULD NOT JUST BE *GONE*.

Luna shook her head. No, no way. He would not just leave. "No."

Esme tilted back her head. She wore an oversized straw hat. One that somehow managed to look stylish and elegant on her. Her big sunglasses perched on the edge of her delicate nose as she stared up at Luna.

Luna shook her head once more. "I'll go meet him in the bungalow." He must have gone to change, and he'd left his friends on the beach to keep an eye on her. She didn't need eyes on her, though. The little island was safe.

Luna grabbed for a towel that she'd shoved into her bag.

Esme's hand flew out and curled around her wrist. "Your husband was called away on business," she said, her voice a little too loud.

A waiter bent near Tyler. "Sir, do you need another drink?"

Luna jumped. She hadn't even seen the waiter approach.

Tyler nodded. "Yeah, why don't you bring a round for

everyone?" His rumble in response, then as the waiter hurried away, Tyler added, "We're probably gonna need them."

"Let go of my wrist," Luna told the other woman.

Esme immediately did. "Why don't you swim some more? I think a storm is coming. You should enjoy the day while you can."

Luna felt like the storm was already there. "I don't want a drink." Definitely not. "I don't want to swim again. I want to talk with Ronan."

Esme and Tyler exchanged a long look.

"He wasn't called away on work." Luna put the mask and snorkel into her bag.

"He was." A quick response from Tyler. "Unavoidable work."

Her stomach twisted. She'd been leaning over the bag, but at his words, she immediately shot upright as fear flashed through her. "Just what kind of *unavoidable* work?"

* * *

IT DIDN'T TAKE LONG to pack. He'd always been a minimal kind of guy. Basically, all he needed was a weapon and a fake ID and some cash. All stuff that he'd long ago learned to keep in a convenient go bag.

He'd had one of those bags on the island.

Gray believed in go bags, too. They all did.

Within five minutes, he was walking along the dock. At the end of the dock, a private boat waited, a boat that shuttled guests back and forth to Key West. He'd known that the boat left promptly at noon. Check-out time for departing guests. The boat would return—again promptly— at four p.m. with the new arrivals.

He would not be returning.

As soon as Tyler had told him the news about the hit, Ronan had realized he had to act quickly if he wanted to catch the departing boat. There had been no time to second guess. To hesitate. To give in to the urge to stay with Luna.

To make a life with Luna.

No, her life will be better without me. Hell, she couldn't even have a life, not a real one, until he eliminated the threat from her past.

He hopped onto the boat. The last passenger to board. The attendant moved to begin untying the ropes that bound them to the dock. Ronan didn't take a seat with the other guests. Instead, he turned and stared back at the island.

He hadn't turned to stare back at Luna. He couldn't. It hurt too much to see what he was losing. But he couldn't see her from this position. She was probably still swimming on the other side of the little island. Luna had no idea that he was gone.

When he already felt her absence like a giant hole in his chest.

The boat began to pull away. He lifted his hand. Curled it around a long pole near his head as he held his balance.

"Where is your lovely wife?"

The voice had his jaw tensing. A voice he recognized. The club owner who'd wanted to book Luna as a singer.

Ronan turned his head. Slowly. He'd kept on his sunglasses, and behind the lenses, his gaze raked the man who had inched up beside him. "*My* lovely wife is enjoying the beach."

The guy didn't heed the warning that Ronan knew had been in his words. Instead, the fool sidled a bit closer. "My Monique is still on the island, too. She's enjoying the spa. Loves her a good spa day." He flashed a broad grin. Like

Ronan, he also had on sunglasses, though his sat slightly askew on his nose. "Had to go back early for some business in Miami. Always a few fires to put out, am I right?"

"I'm on my way to put out one right now." Permanently.

"Then you'll be coming back?" A pushy question from the man who now apparently wanted to be his new best friend.

I won't be coming back. I won't be seeing Luna again. Because he couldn't see her and walk away a second time. That would be too hard.

Her father fucking left her, and I just did, too.

How did you destroy someone's love? By breaking the person's heart into a thousand pieces. "Of course," Ronan finally replied because an answer was needed. "Not like I'd leave my wife."

"If I left mine..." The man leaned conspiratorially toward Ronan. Harris—Harris Croft had been the name on the card he'd given Ronan. "If I left my Monique, she'd skin me alive." He shuddered. "Then, since we don't have a prenup, she'd take every dime I possess and have me begging her to take me back. That woman is a shark." An exhale. "I love her so."

"Um. Fantastic for you."

Harris eased back. "Guess you feel the same way about your wife, huh? Some women are just worth everything."

"My wife is definitely worth everything to me." He realized the statement was one hundred percent true as soon as the words left his mouth. Luna was worth everything. He would do anything for her. Even walk away.

"Did you, ah, get a chance to talk with her about my offer?"

The offer of a dream job for her. "You know what? Maybe she will take you up on that offer soon." Once she didn't fear being killed every moment, she could live. "Stay tuned on that one." He'd be sure and give Gray the man's number and name. Maybe Luna could contact him when everything was over.

Harris clapped. "That's great news! That's—"

They hit a particularly hard wave. Harris bounced. He also grabbed out for the bar that Ronan had been holding.

"Steady," Ronan warned him.

He realized that Harris was looking at his left wrist. Ronan hadn't put on his watch, the big watch that could mostly shield his tattoo. He'd been in too much of a hurry to leave. The dark snake was on full display.

Ronan's other hand came up and gripped Harris's shoulder. Harris flinched.

"You good?" Ronan asked him.

Harris nodded and hurriedly let go of the bar. "I-I didn't expect such rough water."

"A storm is coming," Ronan told him as he released the other man.

Harris turned his head to look at the darkening clouds. "I want to be back with Monique this evening. Got to hurry so I can get on the return boat."

"Um."

"You doing the same? Hurrying back?"

The boat bounced again. Harder. Ronan didn't answer Harris's question.

"That's, ah, some tattoo." Harris swallowed. Looked a little green. "You must really like snakes."

"Fucking love them." Enough chatting with the guy. He looked toward the little island. Only he could barely see it now. "Snakes are my damn favorite."

* * *

THE BUNGALOW WAS EMPTY. More than that, it felt cold. Silent. The candles had all been removed. The rose petals cleaned up. No more champagne chilled beside the bed. In fact, the bed had been neatly made. The housekeeping staff had clearly buzzed in and out, setting everything back to order.

Ronan's clothes still hung in the small closet.

She touched one of his shirts.

Gone. He left.

There was a knock at the door. She'd expected the knock to come. Not like Esme and Tyler were going to leave her on her own, despite her pleas for some privacy. She released the shirt. Squared her shoulders. And headed for the door.

Her steps seemed to echo in the little bungalow. Why did it hurt so much, knowing that he'd left? She'd understood that they didn't have forever. He'd never said he loved her.

She'd only known him a few days.

Didn't matter how long it had been, though. *I love him.*

She opened the door.

"Hi, new friend!" Esme shrilled brightly. She barreled inside and embraced Luna. A warm, strong hug. And damn if Luna didn't need a hug right then and there. Her hands rose, and, for a moment, she hugged the other woman back just as tightly.

"It will be okay," Esme whispered into Luna's ear. "Don't give up on him. Some men just will not rest until they've eliminated the threats to the ones they love."

But he didn't love her.

She pulled from Esme's embrace. "What threat?"

Tyler shut the bungalow door behind Esme. He crossed his arms over his chest. Luna had the feeling he was a giant, immovable object intent on blocking her path. "You're not gonna like this," Tyler warned her.

"I was just told Ronan left me. I already don't like things." Her chin notched up. "It would have been polite to tell me goodbye."

"It would have been painful," Esme corrected with a shudder. "Goodbyes are the worst. Especially when you realize you've fallen in love for the first time in your life."

Her gaze cut right back to Esme. "How do you know I love him?"

"*Mon amie,* it is on your face when you look at him. In your voice when you say his name." A sigh. "Love can hurt. But it can also bring so much joy."

Did she look joyous right then? Joy was not the emotion pouring through her. "I'm assuming you two are my new guards?"

"I am your new friend," Esme stressed. "Perhaps I will become your very best one." She offered a wide smile. "I am a very useful friend to have. *Je promets.*"

Luna's lips pressed together. Her right foot tapped on the floor. "I feel like you're both stalling. Just as I felt like you were stalling on the beach." There were no clocks on the wall. No clocks on the whole island. Part of the whole relaxation and time-having-no-meaning bit. No clocks. No TVs.

But she had seen Ronan's watch on the nightstand...

She stopped tapping her foot. "I guess the island's transport boat has left already?" That would have been why they were stalling. To give Ronan time to leave the island.

Tyler inclined his head.

"Am I going to get a new identity now?" She kept her chin up. "A new life some place? Ronan left me because his job was done?"

Tyler and Esme shared a glance. They did that. A lot.

Tyler cleared his throat. "His job isn't quite done. You won't be getting that new ID just yet. Instead, you'll be staying here on the island with us while Ronan takes care of unfinished business."

Goosebumps rose onto her arms. "Just what would that unfinished business be?"

Esme edged closer to Tyler. "He's not supposed to reveal confidential info. Grayson will be a pain in the ass to him if he does." She flashed a mega-smile. "I, however, am under no such restrictions."

She focused on the other woman. Completely. "What is happening?"

"A hit has been placed."

Luna backed up a step. "Marcus knows I'm alive?" He'd put another hit on her already? Her eyes widened in horror and fear and—

"Non. Not on you. The hit is on Ronan."

The wave of shock that rolled through Luna was so intense that her knees almost hit the floor. "No!"

But Esme nodded. "Marcus put a bounty on Ronan's head. Because of that hit order, Ronan knew the sharks would be closing in. He didn't want to risk anyone seeing you with him. So he left. No doubt, he told himself it was so he could better protect you."

Breathing was too hard. Something heavy weighed down her chest.

"He decided to go on the offensive," Tyler added as he continued to be an immovable object in front of the door. "He is going straight for Marcus. Going to try and find the trophies and evidence that will put Marcus away for life. He's ending the threat to you."

By putting an even bigger target on himself?

"He left a message for me to give you," Tyler revealed. "Want to hear it?"

"No," she snapped. "I want to go around for the rest of my days filled with burning curiosity."

He frowned.

Luna lifted her hands into the air. "Of course, I want to hear it!" Had the question even needed to be asked? Her hands fell to her sides.

Tyler nodded. "Ronan said...he said that he wouldn't forget you."

That was something, she supposed. Not like she would ever—not in a million years—be able to forget him. His memory would haunt her far too much.

"He said that, uh, you should go on any adventure you want. Not real sure what kind of adventures he meant, but you should have them."

Her lower lip began to tremble.

"I do enjoy adventures," Esme murmured. "Perhaps I can have some of those with you."

Tyler cut a quick glance at his wife, then focused on Luna. "Ronan wanted you to know that you're gonna be safe."

Because he'd left her with two guards. Check. Her lips pressed together. The better to stop the trembling.

"You won't have to worry about the darkness much longer," Tyler added. "Because Ronan is gonna take it out of your life."

Her heart thudded hard in her chest. She wasn't sure exactly—was Ronan the darkness? She knew he saw himself as the bad guy. But he wasn't. That was certainly not how she saw him.

When he referred to the darkness, had Ronan been talking about himself or...

He's talking about Marcus. He must have been referring to Marcus. But had he been talking about getting Marcus locked away in prison—or killing him? Her heartbeat was way too hard as Luna inched a bit closer to Tyler. "He didn't just...leave me, did he? There's more involved."

"He's gone. He won't be coming back." Final. Then, gruff, "I'm sorry."

She would not cry. She would not break down. Mostly because fear was pushing too hard inside of her. "He went after Marcus."

Tyler's jaw hardened the faintest bit.

"He's out there now, hunting." A stark pause from Luna. "Isn't he?" That must have been what Ronan meant when he said he was taking the darkness out of her life. If he wanted her to have her adventures, then he thought she'd be safe soon.

The only way for her to be truly safe? It would be for Marcus to be gone. *Dead?*

But Tyler wasn't answering her.

Her shoulders slumped. "May I have some time alone?" Did she sound suitably forlorn? She certainly felt freaking forlorn.

"Ronan was never going to stay as your permanent guard. That's not how it works." Again, Tyler's voice was gruff. Incredibly uncomfortable. As if he hated to tell her the cold, hard facts. Or maybe, as if he hated to break her heart. The big guy had a soft spot inside of him.

"Don't be ridiculous, darling," Esme admonished. "You are my permanent guard. That is certainly how it happened for us. Why can't it happen that way for her, too?"

Luna's gaze whipped to Esme.

She found Esme staring straight at her.

234

"If you want something badly enough," Esme said as she deadeye stared at Luna, "you fight for it."

Luna caught herself mid-nod.

Esme winked. A wink that Tyler did not see. Then Esme moved toward her immovable-object husband. She poked at his chest. "She's about to cry," she loudly whispered to Tyler. A stage whisper if Luna had ever heard one. "She doesn't want an audience for her tears. I certainly understand that."

His expression softened.

"The transport boat is gone," Esme told him. "She can't swim from here to Key West. We'll be right outside the front door. She asked for privacy. Let's give her some."

The battle was clear on his face. He didn't want to back down.

His wife poked him again.

Grudgingly, Tyler nodded. But he lasered a hard look Luna's way. "He told me you were a runner."

She tried to look innocent. After all, hadn't Ronan been the one who told her that she could do that look so well? Or, wait, maybe he'd said she had an innocent smile. Not like she could manage any sort of smile right then.

"There's no point in running," Tyler warned her. "Unless you're going to sprout wings, you aren't getting off this island. A storm is rolling in. The water is going to be helluva rough, and we all need to stay inside until dawn."

If only she could sprout wings...

"I can practically see the thoughts spinning in your head. Don't do it." Tyler was adamant. "*Don't.* He's helping you, okay? Let Ronan do his job."

But his job would risk his life. Ronan was risking *his life* for her. She was just supposed to stand back and let him do that?

"This will all be over before you know it." A soft assurance from Tyler. "Soon enough, it will seem like a bad dream."

Parts, maybe. Parts had been a nightmare. But other parts would seem like the best fantasy in the world. Luna released a long, slow breath. She knew exactly what she needed to do. "It's too bad, really," she said, rolling her shoulders.

Tyler's eyebrows beetled down. "What's too bad?"

"That Ronan didn't give some big, heartfelt confession of love for you to deliver to me. Would have been nice." A million times better than nice. "Thanks for telling me what he actually said." She swallowed. "Thanks for your help. Both of you." *Now please exit the bungalow so I can get the hell out of here.*

She wasn't going to let Ronan risk himself for her. She'd get off the island. She'd call Grayson. They could come up with a new plan that involved Ronan being safe. In no world did she want Ronan potentially dying for her.

Tyler turned away. He reached for the doorknob but stopped before actually touching it. "Sometimes, you don't have to say a word in order to make a confession."

What did that even mean?

Tyler glanced back at her. "Ronan didn't say he loved you."

Wonderful. Another knife straight to her heart.

"But he does."

Oh, that was sweet. She had to blink away tears. The U.S. Marshal was trying to make her feel better by lying to her. "It's okay," she assured him. "You don't need to tell me that story. I love him, and my feelings won't change."

His expression just hardened more. His lips parted.

"Privacy," Esme said, tone brisk. "Don't you see the

tears in her eyes? *Let's go*." She reached around him and opened the door.

"Some people don't mind crying when others are around, Esme," he muttered.

"And some do. Come on." She dragged him out.

The door clicked closed.

A lone tear slid down Luna's cheek. Then she spun around and ran toward the bedroom. She threw on fresh clothes as fast as possible. Not like she wanted to leave the island in her bathing suit and cover up. And she *was* leaving that island.

Ronan didn't get to risk his life for her.

She was not going to hide while he faced all the danger. Maybe she could meet him in Key West. Stop him before he jeopardized himself.

Jeans, t-shirt, underwear, tennis shoes. She threw them all on and then grabbed for the sliding glass door in the bedroom that led out to the beach. A beachfront view that had been killer. She slid that door open soundlessly. Barreled forward.

And screamed when she hit an immovable object.

Tyler's hands closed around her upper arms. "I told you," he sighed. "Ronan warned me you were a runner."

Chapter Twenty-One

THE CLUB OWNER KNEW WHO HE WAS.

The boat slowly inched toward the dock. The crew members threw off the lines, securing the vessel as it bobbed in the rough water. Raindrops fell, pelting down on Ronan as he waited for the all clear to be given to the passengers.

Harris Croft twisted his hands in front of his body. He'd already lined up to get off the vessel. He kept casting nervous glances Ronan's way.

Whenever he caught one of those glances, Ronan just stared back. He'd ditched his sunglasses. Not really a point in wearing them in the rain. So he laser-locked his stare on the other man.

"All clear!"

The passengers began to disembark. Harris nearly busted his ass as he jumped on the slippery dock and hurried away. Ronan followed. Much slower, but he didn't let his prey out of his sight. He tracked Harris to the nearby parking lot as the guy headed straight for a G-Wagon. Harris fumbled with his keys.

Ronan closed in behind him. "Do we have a problem?"

Harris jumped. He spun around. "N-no!" Wide eyes. Shaking voice.

In other words, definite problem.

Ronan inclined his head. "You seem very nervous, Harris." Understatement.

"I just want to get back to my wife," Harris assured him. "Storm came in too fast. I-I might have to fly to her."

Lightning flashed overhead. "You really want to be in a little seaplane, in this kind of weather?"

"I just want to get back to my w-wife." A pause. "I'm sure you know how that feels."

The jerk knows who I am. Or maybe, *what* Ronan was. "You liked my tat. I noticed you staring at it."

Harris bumped into the side of the G-Wagon. "I don't know that 'like' is the right word..."

Fair enough. He'd seemed terrified of the tat. "You've seen one of these tats before, haven't you, Harris?" A very distinctive snake design.

"I just want to get back to my wife." Adamant. And not exactly a yes or a no.

Voices rose around them. Other passengers. Random visitors to Key West. The lot was too busy. Not like Ronan could knock the guy out and shove him into a vehicle with all of those people around. And they both knew that truth. Harris was safe, for the moment.

He smiled and backed away from Harris. "I'll be seeing you again," he assured Harris.

"Please don't," Harris whispered. "Please don't see me again." He yanked open his door. Jumped inside. A few moments later, the G-Wagon fishtailed out of the lot. Ronan watched the vehicle go.

Then he felt a tap on his shoulder. He didn't turn around. Why bother? This time, the tricky bastard had not snuck up on him. Ronan had been fully aware of his approach.

"You're scaring the locals," Kane Harte informed him.

"I certainly hope so."

"Want to tell me why?"

Sure. "Because that man is going to sell me out and deliver me for an up close and personal kill to Marcus Aeros." He watched the taillights as they bobbed and weaved in the distance.

"You don't say." Kane didn't seem particularly alarmed. "In that case, maybe we should follow him?"

A nod. "Maybe we should."

"I've got extra weapons in my car."

"I was hoping you'd say that." You could never have too many in situations like this one. "Statements like that are why you could be my very best friend in the whole world."

"I'm not going to tell Gray you said that."

"Don't. It would just hurt his feelings."

* * *

"YOU ARE NOT SERIOUSLY STAYING with me the entire time." Luna sat in the oversized, rather lush chair in the bungalow's small den. She took turns glaring first at Tyler. Then at Esme.

Esme waved happily back at her.

"We are seriously staying with you," Tyler affirmed. There was no happy wave from him. Just a glower. "Because the minute we leave you alone, you'll run."

"Where will I run to?" She tried to sound reasonable. "The boat is gone."

240

He raised one brow. "So, here's the deal. You think you're gonna cut out and save him, don't you?"

"I think..." *There's a seaplane on this island. Maybe I can bribe the pilot to fly it out.* She'd seen the seaplane when she'd been out snorkeling. "I think I don't want Ronan risking his life for me."

Esme's warm laughter filled the air. "Oh, *mon amie*, risk is his job. It's what he does. He would risk himself for a stranger." She wagged her index finger at Luna, as if Luna had just made the most hilarious joke ever. Spoiler, she had not. "Of course, he would risk himself for you."

Her hands grabbed for the arms of the chair and dug in a bit too hard. "I don't want that. I don't want him getting hurt because of me."

"Ronan has training. Years and years of covert, dangerous training that has honed him into the hunter he is today." There was no warm laughter from Tyler. There was pretty much no warmth from him at all. Except when he looked at Esme. However, he wasn't looking at Esme right then. His eyes were on Luna. "You have zero training, drama teacher."

"You don't have to be mean, Tyler." A rare chide from Esme.

"I'm not being mean. I'm being honest. She has zero training. She runs out, she tries to trade herself for him or do some other stupid shit—"

Luna flinched.

"Then she dies," he said, a blunt and brutal summary. "Did you hear me, Luna?"

Yes, her hearing was quite good.

"You will die if you do that crap. Not a pretend death. A real one. And it's very possible that your attempt to save my friend will result in him losing his life. I don't want

Ronan dying. Yes, he can be a pain in the ass to me, but I'm quite fond of him. So I will do nothing to jeopardize him. Kane will be his backup. They'll handle the situation, and when we have the all clear, you will get your new life." A roll of one shoulder as he began to prowl around the bungalow. "Or maybe you'll even be able to get your old one back. Who knows?"

Her old life didn't include Ronan. Then again, neither did her new one. "I don't want to put him in more danger." That was the last thing she wanted.

"Good. Then we'll all sit our asses down and we'll—" A knock interrupted Tyler.

She didn't point out that her ass was already sitting down. Luna thought that was obvious.

At the knock, battle-ready tension rolled through Tyler. He grabbed a gun from the nearby table—he'd placed it there earlier—and padded for the door. "Are we expecting guests?" A lethal intensity underscored his words.

Esme cleared her throat. "*Oui.*"

He fired a glance her way.

"We're going to be here for a while." She shrugged. Appeared vaguely guilty. "I ordered some wine. Non-alcoholic cider. Cheese. No reason things have to be unpleasant." She tapped her index finger against her lower lip. "Chocolate will be in the delivery, as well."

"Esme..."

"It's painful enough for her." Her gaze darted to Luna. "Let's make the best of things, shall we?"

Grumbling, he went to the door. Tyler checked before he opened it, and sure enough, an attendant delivered wine and apple cider, three glasses, cheese, and an assortment of decadent chocolates. In moments, the treats were organized and the server was gone.

Luna made no move to approach the delivery.

"Do you trust Ronan?"

Luna glanced up as Esme closed in on her. The other woman could sure move soundlessly when she wanted. Luna admired that skill.

"With your life, I mean? Do you trust Ronan with your life? Not necessarily your heart because I suspect he's broken that, hasn't he?"

A lump rose in her throat. Luna choked it down. "I trust him."

"Then know that he will be safe. We will stay here with you. And before you know it, Ronan will return to you."

Luna shook her head. "He's not coming back to me." *Tyler is right. I can't just run out wildly. I can't save Ronan. I wouldn't know what to do. Where to go. I'd put a bigger target on my head, or God forbid, on his.* Panic and pain had been driving her. "I don't want to ever hurt him."

Esme reached for her hand. "He will come back."

"He never said he loved me." Maybe if they'd had more time together...

"Why would he have to say the words? Saying them doesn't make the emotion more real. Perhaps you should look at what he *did* instead."

Luna blinked. Tugged her hand from Esme's. "He *left* me." That was what he'd done.

"That was a bad choice of words on my part." Esme grimaced. "Shall we have something to drink?"

No, the last thing she wanted to do was drink. What she wanted was to speak with Ronan. To tell him that his life was important. To warn him not to risk himself for her.

But he was gone.

And she was trapped.

* * *

"I-I HAVE INFORMATION THAT YOU WANT." Harris Croft gripped his phone a little too tightly as he stood behind the desk in his Key West office. The club was closed down. It didn't usually open until 8 p.m., and it was still early afternoon. No staff members buzzed about the place. No waitresses. No security. His breath rushed out. "I know you wanted him dead, but I'm not a killer. Consider me an... intermediary."

He heard laughter on the line. It was the kind of laughter that could chill a man's soul. He'd had a few interactions with Marcus Aeros over the years. Each interaction had left him more and more certain that he did not want to ever get on the guy's bad side.

According to the gossip, Marcus Aeros had a very, very bad side.

You wanted men like him to owe you favors. You didn't want them to have you locked and loaded as a future target. Marcus's targets had an unfortunate tendency to wind up dead.

"I know you put out a hit on Ronan Walker." Did his voice tremble? Harris hoped to hell not. "You gave a description of the man. Sent his photo." Maybe Harris had some bad connections in this world. So what? If you were gonna be a club owner in the Keys and Miami, you didn't just mix with the *good* people out there. Business had to be handled.

That was what he was doing right then. Handling business.

Marcus hadn't spoken since answering the call. Harris had identified himself, then had quickly mentioned their previous interactions so the other man wouldn't hang up on him right away. Once upon a time, Marcus had wanted to invest in one of Harris's clubs.

But at the last minute, Marcus had gone with a different hotspot. One in Vegas, not Miami. And Harris had been thrilled to avoid that particular business tie.

Yet, here we are...

"Marcus?" Harris's breath rushed out. "Are you still there?"

"I'm waiting to hear more." The words were almost bored.

So Harris talked even faster. "I-I saw him. The man you're after."

"I don't know why you think *I'm* after anyone."

His mind spun. "I have connections. I know what's going down. You're the one who put the target on Ronan Walker."

No confirmation. No denial.

"I'm calling you because I want payment."

"Do you?" Again, *bored*.

"I know where he is, okay? Exactly where is he. I-I saw his tat, and I know it's him. He fits the description perfectly." His gaze stared straight ahead as he continued. "Minus the beard. He's ditched that. He and his wife were at—"

Harris stopped.

Because a gun had just pressed to his forehead.

His breath fizzled in his chest as Harris gazed at the man who held the gun. *Ronan Walker.*

"Wife?" Marcus asked slowly.

"Uh..."

"Where did you see him?" Marcus wanted to know.

"Where did you see *her*?" Suddenly, he didn't sound bored at all.

"I saw him right here, in Key West." *Right in front of my damn face.* The gun muzzle pressed harder into his forehead. Shit. This was not going to end well. It could not.

"You're not going to kill him?" Curious.

Oh, I think I might be the one in danger of dying. "Not my style. Like I said, consider me an intermediary." An intermediary who wanted to extricate his ass from the situation as soon as humanly possible.

"Don't like to get your hands dirty, is that it?"

He'd prefer not to get them bloody, thanks. "I'm telling you where he is. All I want is a finder's fee." And to keep living. That would be great. "You take care of the rest. Hell, if you name the location, I can serve him up to you on a platter. I've got people who can deliver him to you. I'm just not pulling the trigger." Harris really, really hoped the man in front of him would not pull the trigger, too.

Soft laughter spilled from Marcus. "So many people calling me lately..."

What did that mean? Had someone else already claimed the hit?

"I'll remember what you did," Marcus assured Harris. "You'll certainly be paid back."

Was that good? Or bad? It felt bad. So bad.

"Shut your club down for the night. Have him waiting for me there."

"I don't want to be around when you, ah, kill him—"

"Then don't be there. Lock him down. Secure him. I'll personally handle Ronan while you go somewhere with that pretty wife of yours."

His jaw clenched. He hated it whenever Marcus mentioned Monique.

The call ended. He slowly lowered the phone and put it on his desk. Super slowly so he didn't set off the menacing figure in front of him. "Happy?" Harris croaked. His throat had gone bone dry. "I did what you wanted. He will *personally* handle you."

"Happy doesn't quite cover it," Ronan Walker growled. "You weren't supposed to mention my fucking *wife*."

"Well, it's not like I had a freaking script to read!" Sweat trickled down his back. The sweat trickled harder when the second guy stepped out of the shadows because Ronan hadn't come alone when he'd broken into Harris's office. He'd brought his hulking, scarily intense buddy with him.

They'd ordered him to make the call. Told him all that BS to say about knowing there was a hit on Ronan. He hadn't actually known jack. He didn't play around in the world of killers.

Well, okay, he *had* known one thing. He knew the tat that Ronan sported meant serious trouble. As soon as he'd seen it, he'd wanted to haul ass away from the bruiser.

His instincts had been right, of course. Trouble stared back at him. "Will you please remove the gun from my head?" He'd had the call on speaker the whole time. Both of the men before him had heard everything. "I did what you wanted."

"You mentioned my *wife*."

"You didn't say she was on his hit list! So what if I mentioned her?"

But Ronan and his buddy shared a long look.

Harris's knees shook. "I don't want to die. Look, just let me leave, please?" He wasn't above begging. "I have a wife, too. I want to get back to her. I need to get back to her." His heart thudded hard in his chest. "You stay here. He'll come for you tonight. I will be long gone."

"How do I know that if I let you leave, you won't immediately call Marcus back and sell me out?" Ronan asked.

"Fair question." Harris wet his lips. "I don't suppose you'd take me at my word?"

Ronan shook his head. But he did lower his gun. Thankfully.

Harris pulled in some seriously deep breaths.

Only to see Ronan's buddy haul out a pair of handcuffs. *Oh, no.*

"Afraid you're gonna be locked up until this is all over," the guy told him in a voice that a bear probably would use. If fucking bears could talk. "For your own safety. And ours."

A cuff snapped against Harris's wrist. A chill skated down his sweaty back even as he said, "I don't think this shit is legal."

"Do we look like cops to you?" Ronan asked.

No. "You look like trouble."

"It was the tat, huh? You've seen one of those before. You knew what the tat represented."

The other cuff snapped on his wrist. "Yeah, I've seen one before. It's the whole reason I didn't hire the guy, despite his talent. Knew he'd probably slit my throat if he got pissed at me for something." Harris hadn't always been living the high life. He'd done time in some hellholes, and he knew all about those distinctive, freaking snake tats.

Ronan had gone statue still. "What guy?"

Harris squinted at him. Seriously? "You talked to him on the island. When I saw your tat—hell, I figured you two were there together for a reason. I want my Monique out of that place, understand? If you're not letting me go back to her tonight, then you get her secured." His shoulders straightened. "I did my part. Now you do something for me.

Get my wife off the island. Protect her." She was the best thing in his life.

"*What. Guy?*"

It dawned on Harris that Ronan had no idea about the danger that waited on the island. So he started talking, fast.

Chapter Twenty-Two

"IT'S ALL RIGHT."

The low voice pushed through the darkness. Luna tried to open her eyes, but she couldn't. They were far too heavy. Weighed down. Only *she* wasn't weighed down. If anything, Luna felt as if she was flying.

No, not flying, being lifted up.

Worry pulsed through her, but she couldn't quite make her body respond to the fear that filled her veins.

"We're going on a little trip."

She shouldn't be going on a trip. She was supposed to be staying in the bungalow. Esme and Tyler were guarding her. She couldn't run out and try to find Ronan. They wouldn't let her. All she had of him—hell, it was his big watch. He'd left it on the nightstand. At some point, she'd put it on her wrist. A piece of him to keep for her memories. A melancholy act. An overly sentimental move. As she'd sipped the wine and nibbled on the chocolates, she'd felt increasingly melancholy. And increasingly sleepy.

She was still sleepy. Perhaps...too sleepy. And shouldn't she be more alarmed that someone was carrying her?

This isn't right. Then, with that realization...*I'm not right. Something is very wrong with me.* Her lashes finally fluttered. She had a quick flash of the bungalow. Esme was sprawled on the sofa, with her head tipped back. Sound asleep.

Not just asleep. Unconscious?

Tyler curled near her. His head slumped forward. He barely seemed to breathe. *Was* he breathing?

Fresh, sharp alarm spiked. Finally, real, bracing alarm. Luna hadn't consumed much wine. Just a little. Had Esme even touched the wine or had she just sampled the cider? Luna couldn't remember. They'd all nibbled on the food. The cheese. The chocolates. And...

"Too bad we can't work together. I really did love your voice."

Her eyes fluttered helplessly closed. By the time she managed to open them again, she was outside. Water was hitting her face. Raindrops? It was the raindrops that helped Luna to keep her eyes open even as she heard a dull whirring.

"But you're not gonna be singing for anyone ever again. Not when he's done with you." After those words, the man who'd been carrying Luna shoved her onto what felt like a cushioned seat.

Her eyes focused for a moment on his wrist as he pulled a belt across her body and secured her in place. On his wrist, she saw a striking snake. "Ronan?" Hope came. Relief. She was safe with Ronan.

Her focus was on the snake. A snake she'd seen plenty of times on Ronan's left wrist. No way could she forget those curving lines and the sharp fangs poised to strike.

"Nah. Not even close."

Her head turned. For a moment, she was eye to eye with

the man. And his eyes were the wrong color. His face was the wrong face.

He smiled at her. "Told you to run from him when you had the chance, sweetheart. You should have listened to me. Now you're going to die and so is he, and I'm going to get one big fat payday."

The words poured onto her, but her mind was just working too slowly. She couldn't comprehend what he was telling her. She knew him, though. He was the—

* * *

"The fucking piano player!" Ronan snarled into his phone. "Listen to me, Gray, we are screwed, do you understand me? I'm not on the damn island, I can't get hold of Tyler or Esme, and there's someone there—*the fucking piano player*—who has to know who I am! He's got the same gang tat."

"Shit," Gray said. Then, "Shit."

Kane was securing Harris. Ronan was losing his mind. Lightning flashed overhead and rain pelted down on him. "The island was supposed to be safe!" More than that. Luna should have been safe. It was the reason he'd been able to walk away. *Luna was safe.* Or so he'd believed. But the acid eating away at his insides told him she was not.

He had to get back there. Immediately.

"Calm down," Gray made the mistake of saying.

"Fuck yourself," Ronan told him flatly.

"Look, don't panic. You know the cell service on the island is sketchy—maybe the calls just aren't connecting. Maybe—"

"Marcus wanted me kept in Harris's club. That means he wanted me out of the way because he's handling other business. It's a distraction. *He's going after Luna.* The guy sounded way too calm on the phone. Didn't ask enough questions. Didn't push enough. Just said he'd be here. Not like he had to arrange things or coordinate or do any shit to fly down. Just that he'd be in the club tonight. *That means he's fucking already here.* Don't you get that?" Or, worse, he wasn't right there in Key West. *He's with Luna. Could already be on the little island while I'm stuck here.* "He could be out there with her now, killing her. Killing my wife! And you think I'm just sitting my ass here? You think I'm going to calm my ass down? You think—"

"She's not your wife," Gray pointed out.

Wrong thing to point out. "I am going to kick your ass." He heaved in a breath. "Then I'm marrying her." The words stunned him as soon as they left his mouth. "I'm marrying her," he said again, testing them this time. Weird as hell, but they felt right. "I am *marrying* her."

"Yeah, okay, I heard you the first time. How the hell is a hitman gonna marry a dead woman?"

"*She's not dead!*" A near roar.

"No, no, she's not. I meant pretend dead. Jeez. She is definitely not dead right now. Let's take more breaths. I'll call the owner of the island directly. *He* has a phone that never fails, especially when the call is coming from me. Unless the weather is shit, of course, and—"

Thunder blasted around Ronan. "The weather is shit."

Gray cleared his throat. "No boats will be running. There's an amphibious seaplane that ferries back and forth sometimes, but no way will it take off in this weather."

A amphibious seaplane—a plane that could land on either water or a typical runway. Hell, yes, that would be one hell of a lot faster than a boat. He'd already wasted too much time trying to make contact with Tyler and

Esme and getting Gray's crazy ass in the loop. "I'm flying out."

"*What?*"

"I'm finding a plane. You're getting me a pilot."

"I...do have a pilot fairly close," Gray's very careful voice. "There's an airport in Key West."

Yeah, he knew about it. He and Luna had passed it when they first came to Key West.

"But the pilot, uh, he's—"

"I can fly," Kane reminded Ronan as he closed in, seemingly coming from nowhere. Typical Kane style.

But his reappearance meant that Harris had been duly secured. One less worry.

Ronan jerked his head in Kane's direction even as he told Gray, "Forget your guy. I've got a fucking pilot. One who won't be scared by the weather." Because nothing ever seemed to scare Kane. "Just have me a plane ready. I'll be at the Key West airport in moments. I'm getting in the air, and I'm getting back to Luna."

"But—"

"I'm going back to her. I think Marcus is down here already." How many times had he said that very thing? "I think the prick is hunting. He's taking her out and then he'll come for me." Or at least, that was what Ronan suspected Marcus would do. But he wasn't going to wait for the attack. And he certainly wasn't going to stay away from Luna when she was in danger. "I have to get back to Luna. Stop being a damn agent. Be my friend. Get me a plane. Get me a path to her."

Silence. Then, "A plane will be ready when you get to the airport."

Damn straight, it would be.

Ronan hung up. He didn't ask more questions about

254

just how the plane would be ready. He didn't need those answers. He just needed the damn plane.

* * *

HER EYES FLEW OPEN.

She'd been dead to the world one moment, and in the next, Luna's eyes shot open. Her body bounced. Jiggled as she moved up and down, but even with those movements, Luna realized she was pinned in...an airplane seat?

Lightning flashed right beside her, and her heart nearly jumped from her chest. She opened her mouth to scream.

A man blasted, "Keep this bitch in the air!" The sharp cry came from a man sitting in the seat that was positioned in front of Luna.

"I'm doing my best," a snarl back at him—a snarl from the pilot. "We shouldn't be up here. This weather is too rough. I warned you it was risky!"

"It's barely a thirty-minute flight! Keep us in the air and then land us, and you will get fifty grand from my new boss. *Fifty grand.* I think thirty minutes of flight time is a fair trade-off for that much cash, don't you?"

More lightning. Luna pressed her lips together and didn't make a sound.

"How is the woman?" The question came from the pilot.

Instinctively, Luna snapped her eyes closed.

She heard rustling. "Still out cold." A pleased retort. She knew that voice. *The pianist. The guy who wanted me to sing with him.* "I don't know how much of the drugs she got. If she had too much wine or too many of those chocolates, hell, she might not wake up at all."

Luna had barely sipped the wine. And she'd had two chocolates. Two.

But Esme and Tyler...oh, no, Esme and Tyler...

"Boss said he wanted her alive, but I'll get paid either way." More rustling. Barely discernible over the whir of the plane's engine. "He wants her. He can do whatever the hell he likes with her. Whether she wakes up or not, I will still get the payday." A hard sigh. "Wish that dick husband had been with her. He's got a bounty on him just as high as hers. Found out about it when I was looking for a little side job. Couldn't believe my damn luck. What are the odds, right? When I saw his tat, I knew the kind of hell I was facing. And only one guy in the gang had a scar like that on his chin. Everyone always talked about Ronan the Relentless. Especially once he started his kill sprees..."

Ronan didn't have kill sprees.

He protected innocent people.

He'd protected her.

"The woman won't give us any trouble," the pianist added. What had been his name? She could not remember. He'd told her, right before Ronan had appeared and, uh, threatened to break the man's fingers.

It won't just be a threat this time. Ronan will fuck him up.

Cameron. That had been his name. He'd said she could call him Cam.

"She doesn't look like the trouble type." The pilot's voice. Maybe a little sad. "Poor woman. What did she do to deserve a hit?"

So the pilot was fine with killing her. A little regretful, but fine. Who were these people?

"She saw the wrong person killing the wrong man." Impatient. "Can you go faster?"

"Not in this weather. I'm trying to not kill us all."

Her eyes opened once more when the plane dipped and swerved. Even as her breath stuttered out, Luna began to plan. Because she was most definitely going to be *trouble*.

* * *

HE WAS AT THE AIRPORT. Only he didn't see a freaking amphibious seaplane waiting to go on the runway. He'd barreled into the small facility with Kane on his heels and the attendant up front had practically run away from them in fear. It had taken too long to arrive at the place. He needed a flight. He still couldn't get Tyler or Esme on the phone, and he was about to lose his mind worrying about Luna.

Ronan's phone rang. He snatched it up and put it to his ear even as he glared through the floor-to-ceiling windows that overlooked the runway area.

"We have a problem," Gray informed him.

"That is not what I need to hear."

"I'm tracking you right now, and according to my intel, you're over a large body of water. You've moving way too fast."

What? He wasn't moving at all.

"Where are you, Ronan?" Gray wanted to know.

"Standing in the damn airport waiting for my plane." A plane Gray had promised him.

Gray exhaled. "Different question. Where is your watch, Ronan? The watch you always wear. The one I use to track your crazy ass because it has the absolute best tech installed on it. Secret shit that the government hasn't made available to the outside sector."

Automatically, Ronan glanced down. No watch. "I left it." When he'd left Luna.

"Your watch is heading toward the airport," Gray told him. "And since watches don't move themselves, I think someone is carrying it. Or wearing it."

He surged closer to the windows and peered out at the storm. Kane followed him, not saying a word.

"Who has your watch?" Gray asked.

"It...could be Luna. I left it in our bungalow." Would Luna have grabbed his watch? Or maybe Tyler?

"The watch is coming in, and it's coming in fast. I want you to stay out of sight until I see what's happening."

*Until I see what's...*He stiffened. "You're here, aren't you, Gray?" Tricky bastard.

"Things are approaching a head faster than I anticipated."

"Did you fucking set up Luna?" Rage threatened to overwhelm him.

"*No.* I didn't. I swear it. But when the hit got placed on you, I knew I needed to move. Figured you might need me. I came on Kane's heels. I'm—shit, I have a visual on the plane. *Do not interfere, understand?* I haven't located Marcus yet. This scene is not secure. I repeat, the scene is not—"

He could see the flash of approaching lights. Ronan hung up on Gray and rushed toward the corridor that led to the runway. Two security guards tried to stop him. Hilarious.

"You don't want to do that!" Kane shouted at them. And before Ronan could knock their asses out, Kane flashed some kind of government ID at them. The men backed off. Ronan ran through an additional screening area as Kane yelled orders at everyone. Official sounding orders. Then Ronan was outside. Rain pelted him and lightning flashed around the plane as it descended. He raced forward.

Only to be hauled back. He whirled, ready to drive his fist right into Kane's face.

But Kane wasn't there. A soaking wet Gray was.

Ronan let his fist fly. It slammed right into Gray's face. A rapid hit. Gray swore but didn't let him go. "*Dammit, don't compromise this even more.*"

Kane appeared. He grabbed Ronan's right arm. Kane and Gray dragged his ass to the shelter of a shadowy hangar just as the seaplane rushed toward the airport. It dipped, weaved with the wind, and Ronan almost stopped breathing because he thought the plane might crash right in front of him. But it steadied. Slowed as it eased down the runway.

Stopped.

"Do not move," Gray gritted in his ear. "You don't understand the players. I'm trying to keep innocent people alive."

The plane's door opened. The pilot stayed in the cockpit, but one guy climbed out. Ronan couldn't see his face clearly. The prick reached into the rear of the plane and pulled out...

A woman.

A woman's limp body that he slung over his shoulder and began carrying away from the plane.

A woman who didn't fight him. Who didn't struggle at all. A woman—sweet hell, *no.* A woman who was dead?

A woman...who was his Luna because the sonofafucker carrying her had just walked in front of a runway light. Luna's dark hair slid away from her face. Her eyes were closed. Her face slack.

A roar built in his throat, and Ronan broke from Kane and Gray as he lunged for his wife.

Chapter Twenty-Three

"SHE'S NOT DEAD," KANE RASPED AS HE LOCKED HIS arms around Ronan's waist and yanked him back.

And she wasn't.

Luna had just twisted and heaved and lunged to the side and broken free of her abductor's grip. *Good fucking job, princess.* She staggered briefly, and then she was running away from the creep. A creep who'd fallen to his knees because she'd managed to kick him in the groin and elbow him in the face during her escape.

She was running right for the waiting hangar. *Running right for me.* Only his dumbass friends were holding him back. What the hell was that about? And then—

"I will fucking shoot you!" A bellow from the freaking pianist. Because that was the man who'd had her. The man who was now aiming a gun at her fleeing back.

Why was the place so deserted? The storm? Bullshit. Others should be out on the runway. Security personnel who'd been inside. This madness should not be going down.

Not unless someone wants the scene playing out this way.

"Let me go or die," Ronan told his friends. Because if they thought he was just going to stand there and watch Luna get shot...

She'd stopped. Her back was to the piano player. Slowly, she turned toward him. "My husband..."

I'm right here, princess.

And he realized that Gray had drawn his weapon. He'd taken aim at the piano player.

"My husband is going to kick your ass," she promised the fucking piano player. "Then he'll probably wind up feeding you to the gators."

The pilot had climbed from the plane. He was walking slowly behind the piano player. Cameron. Harris had told him the pianist was named Cameron.

"Shoot the prick," Ronan ordered Gray. "Now." Before the fool pianist pulled his trigger on Luna.

"We need him alive for the hand-off," Gray groused. "He's not going to shoot her. My guy said Marcus wants to handle her himself."

His...guy? And then it made more sense. Gray and his schemes. Shit.

The pilot was almost right on top of Cameron. And the pilot was pulling out a weapon...

Cameron spun around. With zero hesitation, he just fired.

The pilot went down.

Gray's hold slackened. Ronan flew from his friends and hurtled toward Luna even as Cameron laughed in the rain and turned back toward her with his gun aimed and up and —Ronan shoved her out of the way. She never saw him coming. He pushed her to safety and leapt at Cameron even as the sonofafucker was firing.

On the damn runway.

261

In a place that should have been so secure and safe.

With federal agents *right* there.

Ronan felt the bullet blaze over his arm. He didn't care. He hit Cameron. The piano player fell back and landed onto the runway. Ronan sprang down at him. His fist slammed into Cameron's face over and over again.

Cameron tried to swing up his gun.

Ronan caught it. Caught the guy's fingers. Rammed them onto the hard runway and heard the bones snap. He smiled down at his howling prey. "Didn't I warn that would happen if you touched her again?" Only this jerk had done more than touch her. He'd kidnapped Luna. Aimed a gun at her. Ronan was through holding back. He was sending this creep to hell.

"Ronan, *stop!*" Gray's bellow. And, of course, killjoy that he was, Gray appeared like an avenging angel. He had his weapon up and pointed at Ronan.

Friends don't do this shit.

"I need him alive," Gray added. "You can finish whatever this is when I'm done with him, okay? But first, he has to take us to Marcus. End goal, man. End goal."

Ronan felt a featherlight touch along his back. His head whipped around.

Luna stared at him.

He stared back at his end goal.

Without a word, he leapt to his feet and pulled her against him. His head lowered over hers. His body curled around hers.

And all the agents who'd been hiding around the airport finally sprang from their hiding spots.

Too little, too fucking late, assholes.

* * *

"I KNEW Luna was in the air shortly after the plane's liftoff." Gray sat behind some random desk in a random office at the small airport. "Didn't quite understand why I was getting data telling me you were on the plane, too, but I guess that makes sense now, huh? She was wearing your watch."

Ronan was sitting in the chair across from him. He had Luna on his lap. She'd tried to move—twice—and twice he'd hauled her right back into place. He couldn't stop touching her. Not yet.

Luna raised her left wrist. "I borrowed the watch. Don't even know why." Her head turned. She stared straight at Ronan. "That's a lie. I wanted a piece of you. I put on your watch because I was hurting." She swallowed. "You left me."

"I was *protecting* you."

"How'd that work out?" she asked.

Fucking *poorly*.

"The pilot is going to be okay," Gray rolled right on. "No worries. Save your concern."

Ronan spared him a glance. "He was wearing a bullet-proof vest. Of course, he's okay. He was one of your guys. You had him stationed on the island—as what? Backup in case I screwed things to hell?"

Gray shrugged. "I like to have agents in place in case of emergencies. I thought he'd help Tyler when you left, but then, he was approached by our piano playing asshat with an offer of fifty grand if he made an unscheduled departure from the island. Considering the hit that had been placed on you and the fact that Marcus ditched the surveillance crew that I'd had shadowing his steps, I thought my guy should take that flight and see what developed."

"Cameron drugged me." Luna shook her head. "Me and

263

Esme and Tyler. How are they? Are they going to be all right?"

"Tyler and Esme are both currently pissed as hell, but they are recovering well. A doctor from the retreat is with them. You can rest easy on that score. They'll be transported from the island as soon as the storm passes and taken to a local hospital for a complete evaluation. By then, of course, the exchange will have been made."

The exchange. Ronan narrowed his eyes. "You didn't want me killing Cameron because you want him to lead you to Marcus."

A nod. "Your earlier suspicion was correct. Marcus is here, in Key West. If we catch him in the act..." His gaze dipped to Luna. "Then we catch him paying for an abduction, we get him for attempted murder...and maybe we even find his freaking trophies. In short, we nail him to the wall permanently." His hands flattened on the desktop as he leaned forward. "We do all of that, and Luna gets her life back."

"Maybe Luna doesn't want to be risked like that," Ronan snapped. "Maybe Luna—"

"Maybe Luna doesn't want *you* to be risked, but you didn't give her a choice, did you?" Luna snapped right back.

It was in that moment that Ronan realized Luna wasn't scared. She was hotly and completely furious. With him. "Uh, Luna..."

"Not a word did you say to me before you left! Not. One. Word." Her eyes flashed. "You left while I swam!"

"I told Tyler what to say—"

"You could have said something to me. As in, directly. You could have waited one whole minute and said, 'Thanks for the great sex, Luna.'"

Gray coughed.

"'Thanks for the great sex, but I'm off to do my job and we're done, and maybe I'm putting a big old target on my back.' Just FYI. You could have said all that." The angry words erupted from her, rapid-fire.

His hold on her waist tightened. "I didn't want to say goodbye."

"So you left me swimming. Walked away and didn't look back."

"If I had looked back, I wouldn't have been able to leave you."

Their gazes clashed.

Gray coughed again. "So, um, there are a lot of agents involved, it's a multi-agency partnership—"

"Yeah, I saw them lurking around and doing jackshit while a gun was aimed at Luna!" He'd realized the place was a freaking Fed trap when he'd gone too easily through the airport. Plus, Kane had been shouting way too many orders for someone who was supposed to just be pulling free agent status. He'd have to hash things out with Kane soon enough. "Kane was involved in this mess with you. Tell me, are all my friends assholes?"

"Yes, we are." Gray had finally stopped coughing. "But if you want to pick one friend to receive the most of your rage, pick me. I was the one pulling the strings."

"Aren't you always?" Ronan knew the man lived to scheme.

"Kane kept telling me this was all a mistake. He didn't want to keep any secrets from you. But there wasn't a ton of time for big reveals." He released a long breath. "The Feds stationed here at the airport were waiting on my command. I get you're pissed, but I made the best judgment calls I could. I *have* to stop this twisted freak. I've lost *two agents* trying to take down Marcus Aeros." His voice was deadly serious.

Both Luna and Ronan studied Gray in silence.

"I have been working to bring him down for a long time." His nostrils flared. "And, Luna, when you came to me, I already had people trying to gain access to his inner circle. I couldn't move right away with your intel because I had to make sure they were safe. I am trying to get through his minefields with a minimum body count. Yes, I've kept secrets. From you both. Hell, I keep secrets from everyone. That's what I do. That's how I stop the monsters that most people will never, ever know about in this world." The faint lines around his mouth seemed to deepen. "Marcus Aeros needs to be stopped. The people he's killed? Their loved ones need closure. I don't want him getting off on some damn technicality. I want him rotting in a cell for the rest of his life."

"Funny. I want him rotting in the ground," Ronan returned.

Gray leapt to his feet. *"Don't forget who you really are, dammit!"*

Ronan knew exactly who he was. Maybe Gray was the one who had forgotten.

Once again, Luna tried to rise.

He just tightened his hold on her. "You're not getting away."

"You're the one running, Ronan!"

"Not any fucking more."

He felt her start of surprise. They'd get back to that issue in a moment, but, first, Gray needed to understand a few very important facts. "I'm not handing Luna off to anyone so they can deliver her to Marcus. Certainly not to that prick piano player." Cameron would never touch her again.

"You broke his fingers." Gray looked and sounded less than pleased.

"He deserved it." Really? Was Gray gonna argue that point?

Oh, right. Gray was the uptight and upright FBI guy. He probably was gonna argue.

"Noted," Gray said. Just that.

Ronan blinked.

"But I need to use the guy," Gray added grimly "He is the one Marcus is expecting for Luna's handoff."

"Big fucking deal. Get him to give you the location of the meetup for Marcus, then swarm the place."

"He *won't* give up the data. Agents are trying, but he's refusing to cooperate."

Someone save him from good guys who couldn't get shit done. "Give me five minutes alone with him, and I'll have the address." Ronan thought about what he'd just said and amended, "Nah, I only need two."

"Ronan, I can't let you attack a prisoner!"

"I won't put a finger on him." True story. "Scout's honor."

"You were never any kind of scout."

Another true story. He hadn't been. "That's right, and Cameron knows exactly what your men are. They're the scouts. The law-abiders. He knows they will keep him alive. He has no such certainty when it comes to me. He's scared of me, and he should be, and I *will* make him talk."

Gray considered Ronan's words. Weighed them a little too long before he grudgingly nodded. But then he said, "A location isn't enough. If I go in with sirens screaming, I won't get the intel we need. The guy will instantly panic and split. He's gonna have guards all around him. Probably at the perimeter of any building he's using."

Yeah, he would. Marcus would be a cautious prick.

"He's expecting Luna to be delivered to him." Gray's gaze dipped to Luna. "He'll have any guards demanding to see her. If they don't see her, there will be no access to Marcus. He'll get a warning that something is up. He'll be in the wind. And—"

"He'll keep hits on me and Ronan," Luna finished.

Another nod from Gray. "We don't want Marcus walking—"

"Then I'll be given to him, exactly as promised," Luna cut in to say. Why the hell did she have to sound so brave and determined? "His guards will see me. They'll make sure I am sent straight to him. I can be wired or loaded down with whatever tech you need in order to get his confessions recorded. We'll lock him away forever. Then I'll be free."

Free of me. "That's not an operational plan," Ronan growled. "Because maybe he sees you, and he shoots you on sight. Did you consider that option before you decided to risk yourself?"

She was staring straight at him again. "Then maybe I need a bulletproof vest."

Maybe she needed a lot more than that. "Doesn't help if you get a bullet to the brain."

She flinched.

"Well, if *you* trade her..." Gray's ever-so-careful words. "Then you can make sure she doesn't get a bullet to the brain."

Sonofa— "That was the master plan you were working on for the last few moments, huh?" He'd practically felt

Gray's mind spinning. "For me to take Luna in? For me to take the place of Cameron as the bastard selling her out?"

"I do think Marcus will be delighted to see you." Gray lowered back into his chair. "Delighted or he'll piss himself in fear. Whatever. But if you go in, you can protect her. You can get Marcus's confession. You can end all of this for her. Give her life back to her."

He wanted Luna to have a life. He also wanted a life with her. "I'm done."

Luna sucked in a breath. And, fourth time—she tried to rise. He pulled her right back.

Seriously, what the fuck? "I'm not done with you, princess. I walked away once. Pretty sure if I try it again, I might as well cut out my own heart and toss it at your feet."

Her hands rose to grab his shoulders and hold on tightly. "What are you saying?"

Oh, Ronan thought that he'd been pretty clear. But he'd try again. "Gray, I want out. I want to be clear of this life." The words were for Gray, but he could not look away from Luna.

"Why?" Luna whispered.

"Because I think it's time for some adventures."

Her lower lip trembled.

His head leaned toward her. Right before his mouth pressed to hers, he confessed, "I love you, princess."

Chapter Twenty-Four

"I'll give you two minutes with Cameron. Two," Gray stressed. "But you can't leave a mark on him."

No marks would be necessary.

"I'll get things arranged." Gray stalked out of the small office. Shut the door behind him. And, finally, Ronan could be alone with Luna. His Luna. His—

"What in the hell, Ronan?" Her fingers bit harder into his shoulders. "Now you say you love me? Now? When we're about to go out and have some intense face-off with the man who wants us both dead? You choose now as your moment?"

She was so freaking beautiful. Her hair was still wet from the rain. Her clothes slightly damp. She glared at him. Her eyes shot fire. And all he wanted to do was hold her and never let go.

After I permanently eliminate all the threats to her.

"Ronan!"

"Sorry. Got lost in your eyes."

Those eyes shot even hotter sparks at him. "Don't you dare try to charm me right now. You left me. I thought I'd never see you again. I've been drugged. Kidnapped. And *now* you're saying that you love me? I'm supposed to believe you?"

Hell, yes, she was. "I loved you when I left." It had been one of the reasons he left. "I wanted you to have the life you craved. Wanted you to sing and shine on a stage. Or get back in the classroom with your kids if that was the choice you wanted. Nothing should stop you from living." She'd been stopped too much in her life. "That was one thing I could do. Eliminate the threat to you." It was precisely what he would do.

But he'd realized—when he saw that prick carrying her across the runway—that the only way to be absolutely sure Luna was protected for the rest of her days and nights... well, she'd need a bodyguard. Someone with a very personal and vested interest in keeping that hot body of hers safe. *She needs me.*

Gray would have to pull off a miracle for him, though. Too many people hated Ronan Walker.

So I might just have to become someone else. For her, he would. "I love you," Ronan said the words again. The first confession had felt rusty. Stilted. This flowed more. "I love you." Certainty. He started to smile.

A tear slid down her cheek.

His smile died. "Luna?"

"I love you, and I don't want you in danger."

"I can handle danger."

"Yes, you say that, but when I was on the island and you were gone, I kept imagining you getting shot. I imagined you dying because you were out there fighting my battles!"

There was no other battle he'd rather fight. "I'm not dying." Not when he had a life waiting for him. "Can't say the same about Marcus."

271

Her eyes widened. "Ronan—"

His mouth went to her ear. "James," he rasped.

"What?"

"That's my real name." James Ronan Turner.

A knock on the door. "You have two minutes with Cameron!" Gray fired out. "Hurry! We've got to get moving! Marcus will get spooked if Luna isn't delivered soon."

Luna swallowed. "You're going to be with me for this big showdown scene."

"Every step of the way."

Her gaze searched his. "You love me?"

"With every bit of my dark, dark heart."

Her right hand let go of his shoulder and rose to press against his cheek. "I love you with every bit of mine, too." She kissed him. Soft and sweet.

He kissed her. Hard. Demanding. Deep.

"Ronan!" Gray threw open the door. He glowered when he saw them, basically mouth to mouth. "Seriously?"

Yes, seriously. Always. But he let go of Luna. She rose to stand beside him. Her hands twisted. He stood and towered over her. "How many kids shall we have?"

Her eyes widened.

"Think about it. I'm good with zero, if that's what you want. If you want twelve, I'm good with that, too." Then, whistling, he turned away and headed for the door.

Gray stared at him as if he'd never met Ronan in his life. Total stranger. "Who are you?" Gray demanded as Ronan passed him.

"Your time will come," Ronan warned him. Ronan could pinpoint the exact instant when his own world had realigned. It had been when Luna was pulled from the damn plane, and he'd thought that she was dead.

Everything had stopped.

If she *had* been dead, he would have made that runway into a freaking bloodbath. "Take me to Cameron."

Gray led him through the twists and turns in the terminal. Two stuffy Feds waited near a closed door. Gray opened that unassuming door. Waved Ronan inside.

Ronan strolled in with a smile on his face. Cameron was cuffed to a chair. His face was battered to hell and back. Honestly, why was Gray so worried about him hurting the guy in this little interrogation scene? Who would notice a wee bit more damage? But, a promise was a promise so...

"Give them privacy," Gray barked to the guard-slash-agent who'd been stationed with Cameron. The guard immediately filed out. So did Gray. The clicking of the door as it shut seemed overly loud.

Cameron smirked. Or smirked as much as he could with that bruised and swollen face of his. "I'm not telling you *jack*," he spat.

Ronan eliminated the distance between them. When he was right in front of Cameron, he tilted his head down. He eyed his prey. "How are those fingers feeling?" he asked, voice pleasant.

"You fucking *broke* them!"

"Yes, I did. You touched something you shouldn't have touched. But, I was thinking about it...and I think I've come up with a fun idea for us." He pulled out his knife. No one had bothered to pat him down. Their mistake. Or, had it been a mistake? Gray knew him well, after all. "Did you know that Marcus once asked me to cut off one of Luna's fingers in order to prove that she was actually dead?"

Cameron licked his lips. "What the hell are you doing with that knife?"

"I'm planning to cut off one of your broken fingers," he

273

explained, slowly and patiently. "Actually, I'm not going to stop with just one. I will cut them all off. Each time you don't tell me what I want to know, I'll cut off another finger."

Cameron's eyes were the size of saucers. "You can't do that shit! You're a—"

Ronan tapped the knife to his chin. "What am I? A cop? Nope. A Fed? Nope again. A hitman? Ding, ding, ding." He lifted his left wrist and turned it so that Cameron had to see the striking snake. "You know what this symbol means. It's what tipped you off about me. You know that I might have cut some deals with the Feds in order to save my ass, but you also know that I don't give a shit about their rules. They actually like that, truth be told. They need someone to break rules while they keep their precious hands clean."

Cameron gulped.

"Me? I don't mind some blood. I'm also feeling particularly pissed because you drugged my friends and my wife, and, FYI, no one does that shit and gets to walk away. So, which finger should we start with?" He lowered the knife.

"No, no—*no!*"

* * *

WHEN THE SCREAMING STARTED, Gray straightened his shoulders. He also moved to stand in front of the door because the green agents looked so shaky and uncertain. Why did he keep getting the new recruits? Such a pain in his ass. "Go scout the area," he told them. "Check for threats." *Go do some other damn thing.*

"Sir, there is screaming."

"I hear it."

"We should investigate—"

The screaming stopped.

He stared at them. Then shooed them away. "The area needs scouting, remember?"

"He can't hurt a prisoner!"

Oh, right. Fine. Someone needed to peek inside. Obligingly, Gray swung open the door.

Ronan stood by the prisoner. No weapons in his hand. In fact, his hands were crossed over his chest. Ronan smiled innocently. Or, he probably thought it was an innocent smile. Gray let the agents look, then he closed the door again. "Satisfied?"

They trotted off even as Kane sidled up. Kane peered at the closed door, then at Gray. He sucked in the side of his cheek and finally asked, "How pissed at us is he?"

"Probably a fifteen."

"On a scale of one to twenty?" Kane nodded. "I'll take that."

"On a scale of one to five."

Kane flinched. "He's gonna try and kill us while we sleep then, huh? This is on you, man. I warned you not to keep secrets from him but then you fucking blasted your way past me, and now *I'm* the bad guy, too, and—"

"Secrets are a pain in the ass. Sometimes, though, you have to keep them." Soon enough, there was one secret in particular that he would have to reveal to Kane. A few bits of new intel had been giving him cause for concern. Currently, the situation was still under control, but the more Gray learned, the more worried he became. The worry he felt centered around a witness who had once gotten extremely close to the so-called Heartless Kane Harte.

So-called...because Kane actually did have a heart. He'd

just given it to a woman long ago and then let her walk away. Or perhaps, *let* hadn't really been part of the equation. When Anastasia had entered witness protection, she'd been taken from Kane.

Perhaps he should go ahead and give Kane a heads up about the new developments that seemed to be happening with her. Not like he wanted two of his best friends both pissed at the same time. Dealing with a furious Ronan was hard enough. Dealing with a rage-filled Ronan *and* Kane? That could be a nightmare situation. "So, Kane, you need to—"

The door opened. "Got the meeting address. Got the meeting time. Let's roll." Ronan was completely cool. No, more like ice.

Gray peered around him to assess the prisoner.

Cameron was crying.

"What did you do?" Gray wanted to know. "And is it going to bite me in the ass?" Though he had already started to think that maybe he needed a change from the FBI. So many suffocating rules all the time were annoying the hell out of him.

And there is so much darkness growing in me.

"Didn't have to do a thing. He was happy to talk with me. We were in the same gang once upon a time. Brotherhood and all that."

"He's a fucking psycho!" Cameron shouted. "He's the one who belongs in handcuffs!"

Ronan winked at Gray. "I'm a psycho who knows where Marcus Aeros is lurking. Let's get the party moving." He stepped forward. Then stopped. "By the way, there is a price for tonight's work, Gray. I'm not doing this shit for free."

Oh, he'd never doubted that he would owe a debt.

"When I said I wanted out, I meant it. I will not be separated from Luna again. Make that happen."

Sure. He'd just wave his hand and make a miracle happen. No big deal. He'd turn a hitman into an upstanding member of society in a blink. No sweat.

Ronan had already passed him.

"You needed to tell me something?" Kane asked.

Yeah, he did. But... "Hold the thought?" Because maybe he should put out one fire at a time. If he told Kane now, Kane might run straight for Anastasia. Such a move could prove unnecessary at this time. Better wait longer and see what additional developments occurred. And, hell, Gray could use his backup. He trusted Kane a thousand times more than he trusted any FBI agent. He was well aware that this night's mission could explode in his face. And if things were going to explode, Kane was always exceedingly good at handling the fire.

Plus, if he needed to work a miracle for Ronan, Kane was just the man to help with that particular job.

* * *

SHE STOOD in front of the open trunk. Her hands were cuffed. A knife was strapped to her ankle. A taser hidden in the pouch of her borrowed sweatsuit. And—

"A gun is right here," Ronan told her. He pointed just behind the left taillight. "You remember how to get out of the cuffs?"

Luna nodded. She'd had to prove—three times—that she could get out of the trick cuffs. A quiet and very watchful Kane had provided the cuffs.

"I'll be driving the car. I'll be with you every second." A promise from Ronan.

They were outside of the airport. The rain had let up, but every now and then, a rumble would roll through the air. The lightning was in the distance now. And they had a killer to go see.

"Luna..." He pulled her close. "I can face him alone. You don't need to do this."

A point he kept making, but she shook her head. "You got Cameron to give you all the instructions for the trade-off. I'm supposed to be in the trunk on arrival." The car they were using had been waiting at the airport just for Cameron. Marcus and his guards would be expecting this particular vehicle. "The guards will check to see if I'm there. If I'm not inside, you won't get past them." She had to go with him.

He needed her to end the nightmare.

"I just want you safe," Ronan said.

"I am safe with you." Even locked in a trunk. Though it was not exactly ideal. Far from it, in fact.

But...she'd run on her own for weeks. She wasn't alone any longer.

She had Ronan.

He had her.

He pressed a kiss to her forehead. "What's the first adventure you want to have when this is over?"

"Let's watch the sunrise together."

"Done."

Her eyes squeezed closed. "Now put me in the trunk."

His body tensed. But he did it. He lifted her up. Settled her inside the rather spacious trunk. If, you know, a trunk could be spacious. She looked up at him as she curled on her left side.

"It's the second time I've done this to you," Ronan said. His voice had gone extra gruff. "Second and final."

"At least I'm conscious this time." Speaking of conscious, she'd spoken briefly with Esme. Her new friend had been enraged about the drugging incident. Luna had the feeling that Esme might be getting some payback of her own against Cameron very soon.

Ronan's hand rose and curled over the trunk's open lid. "You're going to be fine, Luna."

She nodded. "So are you."

His jaw hardened. "I love you."

Then he shut the trunk.

Darkness filled the interior.

I love you, too.

279

Chapter Twenty-Five

HE'D DRIVEN THROUGH THE DARKNESS. SNAKED ALONG the old road until he reached the boat storage facility. Guards were stationed at the high, chain-link fence that started at the edge of the property. He'd expected the guards. They were waiting just as Cameron had described.

Cameron had been so very helpful with his information. He'd just needed the right motivation in order to be a real team player.

Ronan slowed the car. Rolled down the window.

"What do you want?" A burly guard. Hair wet from the earlier rain. A cigarette dangling from his fingers.

"Got a delivery."

The man poked his head in the car. "Don't see a delivery."

"That's because she's in the trunk."

A cold smile. A nod. Then, "Show me."

How about I kick you in the dick instead? But, no, that wasn't part of the plan. Ronan reached down and popped the trunk. "Go see for yourself."

Grunting, the burly guard did just that, leaving a wave

of cigarette smoke in his wake. He strode to the back of the car. Laughed. Then slammed the lid closed once again before coming back to Ronan's side.

"Boss is inside. Things are ready for the woman."

So this prick knew that Luna was to be tortured and killed, and he had no problem with those plans. Not him and not the silent guy who stood just a few feet away. Good to know. Ronan hoped the Feds locked their asses away and that they never saw the light of day again.

The silent guy pushed open the chain-link gate. It rolled on wheels, screeching.

Ronan drove along the narrow path, pulling right in front of a two-story boat storage facility. Lights shone from inside the cavernous warehouse, and he eased the vehicle past the open doors, parking right inside. Ronan killed the engine.

When he exited the car, he had the hoodie up on his borrowed sweatshirt. He wore jeans, and his gun was tucked into the waistband, hidden right under the thick shirt. Another gun was strapped to his ankle. That one was hidden beneath the left leg of his jeans. He also had two listening devices strategically placed on his body. Two because Gray believed in being thorough.

Three figures moved toward him. Two were big, rough-looking men. Tattoos on their necks. One with a scraggly beard. The other with a thinning hairline and eyebrow piercings. Between those two men? Marcus Aeros.

In the freaking flesh.

And Marcus was staring at Ronan with absolute horror on his face.

Ronan smiled at him. "So, I heard you wanted to see me."

"Shoot him!" Marcus screamed.

His two guards fumbled for their guns. "Why would you want to do that?" Ronan asked. "Especially when I brought your target to you."

"*Stop!*" A roar from Marcus.

Shoot. Stop. Make up your mind, Marcus.

The men stared in confusion.

"You're a fucking idiot," Marcus told him. Then he laughed. "Don't shoot him. I want to play." He shoved the man with the thinning hair and eyebrow piercings. "Go search him. Take away every weapon he has."

Ronan stepped away from the car. "Is this any way for a businessman to act?"

"Businessman, my ass," Marcus threw back. "You *killed* my cousin."

"Well, in my defense, he was trying to kill me. I get annoyed when people do that shit. Lethally annoyed."

The goon who'd been sidling toward him stilled.

In the next breath, Ronan had his gun out. And aimed right at Marcus. "I can kill you before they can shoot me." Not bragging. Just stating a fact. "But I didn't come here to kill you. I came here to do business."

"You lied!" Marcus heaved forward. "You said you killed Luna Black! You didn't!"

"Ah, that's right. You hired me to kill her."

"Damn straight, I fucking did!"

Confess, confess, confess.

"Only you didn't do the job. I got word that she was still alive. Pretending to be your wife or some shit." He laughed. "I put hits on you both. Don't know why your fool ass is here or what happened to Cameron, but I am sure as hell gonna enjoy what comes next." His grin stretched from ear to ear. "You are going to beg me for death before I am done with you."

Doubtful. "I don't typically beg for anything."

"You will," Marcus assured him. "They all beg. By the time I'm done cutting them, by the time I throw them in the waters I've already chummed, people beg! They bleed and they beg, and they don't come up from the water. That's gonna be you. A watery freaking grave. You and that bitch."

Oh, now why did you have to call her that? "I was trying to have a civilized conversation."

"Uh, boss?" It was the hulking goon. The one who was nervously eyeing the car. "Is there a woman in the trunk? Should we get her out?"

"Yes." A decisive nod from Marcus. "Get her out. Let's play."

No one is playing with Luna. "I'm sorry, but there seems to be confusion here. See, I wasn't paid for killing Luna Black. So Luna Black is still living." He kept his weapon up and aimed at Marcus. "And no one else will be killing Luna, either. *Not until I get my payment.*"

Marcus gaped at him. "Are you serious? That's why you're here tonight? You came for your money?"

"I'm here tonight for three reasons." His gun never wavered as he talked his ass off—and got Marcus to keep right on confessing. The Feds had damn well better be getting every word. "Reason one, I want my money."

Marcus grunted. "You didn't kill her! You don't get paid unless Luna Black is dead!"

"Reason two, your dumbass took out a hit on me. On *me*. No one calls in a hitman on the hitman and just gets away with that crap."

Marcus backed up a step. "What in the hell else was I supposed to do? You knew I had sent Kurt after you. Not like you were gonna let me live—"

"Reason three, I needed a confession."

Marcus shook his head. "What?"

"Confession. It's good for the soul. And you just made yours." A rather perfect one. "Ready to rot in jail?"

"*Shoot him!*" Marcus screamed as he seemed to realize that, yep, he'd just confessed his crimes, and this night was not going to end as he'd hoped.

But before the jerk guards could fire at him, Ronan pulled the trigger on his weapon. One bullet hit the goon on the left. A fast shot to the shoulder. The other took out the man on the right. A leg shot that had him falling to the ground and howling in pain.

Marcus didn't fight. He turned and ran like the coward he was. Ronan wanted to give chase but...

I'm not leaving Luna in the trunk.

He rushed to the back. Had the lid open and Luna—her cuffs were already off. She jumped out with a gun gripped in her slightly shaking hands. "Only shoot bad guys," he directed as he steadied her on her feet.

Her eyes were huge.

"For the record, I'm not one of them." Not any longer. "Stay the hell behind me. *Let's go.*" Because Marcus wasn't getting away.

They raced through the boat storage warehouse. He paused just long enough to kick the weapons away from the wounded goons. Then he was going through the maze of boats with Luna right on his heels. Faster and faster. They looped around corners. Ducked under boats.

He caught the movement of a shadow up ahead. He heard shouts from behind him and figured the FBI was taking care of Marcus's men. They would have swarmed the facility after hearing Marcus's confession.

Down, down you go.

Marcus wouldn't escape justice.

He wouldn't escape—

A boat engine growled to life. The back door of the warehouse hung open, and Ronan flew through it. Luna was with him every step of the way.

Marcus had jumped into a thirty-foot sports yacht. The fucking idiot had forgotten to untie one of the ropes that bound the boat to the dock. The engine was roaring, the water was foaming, and the wood on the dock began to groan and heave as it fought the pressure from the rope and boat.

Ronan didn't slow down. He rushed forward and jumped onto the boat. He grabbed for Marcus and spun the bastard around, but when he spun Marcus, the sonofafucker sliced at him with a big-ass fishing knife.

The blade sliced right across Ronan's left arm, cutting far deeper than it should have.

"You're gonna chum the waters," Marcus yelled at him as he slashed again with the giant fishing knife. This time, the slash was across Ronan's right forearm as he tried to block the attack. The gun dropped from Ronan's fingers as the knife kept coming at him. Marcus raged, "You sonofabitch, you're gonna chum—"

"Ronan!" Luna yelled. He heard her feet slam into the deck as she jumped onto the boat.

He didn't look back. He did raise his hands to grab that bloody knife. Why were pricks always stabbing at him? Adding new scars to his collection? Ronan grabbed the knife.

He heard wood shattering. The boat bounced. Surged forward.

"Ronan!" Luna's desperate voice. So close. "Ronan, I have a gun. I can take the shot!"

Unnecessary. Because he twisted that knife and shoved it into Marcus's throat. Marcus couldn't even scream.

"How about you chum the waters?" Ronan asked.

Free of the dock, the boat hurtled forward because Marcus had set it at full speed. The sudden burst of speed had Marcus tumbling into Ronan. They collided hard. Ronan shoved the bastard away, but Marcus hit the side of the boat. He was clawing at the knife, eyes horrified as blood poured from the wound. In the next breath, Marcus toppled over the side of the boat.

Ronan grabbed for the wheel. Stopped the boat as he yanked out the key. He whirled for Luna and tossed the key her way. "Princess, I need to—"

She'd slipped and fallen on the boat's deck. Luna was struggling to rise.

"Freeze!" A shout from the dock. "FBI agent!"

Ronan reached for Luna.

And the shadowy FBI agent fired. The trigger-happy sonofafucker fired. The bullet slammed into Ronan's chest. One bullet. Another.

His mouth opened in a bellow. The sound echoed around him.

He stumbled back. Hit the side of the boat.

And, just like Marcus, he toppled over and fell toward the waves.

"*No!*" Luna's scream was the last sound he heard before the water covered him.

* * *

LUNA DROPPED HER GUN. She jumped into the water. Ronan had been hit. He'd gone beneath the waves. She was *not* leaving him there.

The water was icy when she pierced the surface. She sank deep because it pulled greedily at her. Her arms shoved frantically at her sides, and her feet kicked. The bulletproof vest she wore seemed to weigh her the hell down and she wanted it off, but she was too busy looking for Ronan. Searching desperately in the dark. But she couldn't *see*. Too murky and black. Not like the crystal-clear waters they'd had before when they swam in the picture-perfect spring.

This water was dark like a grave. A watery grave. She was not going to leave Ronan in the grave.

Something grabbed her. A hand. It closed around her shoulder, and relieved, so eager, she spun around to see—

A diver. A diver was right in front of her. Bubbles drifted past Luna's face. The diver held a flashlight, shining it upward.

Luna tugged against the diver's hold. Her lungs were burning. But the diver didn't let go. The diver kicked and propelled them upward, and they broke the surface of the water. As soon as she pulled in a gulp of air, Luna cried, "Ronan!" The waves hit her.

Voices rose and fell.

More lights. So many more lights. From the dock. From the water. The agents were already *everywhere*. She spun in the water, searching, desperate. "Ronan!"

Luna was still screaming his name when she was hauled onto a rescue boat.

* * *

THE BODY WAS PULLED out of the water. Bagged. Loaded onto a gurney. The Feds fanned out and searched the facility. They also kept sweeping the water.

The waves were strong. The currents powerful.

"He could have been dragged out." Grayson's solemn voice.

The EMT near Luna put a blanket around her shoulders. The blanket did little to chase the chill from her body.

"We'll keep searching," Grayson assured Luna.

The body they'd recovered was being wheeled by her. Her gaze slowly followed its progress.

"Marcus Aeros will never hurt anyone else again. Even before his death, Ronan got him dead to rights with the confession. He was either going to jail or going to hell." Grayson ran a hand over his face. "Guess hell decided to claim him."

Ronan had sent him to hell. "Ronan was bleeding when he went into the water."

"Yes."

"You're going to keep searching the water."

"Yes." Low.

The EMT moved away. The body had been loaded into the back of a black van.

She pulled in a breath. "Who fired the shots at him?"

"The agent...misunderstood the situation. Thought that Ronan was going to attack you."

Her head turned toward him. "Who fired the shots?" Agents milled around them. So many eyes and ears.

And no Ronan. No dangerous, intense Ronan.

"You get your life back, Luna. This time tomorrow, you'll be sleeping in your own bed."

Alone.

"You can have those adventures Ronan said you wanted. Guy told me that you had big adventure dreams."

Tears slid down her cheeks. "They pulled me out of the water."

"You were kicking and screaming the whole time."

Yes. "I didn't want to leave him."

He reached for her hand. Squeezed it. "Sometimes, we don't have a choice."

Ronan, I love you. She broke. Right then and there, with the FBI agents watching her. With EMTs and local cops milling around. Luna put her hands over her eyes, and she cried for the man she already knew was dead.

Ronan Walker. Hitman. Temporary Husband.

The love of her life.

* * *

"She knows," Ronan said. He had to keep saying those words. His sorry ass had been dragged out of the water by one of the divers that Gray had strategically positioned near the dock. That was Gray, always thinking ahead.

He was being stitched up by Kane. Mostly stitched. Someone was doing a piss-poor job of stopping the blood flow. *That someone was Kane.*

"She knows," Ronan said again because Luna had understood exactly how his story would end. There had never been any chance that Ronan Walker would walk out of this final scene alive. One of the many reasons he'd insisted on playing the story this particular way. He'd needed a public death. "She knows but she is seriously a fantastic actress." Consider him impressed.

Luna was crying. Her shoulders shaking. Gray awkwardly attempted to comfort her. A few big slaps on her back. Then Luna threw her arms around him, dislodging the blanket that had been placed around her shoulders, and she held him tightly.

"Could be an adrenaline crash, too," Kane noted as he poked again with a needle. "The woman has been through a whole—"

Ronan's head turned. He stared at Kane.

"She's a fantastic actress," Kane agreed. "Probably should get an Oscar or some shit like that. Breathtaking. Believable. Amazing."

Ronan nodded. Damn straight.

"Though I didn't realize she'd be jumping in the water after you..." Kane mused "That was taking things to a whole other level. Guess she went full method actress or something?"

He hadn't known she would go in the water, either. An unexpected Luna twist.

His head turned toward Luna. He wanted to go to her right then. To be the one holding her. But...

Ronan Walker had to die.

So he was damn well going to the grave. In this case, it would be a watery grave.

His jaw hardened. "See you soon, princess. See you very soon."

Chapter Twenty-Six

"WHAT HAPPENED TO THE SINGING TELEGRAM business?"

Luna glanced up from her desk. All of her students had cleared out, and she'd just been finishing the final details on the programs for Friday night's events. She hadn't even heard her door open.

But Grayson stood there. His hands were shoved into the pockets of his black pants. His eyes were on her.

Luna exhaled. "That business was a little too high risk for me. I came back to teaching." For a time.

"Heard that you had some offers to sing at clubs in Miami and Key West." He ambled closer to her. "Harris Croft and his wife told me—just two days ago—that they were hoping you'd change your mind and come work for them."

She shut her laptop, pushed back her chair, and rose to her feet. "I'm afraid Key West holds too many painful memories for me." The school day was over. She should get going. Head back to her empty home.

291

Two months. Two months had passed since that last, terrible night.

Two months that had left her heart broken.

"Understood." He stopped in front of her desk. "We found the trophies."

Her brows lowered.

"Marcus's? We've kept the details from the media because we're still trying to ID all the vics. But I searched all the boats that Marcus owned. Found pay dirt at one docked in Pensacola Beach. In the bedroom of his yacht, I discovered his mementos. Realized I should search all his boats because of his damn obsession with chumming waters. Figured he must have killed plenty of his enemies out at sea, and I was right."

Her stomach rolled.

"Wanted to give you that news personally. Wanted to check on you and..." An exhale. "I actually wanted to hire you."

He could not be serious. "Excuse me?"

Grayson reached into his pocket and pulled out a card. "I've got this friend...A real melancholy asshole—uh, I mean guy. He lost the only woman he's ever loved, and he just hasn't been the same since she left his life."

Her fingers were shaking when she reached for the card.

James Turner.

An address was neatly printed beneath his name.

"Thought he could use a little sunshine. You know, of the singing telegram variety. I can promise, you won't witness a murder if you stop by his place."

She dragged her gaze off the card and up to Grayson's face.

"Though you might just come face to face with a dead

man." A murmur from him. "The choice is yours, though. Maybe you don't want the job. Maybe you changed your mind in the last two months. Maybe it was the heat of the moment and adrenaline and a thousand other things making you feel the way you did."

Luna shook her head.

"Is that a no? You don't want the job? Completely understood." He reached for the card.

She snatched it back. "I think I can handle one final job."

"This friend...he may be leaving town fairly soon. He has plans to open a night club. He'll probably need a top-notch singer for a place like that, though. If you've got any ideas on who he can hire, be sure to tell him." A faint smile curved his lips. "Tell him that he's one lucky bastard, too. Fresh starts and second chances are hard to come by." With that, Grayson turned and walked away.

He hadn't even reached the door when she blew past him.

"Luna?"

She didn't stop. How could she? She had a very important job to do.

* * *

SHE MIGHT NOT COME.

Ronan stared through the massive window and out at the night. A temporary home. A condo in a high-rise that belonged to a friend, of sorts.

She might not come. Two months had passed. He'd thought about her every single day, but maybe Luna had changed her mind. Maybe she'd decided she didn't really love a grumpy asshole who knew too much about death.

Maybe she'd already found some other lucky bastard who wasn't so well acquainted with darkness.

His jaw ached because he'd clenched it so tightly.

She might not come. Her feelings could have changed. She wasn't living in fear any longer. Maybe the adrenaline and terror had been driving her before.

Maybe she'd started having adventures with someone else.

Maybe...

There was a knock at his door. Hesitant.

His eyes squeezed shut. Relief made him dizzy. But... what if that wasn't Luna? What if it was just Gray, telling Ronan that he was shit out of luck?

His eyes opened, and he whirled to lurch for the door. Surely, Gray would have just called with that bit of news, right?

He unlocked the door. Grabbed the knob. Hauled the door open.

A swarm of red balloons immediately slapped him in the face. He batted them away, desperate to see—

"Hi."

Luna.

She smiled shyly at him. "I heard that you need a pick-me-up."

Warmth flashed from his chest through his whole body. He felt a wide, wild grin curving his lips, and he grabbed for her. Ronan picked her up and kissed her and held her as tightly as he could even as the balloons bobbed and weaved around him. He kicked the door shut. Some of the balloons stayed outside. Some remained in the condo. "You got me balloons," he rasped against her delectable mouth. No one had ever given him a balloon. Hell, come to think of it, he didn't think he'd been given any gifts at all since his mother had died.

No, not true. Luna is the best gift of all.

"You got me my life back," she said. Her arms were around him. Holding him just as fiercely as he held her. "I missed you."

He'd craved her. How the hell was he supposed to sleep at night if she wasn't sprawled on top of him? The answer... he hadn't slept. Every night, he'd been restless because he needed her.

Now he had her.

He would not be letting go. "You jumped in the water."

"You were only supposed to fake die. But you were *actually* bleeding when you went overboard. I was worried. I panicked. Lost my sanity for a moment." Another kiss. "Don't dare fake die on me again."

They were done with that. Both of them. "Didn't know how it would go down." He truly hadn't. "Just knew that after I told Gray I wanted out..." He had to stop talking and kiss her again. "He'd take me out. Others would see it. My death would be witnessed." Several of Marcus's thugs had been blasting the story of Ronan's death through the jail grapevine by the next day.

Ronan had warned Luna that his "death" would be coming. No way had he wanted her to think he'd be leaving her.

No more ever walking away without a goodbye again. Lesson learned.

"The rubber bullets came in a flash," he added. He strongly suspected that Gray might have been the one to fire. "But when they hit, I knew I could go overboard." He had. Kane had been in the water with a diver, and they'd swept his ass away from the boat.

He hadn't seen Kane much in the last two months. Something that worried the hell out of him. But, then again, he had been declared a dead man so...

Ronan pulled back.

His eyes darted over Luna. Somehow, she'd grown even more beautiful. "You didn't change your mind?" Gruff.

"About what?"

A deep breath. "About loving me."

A negative shake of her head.

His shoulders rolled back as he lost the weight that had been dragging him under.

But then Luna's gaze swept over him. She frowned and reached for his left wrist. She turned it over. "A new tat?"

Yes. A moon, one surrounded by dark clouds.

"I've got this woman I love," he said, probably sounding awkward as hell. "Thought she might like it."

A delighted smile curled her lips. "You got a tattoo for me?"

"I covered up something I hated with something I loved."

Her gaze lifted. Her smile was still on her precious lips.

"I love you, Luna. I always will." A pause. "Ready to have some adventures with me?"

"I think a sunrise is waiting for us." Soft.

"I think a whole life is waiting for us." Ronan was gone. He was ready to be James. Ready for anything and everything that she wanted them to experience together. His job? From this moment forward, his job was to make her dreams come true. To love and protect Luna for the rest of her life.

Done.

She threw her arms around him again and kissed him so sweetly. She pushed away the dark and brought the light back into his life. And he knew with complete certainty that Luna was far more than a target.

She was life.

His life.

Turned out, he was the lucky bastard who would spend his days and nights with Luna.

Some days, it paid to be bad.

"Guess what?" Luna whispered as she gave his lower lip a sexy little nip. "I brought handcuffs."

Laughter boomed from him. So did desire. He scooped her into his arms, batted away more balloons—hell, some of them were heart-shaped, freaking adorable—and he carried her toward the bedroom. He had lots and lots of plans for Luna.

Some of those plans would definitely involve the cuffs.

And the engagement ring that he had tucked away in his pocket...An engagement ring that he'd be giving her when they watched the next sunrise together.

Epilogue

"So...THE HITMAN GOT A HAPPY ENDING, HUH?" KANE's voice was low as he lifted his beer bottle and saluted Gray. "Good for him."

Gray eased onto the barstool beside Kane. "How'd you know?" He hadn't told Kane. Not yet.

"Clearly, you have not checked the group text. Guy just invited us all to his wedding."

No, he hadn't checked the damn group text. He'd been...occupied. Gray glanced around the dimly lit interior of the small bar. Only one other patron. The guy who appeared to be passed out in the corner.

"Tell me, Gray, do you ever get tired of scheming? Ever get weary of moving people around like chess pieces?"

Only every other day. "We need to talk, Kane."

"Yeah, figured we did, or you wouldn't have requested this little meeting." He put down the beer. "Let me guess, you have a problem that you need handled."

Gray nodded.

"And you need someone outside of the FBI's normal

parameters who can do the dirty work for you? Got to say, man, you are lucky you have friends who enjoy fucking around with danger."

Gray's fingers tapped against the bar.

"But maybe I'm tired of dicking around with danger," Kane continued, voice thoughtful. "Maybe I wonder about that whole happy ending lifestyle now that both Ronan and Tyler have settled. FYI, Tyler is still damn bitter and, frankly, I think he's embarrassed as hell that he was drugged while on—"

"It's Anastasia." Tyler and Esme were both completely healthy. He'd been assured of that fact by a team of professionals. They were healthy, but pissed. His current problem centered on... "You remember Anastasia?" Gray knew that the other man did.

The glass beer bottle shattered in Kane's hands.

Right. That response had been anticipated.

"*My* Ana?" The possessiveness was obvious. "Not like I could ever forget her."

He nodded. "I'm afraid...I may need you to pull her out of hell again."

Kane shot to his feet. The barstool crashed to the floor behind him.

Gray wished he'd had a drink. Maybe a drink would have made this conversation easier. Maybe not. He swiveled toward his glowering friend. "He's found her," he said. "And there isn't much time to waste."

Kane grabbed Gray by the shirt and hauled him to his feet. "He's in fucking *prison*."

About that... "He broke out during a psych transport four days ago."

"Four. Days?" Rage burned in the words.

Gray started talking, fast. After all, a woman's life was on the line.

Kane had saved her once before. Gray had every confidence that he would be able to do it again.

Hopefully.

THE END

Want another romantic suspense from Cynthia Eden? Don't miss FORBIDDEN ICE.

SOME OBSESSIONS CAN'T BE CONTROLLED.

FORBIDDEN ICE

New York Times & USA Today Bestselling Author

CYNTHIA EDEN

Solve the case. Save the girl. Stop the killer.

Protect Wren. The minute that Jacob Jones receives the text from his brother, he springs into action. Wren Maye is the golden girl from his childhood, the star of his teenage fantasies, and the one woman who was always off limits to him...because she was his twin brother's girl. Over the years, he kept a careful distance from Wren because he knew she was the one person who could wreck his careful control.

She's in danger, and he's the only one who can save her.

Jacob arrives just in time to stop Wren's abduction. Now he's going to be her shadow because Wren is the target of a killer bent on vengeance. Jacob has always maintained a careful distance between himself and Wren—but there is no room for distance any longer. There is danger. There is desire. There is a vicious obsession that will not end. So now, he's just going to take what he wants. And, yes, he will damn well fight his brother for her. He will fight the world for her. She will be his. No one will hurt what belongs to him.

She thought he hated her. Now he's being her hero.

What is a woman supposed to do? One minute, the delectable Jacob Jones is keeping an icy distance between them, and in the next instant, he's saving her. Kissing her as if his life depends on the task, and swearing that he'll keep her safe from any and all threats. And in order to do that protection bit? He has to assume the role of his brother. He'll be her lover. Or...at least Jacob mistakenly believes that was the role Ebenezer "Eb" Jones had in her life. Newsflash—she has never belonged to Eb. How could she? For years, she's been hooked on Jacob. The intense and brooding twin who knows far too much about darkness.

A killer will use her to get his vengeance.

It is Wren's connection to both Jacob and Eb that makes her the killer's perfect target. He wants to kill her in order to punish the brothers. A life for a life. The twins will pay for their crimes. And they will pay by losing a woman who is so very important to them both. A friend to one. A lover to another. An ice-cold grave for them both to visit as they mourn for what they lost.

Vengeance is best served ice-cold. And desire? It's best when it burns red-hot.

Author's Note: A cold case from the past is about to shatter Jacob's world. If he can't team up with the Ice Breakers and solve this case, he may lose the woman who has been his life-long obsession. The woman who owns his heart. Get ready for another Ice Breaker Cold Case Romance...danger, steam, a hero who will not fight his desire any longer. Be careful when you wake the beast. Because he will fight like hell for the woman he wants.

Author's Note

Thank you so much for taking the time to read WHEN HE HUNTS! I hope that you enjoyed Luna and Ronan's story. The hitman with a (maybe!) heart was such a fun character to write. Thank you for going on an adventure with him. After all, what is life without a few adventures?

If you have time, please consider leaving a review for WHEN HE HUNTS. Reviews help readers to discover new books—and authors are definitely grateful for them!

If you'd like to stay updated on my releases and sales, please join my newsletter list. Did I mention that when you sign up, you get a FREE Cynthia Eden book? Because you do!

By the way, I'm also active on social media. You can find me chatting away on Instagram and Facebook.

Again, thank you for reading WHEN HE HUNTS. Thanks for enjoying romance books! Go make an adventure list and be happy.

Author's Note

Best,

Cynthia Eden

cynthiaeden.com

More Books By Cynthia Eden

Protector & Defender Romance
- When He Protects

Ice Breaker Cold Case Romance
- Frozen In Ice (Book 1)
- Falling For The Ice Queen (Book 2)
- Ice Cold Saint (Book 3)
- Touched By Ice (Book 4)
- Trapped In Ice (Book 5)
- Forged From Ice (Book 6)
- Buried Under Ice (Book 7)
- Ice Cold Kiss (Book 8)
- Locked In Ice (Book 9)
- Savage Ice (Book 10)
- Brutal Ice (Book 11)
- Cruel Ice (Book 12)
- Forbidden Ice (Book 13)
- Ice Cold Liar (Book 14)

Wilde Ways

- Protecting Piper (Book 1)
- Guarding Gwen (Book 2)
- Before Ben (Book 3)
- The Heart You Break (Book 4)
- Fighting For Her (Book 5)
- Ghost Of A Chance (Book 6)
- Crossing The Line (Book 7)
- Counting On Cole (Book 8)
- Chase After Me (Book 9)
- Say I Do (Book 10)
- Roman Will Fall (Book 11)
- The One Who Got Away (Book 12)
- Pretend You Want Me (Book 13)
- Cross My Heart (Book 14)
- The Bodyguard Next Door (Book 15)
- Ex Marks The Perfect Spot (Book 16)
- The Thief Who Loved Me (Book 17)

The Fallen Series
- Angel Of Darkness (Book 1)
- Angel Betrayed (Book 2)
- Angel In Chains (Book 3)
- Avenging Angel (Book 4)

Wilde Ways: Gone Rogue
- How To Protect A Princess (Book 1)
- How To Heal A Heartbreak (Book 2)
- How To Con A Crime Boss (Book 3)

Night Watch Paranormal Romance
- Hunt Me Down (Book 1)
- Slay My Name (Book 2)
- Face Your Demon (Book 3)

Trouble For Hire
- No Escape From War (Book 1)
- Don't Play With Odin (Book 2)
- Jinx, You're It (Book 3)
- Remember Ramsey (Book 4)

Death and Moonlight Mystery
- Step Into My Web (Book 1)
- Save Me From The Dark (Book 2)

Phoenix Fury
- Hot Enough To Burn (Book 1)
- Slow Burn (Book 2)
- Burn It Down (Book 3)

Dark Sins
- Don't Trust A Killer (Book 1)
- Don't Love A Liar (Book 2)

Lazarus Rising
- Never Let Go (Book One)
- Keep Me Close (Book Two)
- Stay With Me (Book Three)
- Run To Me (Book Four)
- Lie Close To Me (Book Five)
- Hold On Tight (Book Six)

Bad Things
- The Devil In Disguise (Book 1)
- On The Prowl (Book 2)
- Undead Or Alive (Book 3)
- Broken Angel (Book 4)
- Heart Of Stone (Book 5)

- Tempted By Fate (Book 6)
- Wicked And Wild (Book 7)
- Saint Or Sinner (Book 8)

Bite Series
- Forbidden Bite (Bite Book 1)
- Mating Bite (Bite Book 2)

Blood and Moonlight Series
- Bite The Dust (Book 1)
- Better Off Undead (Book 2)
- Bitter Blood (Book 3)

Mine Series
- Mine To Take (Book 1)
- Mine To Keep (Book 2)
- Mine To Hold (Book 3)
- Mine To Crave (Book 4)
- Mine To Have (Book 5)
- Mine To Protect (Book 6)

Dark Obsession Series
- Watch Me (Book 1)
- Want Me (Book 2)
- Need Me (Book 3)
- Beware Of Me (Book 4)

Purgatory Series
- The Wolf Within (Book 1)
- Marked By The Vampire (Book 2)
- Charming The Beast (Book 3)
- Deal with the Devil (Book 4)

Bound Series
- Bound By Blood (Book 1)
- Bound In Darkness (Book 2)
- Bound In Sin (Book 3)
- Bound By The Night (Book 4)
- Bound in Death (Book 5)

Stand-Alone Romantic Suspense
- Waiting For Christmas
- Monster Without Mercy
- Kiss Me This Christmas
- It's A Wonderful Werewolf
- Never Cry Werewolf
- Immortal Danger
- Deck The Halls
- Come Back To Me
- Put A Spell On Me
- Never Gonna Happen
- One Hot Holiday
- Slay All Day
- Midnight Bite
- Secret Admirer
- Christmas With A Spy
- Femme Fatale
- Until Death
- Sinful Secrets
- First Taste of Darkness
- A Vampire's Christmas Carol

About the Author

Cynthia Eden loves romance books, chocolate, and going on semi-lazy adventures. She is a *New York Times*, *USA Today*, *Digital Book World*, and *IndieReader* best-seller. She writes romantic suspense, paranormal romance, and fun contemporary novels. You can find out more about her work at www.cynthiaeden.com.

If you want to stay updated on her new releases and books deals, be sure to join her newsletter group: cynthiaeden.com/newsletter. When new readers sign up for her newsletter, they are automatically given a free Cynthia Eden ebook.

About the Author

www.ingramcontent.com/pod-product-compliance
Lightning Source LLC
Chambersburg PA
CBHW010233100425
24902CB00014BA/572